Laikonik Express

NICK SWEENEY

UNTHANK BOOKS

First published in 2011
By Unthank Books
www.unthankbooks.com

Printed and bound in Great Britain by Lightning Source, Milton Keynes
A CIP record for this book is available from the British Library
Any resemblance to persons fictional or real who are living, dead or
undead is purely coincidental.

ISBN 978-0-9564223-2-3
Cover design by Ian Nettleton and Dan Nyman

Cover image 'Laikonik Express' © Ian Nettleton 2011

Dedicated to:

Aidan Sweeney *1928-1966*
Imelda Gallagher *1940-1986*
Helen McSweeney *1931-1997*
Colin Gruzd *1950-2010*

One

The train

Luckless in love, lost in words, Nolan Kennedy got on the train at Istanbul and rode it toward Warsaw. He wore a face, he often got the feeling, that was not entirely his. It would change as he shuttled through the Balkans and got a sense of its history, people's lives falling to pieces leaving the rest of the world with the cursed poetry of it. History to Kennedy was like one of those suburban houses, innocuous on the outside, where axe murders took place.

'Please?' A man shuffled a paper bag at him. 'You like an apple?'

Kennedy put a hand to his chest, Ottoman gesture of reluctant refusal. The guy accepted the rebuke with polite mystification. East of Istanbul you never refused food, but the train was west of the place by then. And Kennedy had never been crazy about red apples.

Messages hared down the nerves behind his face as his brain produced answers to questions he had forgotten. His eyes lit up like a pinball machine as he realised, with a sudden alarm, how wired he was.

Around him were three Turkish men whose tongues worked loose from drinking raki to spout schoolboy stuff about women they would never have. They revealed the harems they kept in their heads, and Kennedy wanted to remind them: *the only regular joes ever got to see the harem women were the eunuchs, you cuntstruck suckers.* Who else was there? Kindly bearers of apples, two Iranian brothers in extra-extra-large. They gave

Kennedy hell in good temper for being an American, fighter of unfair desert wars and non-believer in the only faith. Turks, in Kennedy's experience, never gave a damn about that, and the harem keepers looked on in polite amusement. Last, and least, there was a Bulgarian woman so small she had surely passed herself off as hand-luggage.

Kennedy watched the Orient disappear in the dark. When you were no longer there, he had the idea, it went back to some location in history, wreathed in silk and flowers, drenched in scent and spices, where everything that happened was exotic, but painful too.

The train guard, each time he passed, called out a cheery *Mister President* to Kennedy. He was the comic trophy the guard unveiled to his Bulgarian colleagues when the train passed into their jurisdiction, and he flapped Kennedy's passport as provenance. 'President Kennedy,' they all hooted. Kennedy guessed that kind of humour had to make those winter railtrips pass in just no time at all.

That laughing guard did not think it worthwhile to find the Bulgarian woman a compartment with other women in, Kennedy noticed, like he would have for a Turkish woman. She was not bothered, he could see, but she never spoke and hardly slept, and achieved the impossible, he thought, in not ever really looking any place at all. Her hair was sleeked back into a knot in a housing project facelift, and her face was that of a onetime prima ballerina, a short one who made perspective happen on narrow stages. She kept her feet on a travelling bag, which Kennedy guessed would be full of the kind of lingerie that would grab men who got themselves off from the relevant pages in mail order catalogues. She was done with the Orient, she made it plain, and was not impressed with the men around her for bringing it along with their babble. Feeling thus indicted, Kennedy tried not to look her way, in case she sent him a sneer sharp as a needle in his eye.

In the night, one of the Iranians asked him what he had on his Walkman. Kennedy told him Joni Mitchell, even though this was not the case. But you just could not tell people you were listening to Chinese classical music. 'Johnny Mitchell?' The man seemed as puzzled as Kennedy at having somehow heard of the warbling Johnny. Kennedy bluffed the offer of a blast of the music, which got the man's eyes going, *Catch me on a train listening to your Johnny Frigging Mitchell, pal.*

'Pink Floyd.' The brother pointed at himself.

'Uh, so…you're Floyd,' Kennedy took it, eliciting a contented nod.

He knew he was way gone, and should not talk anymore.

He began thinking that, if it was the Orient that was required, how cool it must be to live in China, the radio blasting that Chinese music all the time. He imagined it following him through some Manchurian town without either trees or colour, where he was on his way to meet the dreamiest girl out of China's multiple millions; there she lounged at the end of a street, under a loudspeaker on a pole, and in a room nearby she would pull her t-shirt over her head and would smell of fresh leaves, taste of ginger and aniseed.

The coke had worn off by morning, leaving Kennedy razzled and fretful. Sofia lay behind the white crystals that hazed the windows, just as they hazed the part of his brain marked *critical faculty*. He had carried his own crystals, needling the membranes of his nasal passages, past all those wiseguy customs and border officials, and that had to be worth something. He fell into the raggedy bullshit smile of the knowing.

He thought of his dad and Neal Cassady, sharing a room and a joint and a girl, smiling that same smile, and not caring what was happening to them. His own smile slipped off his face.

The Iranians alighted at Sofia, and one of them asked for Kennedy's address in the States. Kennedy searched pockets for a business card, could not put his hand on one. He found a pen and wrote, murmuring, 'You going to come visit me?' He saw the crazy dream of the idea in the guy's eye, and as ever felt cruel in encouraging it; as ever, too, he felt unable to kill it. He would see it come home one day in ten years' time, maybe, when, a gift of red apples in hand, the big guy would block out the light in Kennedy's doorway. Or at least Gerry Brook, who lived in Allentown, Pennsylvania, would see it. Alongside Gerry's address, he wrote, *Caught ya in the Rye*, which might make Gerry remember that when Kennedy lent somebody a book he wanted it back, or he would send the defaulter a huge Iranian. Kennedy handed the address over, saying, 'You come on over. Bring the whole gang.'

The man said, '*Inshallah*,' on it. He reached into a pocket and handed Kennedy a little pink embroidered slipper. He shook Kennedy's hand, and then his brother shook it, and between them they had a go at fusing his knuckles for him. Then they headed out into ice-sculpted Sofia.

Kennedy looked at his slipper. It was decidedly Persian, not Iranian. He was going to do *what* with it, exactly? It had a little leather loop. He put it carefully on his Pinocchio keychain.

The proximity of great cities blotted out the rest of the day, and beckoned through the eventuality of night. Kennedy thought how he was fixed on Warsaw instead. Lights came at him to reveal the furniture of towns, brought him on an imaginary journey that stopped dead at some point and eased him back into the forward motion of his actual journey. The train sounded and moved like an entirely different beast, like it was sick of the indigestion the passengers made as they sat in its innards, was preparing to disgorge them with a heave. Next thing Kennedy saw out the window was the Cyrillic script that spelled B-e-o-g-r-a-d, and the peculiar tinge of the night that spelled out m-i-n-u-s-f-u-c-k-i-n-g-t-w-e-n-t-y.

Belgrade

In his hotel room, Kennedy peeled off layers, caught himself in a mirror and suffered the everyday anguish of any high school quarterback going to seed. Guy of thirty he saw, getting fat, but with a head of dark-brown slicked-back hair and all his some-shade-of-white teeth, nostrils flared, contact lenses showing eyes that were a trick-of-the-light brown instead of a washed-out seagreen, his mouth set and sapient, or so he always liked to think. He peered, thought for a second how he might risk getting stuck forever in that pool of glass. He moved away from it, and showered, and covered himself in Chinese lotion that smelled of lemon verbena.

Later, he recalled reading somewhere how the next European war would be fought by economists. They had never heard that one in Belgrade. He could not guess at the deeds that would be hatched out in that unlucky city, the way men in rooms would reshape the Balkans by filling the world's thoughts with the unthinkable. He reflected later how maybe he could have walked the streets, climbed walls, peered into those rooms, glimpsed a mime show of the mechanics of evil. He was too weary though to go out and experience Belgrade, too struck by the idea that the whole place was signposted in the script of Saint Cyril, and that if he wanted to go out he would have to tie a long piece of string to the hotel door so he could find a way back.

Instead he lay down on a bed that reeked both of the business of empire and of whores down on their luck, and read the words, *If Jesus ever came here, it was to be tempted by the devil that time. I happen to think, however, that Jesus kept the idea of this place to Himself just so He could maintain the fiction that Hell was a different place altogether, and not to be found on this globe at all.* They were the opening words of his friend Don Darius's novel, which, back in Istanbul, he had pulled out of Don's trash. He did not like that *however*; it was not a good word for the opening of a novel. He had crossed it out, and yet still always read it.

Hermes, the thought came to Kennedy, *here's the messenger, hoiking words round the globe*, not so much wings on his heels but looking down-at-heel, and suddenly, in that little room, powerlessly tired and lonely.

Bakirköy

Back in Bakirköy, the Istanbul suburb in which Kennedy lived, he had sat in Don Darius's kitchen and read the script of the book until the words had started to fade into the woolly page. Maybe its beautiful prose was blinding him and, while he was pleased about having read it, the thought of never reading anything else was not boosting him, especially as he had not reached the end of the thing.

And he remembered his dad drawling, 'A good book'll make your eyes go blind, man. Know that? Make your brain go ape.' His dad was engaged around that time – nineteen sixty nine, was it, seventy? Kennedy was bad at dates – in tapping out the northern gothic epic that was going to swing American literature round by the neck. He was busy too though with cramming his head and body full of stuff that did not lend itself to the cohesive devices words are. His dad was a true beat, in that he knew the world was encapsulated in words, and not music. Kennedy's dad predicted scornfully how jazz would become the preserve of college professors and their college wives. A true beat, imprinted in his skin and bones the *pentimento* of too much bad whiskey and too many nights in the open, and of the bum jobs he got stuck with when he realised that self-education did not just stop at being hip to time and place. The sad sack wound up having to face it that not all beats could write. And even as he listened to some doctor's deadly spiel, Kennedy senior would be thinking, *I'm fixing to go out tonight, get good and drunk and score, get high and lucky and get laid, yass sir.* He would see the doc drift back into focus, would have to concentrate hard to recall that the doc was talking about the messed-up liver and lungs and lights whose x-rays were portrayed in a box on the wall like an icon from an alien church.

'Hey Dad,' Kennedy had called out in Don Darius's kitchen. 'Where are you now, great father and artificer? You peering over my shoulder, huh? Or rapping out the side of your mouth with Kerouac and Cassady in some corner of the ether, too strung out to know it's me? You wish. But I hope so.'

The big book Kennedy's dad wrote had wound up at Fahrenheit four-five-one, burned in an oildrum outside the trailer of some slattern who had him by the balls. Kennedy did not know why he had torched it, but a pick-list in the face of rejection featured petulance, drunken bravura, maybe a pompous Joycean gesture, or maybe just the need for fuel. The pain of not ever reading a word of it would nip Kennedy only years later as he stood at a roadside out of Syracuse University to hitch home for his dad's own date with fire and pomp. Unlike James Joyce when he did his book-burning, Kennedy's dad had no sister there to reach a hand into history and pluck the words from the flames.

In Bakirköy, Kennedy had sensed that he was about to get together with history, even if Don Darius's abandoned kitchen seemed an unlikely venue. He had put thoughts of Joyce away, and thoughts of his dad. He had upped and pushed the light switch, then found the place was out of juice, and he was not going blind after all. Holding Don's story in hand and mind, he scooted out onto Bakirköy's main drag into crowds at the never-ending pastimes of shopping till dropping, interspersed with yakking till their tongues fell off.

The whole of September's melancholy had tried to drop down on him. When you were teaching overseas, it was the time of year for remembering that friends you had before the summer were no longer there. He went to a place that for obvious reasons was known to foreigners in Bakirköy as Swindle Café. He shoomed through a bunch of coffees and through the rest of Don's book. He noted the piano man get up onto his little podium and launch into easy listening faves for people trapped in bars. He endured it until the man fingered the intro to Lionel Ritchie's *Hello*, then thought, *No – goodbye*, and was out of there.

He had met a crowd he knew on their garrulous way in. An English rose called Janine went, 'Hoy, what's that you got there?'

Kennedy had taken it that she didn't mean the food mixer thing he had inherited from Don, poking out as it was from a big bag, nor the snub-nosed fan-heater that somewhat chaotically accompanied it.

Kennedy recalled how she got pissed at Don one time at a dull dinner party right out of E M Forster, when he dropped the breadsticks and broke them. Don Darius, not Forster. 'Well, nobody can get them in their mouth whole,' Don had reasoned to Janine. 'Except you, maybe,' it had occurred to him, which had at least sparked Kennedy into chuckling. She had looked at Don and Kennedy the rest of the evening in a way that some Brits had, kind of: *Guys who break grissini, huh – bastards*. Kennedy had missed saying to her, *Most places in the world, breaking bread is a sign of friendship*.

'It's a typescript,' he had told her at the doorway of Swindle Café, and she had made a get-a-life face. Kennedy did not care. He had one. They gave no more thought to him, or to what he had in his hand, and nor did he for a while. Then, at some point one sleepless night he realised that a head of steam was building up inside him that would drive him, finally, to Istanbul's Sirkeci station and onto that railroad, the lights of the Balkans shining him through Europe toward Don Darius.

Kennedy had not known that Don was a writer. He had thought Don was simply a bum with the…*mien* of a writer, just like himself. Kennedy would have defied anybody to think of Don typing any kind of prose, let alone the magic kind.

Don Darius had come to teach English in Istanbul after doing the same for the po-faced Saudis, his head screwed up, having, like a lot of the Turks themselves, bought into the hype about Istanbul being equal parts east and west. Of course, it was not the place Don had wanted to be in. In Istanbul, he had become a prey to hurt, and drunkenness, and unhappiness. Kennedy had been one of those who got drunk, at least, with him. Kennedy hurt and got unhappy like anybody else, but it seemed to hide itself when he got drunk, which made him that guy in that story who drank to forget. It was almost like Don drank to remember. It was only when Kennedy read through the first draft of Don's book that he saw some worth in the curse. He turned on the main drag at Bakirköy, looked up for the last time at Don's old apartment, saw Don banging a typewriter in that kitchen, the only room from which his tapping had not raised hell with the neighbours, Kennedy learned later, in his pursuit of the words that made a beautiful thing out of what had once been nothing.

Belgrade
Kennedy's form imprinted itself into the bed as he skimmed the typescript of Don's book one more time. He stopped, agitated. He went back to the opening of part two, which at that time began, *The door opened onto bearded queens in dresses and headdresses, and I found my head bowed before the whole of the majesty of the law,* to take the reader briefly into Franz Kafka. Editors would change the word *queens* to make it *kings* in the published version, unwilling to have it that it was a tortured man's impression of beautiful-eyed men in robes, and not a throwaway remark to suggest they were gay, God forbid. Kennedy sourced his agitation in the knowledge that he might one day have a shot at being one of those monkeys who could sit at a typewriter and come up with Shakespeare after a thousand years, but who would all the same never write prose like Don Darius.

The thought brought him anguish, as it always did. He had a few stories seeing the light of day in various little magazines that, he was sure, only other wannabe story-writers read. He had a novella out, the tale of a gravedigger who fell in love with a mourner who turned up at the wrong funeral, under the imprint of an…eclectic publishing house in Manhattan. He had two abandoned novels in a drawer in his Istanbul apartment, had several more – three, at least – gone on the wind in various parts of the States; there were a hundred more in the wilds of his mind.

He loved Don Darius's book. He hated it too. Whatever he felt about it, there it was in his hand again, running itself across his eyes, and it really was time to put it down.

Inspired by the arabesques Don had doodled down some of his margins, Kennedy got out brush and ink and tapped into his own talents to make barbed wire ladders down a chequered page for a half hour. He came up with thirty halfway good Chinese characters. He wrote them as small as he could with the brush, then mixed ancient and modern and scribed them with a ballpoint pen. He flourished his name, as pleased with it as a kindergarten kid, or a cross-continental train guard. The weight of the day crashed down on him then. The rhythm of the railroad finally died out in his bones. He settled down ready for all the dreams left behind in the room.

Next morning, Kennedy called Don from the station, the Warsaw train muttering in the background. He told Don, 'I got your book.'

In the months that he had had a hold of Don's book, he had never called or written to tell him. Kennedy guessed that he had been working up all that time to this moment of smart-aleck denouement. Out of the silence of a held breath, Don pricked the bubble by saying only, 'Oh, ah, okay,' then asked Kennedy how were things.

'Your *book*, man. It's genius.'

Don said, 'So, what then, you gave up the teaching of English in far-flung parts?'

'I wish.' Kennedy didn't get the orientation of the question, but didn't particularly care.

'You're a literary agent now,' Don deadpanned. 'Huh?'

'Nothing so sharp-suited.'

'You're Ezra Pound, then. Spacer with wild hair and admirer of Mussolini?'

'I know who he *was*.'

'And nurturer of maverick talent. You know Hemingway taught him to box?'

'Christ.' Kennedy wondered how anybody could be roused first thing in the morning and just *have* all this shit in mind. 'Hey,' he reminded Don. 'This is long distance.'

'So, what's happening?'

'I'm in Belgrade.'

'What? Where, you said?'

'I'll be in Warsaw tonight.'

Kennedy liked the way that snapped Don out of the crap – it was early in the frigging morning for him, too – and got Don repeating, 'Are you kidding?'

A train guard, splendid as a Filipino army general, was making little hand-signals; the train was about to escape. Kennedy dropped the phone and left it swinging, let out a bunch of curses. Later, he thought of them slipping with ease into that city of bad plans and worse fortune, but for now he was just running for daylight after that train.

The train

Kennedy's compartment was empty. A Hasidic Jew decked out in New York black had paused in the doorway, had smiled but looked puzzled at the same time. Kennedy was diverted from staring appreciatively at the man's hairdo when the man spoke. Kennedy wavered over the meagre smattering of foreign words at his disposal, then chose English to confess that he didn't speak…whatever language the man was speaking. And wasn't about to learn it just to take part in this conversation.

He waved toward a seat to assure the traveller of its emptiness, and began thinking how maybe, in some culture someplace, it was lucky to meet a Hasidic Jew in the full kit and caboodle. It certainly beat running into an Israeli schooltrip whose kids had the loudest voices in the universe. He turned for a second to right his bag. When he turned back, the man was gone. He turned to his seat in the mood for the absence of conversation, spread his stuff over it and made it his own.

Almost as soon as it was into its stride, the train stopped in a town called Novy Sad. The compartment filled, mainly with men, mainly serious-looking, non-speaking. No officials boarded, no announcements were made that anybody there reacted to. Kennedy fell in and out of sleep.

11

Each time he woke, he seemed to see different people around him. He slept away most of the stop, which, as far as he could work out, spanned more than four hours.

It was evening before he passed through Hungary, and night by the time he reached Czechoslovakia, as it was then called. He talked to his remaining companion, a middle-aged Polish guy who was drop-dead handsome in an old-world kind of suit-and-tie kind of way. He presented Kennedy with a business card etched with the high-sounding name of Zell-Brandenburg. Kennedy thought, as he always did, how people who got business cards made were wasters of the first order for using up all that paper and ink and time and money. It was only polite to reciprocate, though. He rummaged in a pocket in his bag, fished out a card and passed it over.

'Oh.' The man was reading it with some difficulty, looking up to search Kennedy's face. 'Oh?'

If there was a question, Kennedy answered it with only a smile. He had forgotten which other waster had given the card to him along the line.

The man did not dare attempt the name on it. All the same, he wanted Kennedy to come stay with him in his pad in some place near Katowice. 'I am a…bachelor,' he let out shyly. 'You understand?'

Kennedy thought he did, and steered his companion onto safer subjects. Mister ZB was okay about that. Kennedy thought him a thoroughly cool type altogether. They shared intermittent conversations about trains and roads and cities and people and art and sport and books.

In the middle of one of them, the train slapped them to a halt. Polish border control people, looking like uniformed Eastern Bloc athletes, put their heads in the door.

'Plain sailing.' Kennedy sounded pleased as he said it, as if he were still in some pleasing conversation about books, or sport, art, or people or cities or roads or trains. The whole day he had been showing his passport to these officials with not one wisecrack about him being *Mister President* Kennedy. He thought he ought to be optimistic about going for the record.

Sometimes Kennedy thought he looked on the bright side because he was truly an optimist. Other times, he was sure he did it simply because he was some kind of idiot. A stony-eyed guard asked Kennedy for his visa. The eyes came to life under the peaked cap when Kennedy inquired, 'Uh, now, uh, what visa is that you're talking about, sir?' The guard was serious. Kennedy said he would gladly buy one there and then, the way he had done to cross Bulgaria, and Serbia, and...wherever-all. But he was far from the Balkans by then, far from its spirit of spontaneity. Quietly, and without hoo-ha, he offered the fellow twenty dollars. When they were refused, Kennedy thought, *What a jerk.*

He had to face it though that he looked much more like the jerk about two minutes later. The guard was nice and warm on his train, while Kennedy was standing on a track in a frozen no-one's-land siding, with instructions to get himself into Ostrava, the closest Czech town, to buy a visa from its Polish consulate.

'Nothing easier,' Kennedy choked to himself as he scrunched across cinders to the lights of a shack. 'It's done, already,' he yelled to the bureaucracy that slept patiently behind those lights waiting for his time and his dollars, knowing all the same that it was not going to wake up just for him.

The border

Kennedy might not have minded being stranded for the night with a square-jawed Polish artist full of Euro-angst, or an emissary from Bosnia-Herzegovina on his way around the continent to raise money and support for his little country's independence, or maybe Elvis. Either one. His first choice would have been with a beautiful Romanian countess who had pawned all her jewels in Paris, who would take Kennedy into her confidence because she could not trust anybody else, not even Elvis. As it was, he had to settle for a guy with the blackest eyes he had ever seen, and a nose you could slice cheese with, also visaless. Plus an extended family of genuine ragtag Romanies. After some token attempts at charmless panhandling, they left Kennedy and Sherlock alone.

Kennedy dubbed his fellow wise guy thus not only because of the nose and eyes. There was the rest of the gaunt, aristocratic face under a long forehead and thinning, gelled-back hair. He was in tweeds, too, and that topped it off to make him look like he was off to a fancy-dress ball as Sherlock Holmes, the wisest guy of all time.

'You feel free to smoke your pipe, man,' Kennedy said. 'Just tell me, though, if you're going to start shooting off that service revolver of yours.'

Sherlock said, '*Sí.*'

'See...what?'

Sherlock was from near Malaga in Spain. As well as his noble Spanish, he spoke a little French, but that was it. Kennedy was sceptical about how a guy could get around Eastern Europe with no German or English.

Sherlock told Kennedy the names of the countries he had been in – Germany, Austria, Hungary, Czechoslovakia – and the two of them mimed acts performed by travelling fools, about the catching of trains, and the sleeping in rooms, the reading of books.

Kennedy said, 'Cervantes, very good.' Sherlock's face said he had never bothered with Cervantes, not knowing that Kennedy had actually given up in despair at around page sixteen thousand. 'Lorca too,' Kennedy tried.

Sherlock found a frown, said, 'Jack Higgings?'

'Oh, right.' The name was familiar. Kennedy matched the frown. 'What'd he write?'

It looked to Kennedy like some book about a guy who shot people, a lot. They gave up on the discussion of literature.

They had a bench to themselves. Eventually, Sherlock wished Kennedy goodnight and, weirdly, shook his hand, then curled into a babe-like sleep, and he dreamed, Kennedy had to guess, about pursuing master criminals down smoky Victorian alleys. Kennedy read bits of Don's script again, wishing he could have a slug of the bathtub gin that trickled through the text.

Then he too slept. He watched a freaky dream in which Ginger Rogers stood in front of him in spangles and sang a song he recognised, kind of, but for which he could not make out the words. This would not have been so bad, except for his panic that he had lost the ability to understand and speak American. It was going through his dream-mind about how no-doubt-about-it embarrassing it would be to go back to Istanbul and tell that to the principal at the school he taught at. He would have to mime a plea to be given something else to do to work out his contract, keep the yard swept and the latrines sloshed maybe, or maybe dust the five books they kept in what they were fond of referring to as the library. Ginger's face was up close to his, made grotesque with her throwing her eyes up to Heaven the whole time she sang, to make her irises almost vanish.

Even in the dream, he could see this as a vision born of anxiety, to do with being stuck in a place where he knew maybe two words of the language: nightmare on Czech-Polish Border Street. A freight train came and obscured Ginger's face, and its rattle made the music fade, and then Kennedy was sitting up, or was dreaming of sitting up, watching a long line of wooden-sided wagons slide by in the dark, and as he began to count them he was lying down again, his eyes closing, the screen in his brain going blank.

Next morning, Kennedy thought it would be swell if they could get a hold of one of those little hand-pumped platforms on bogies, so they could screech along the rails to Ostrava in pure Stan-and-Ollie style. Not having intended to stay in Czechoslovakia, he had not one red cent of Czech money for trainfare into Ostrava. He tried anyhow with the babooshka in the ticket booth as soon as she showed up. He hailed her with, 'Hi, madam, what kept you?' She glared from under Brezhnev eyebrows. He said in his smoothest Boss Cat tones, 'Ostrava, my good lady, in dollars, if that's okay.' It was not. About to protest, Kennedy guessed right away that she simply did not want the hassle of foreign currency, and he refrained from giving her a hard time about it. As if he would, in any case, woman with eyebrows like that. That was not going to get him anyplace soon, though.

'Sherlock,' he begged, and he made a mime. 'Can you please sub me?'

Sherlock mimed back, *Elementary*, and it was done.

Pretty soon they were on a one-car shuttle full of blue-overall-clad Casey Joneses, or else people who really had to get into town at a quarter to six in the morning, whose missions were so important they could not roll over and stay in bed another hour. In this select company, which reeked of both coal and aftershave, they clattered into Ostrava.

Ostrava

Surprisingly, for a town nobody had ever heard of, Ostrava had an airplane hangar of a station. Over the PA system Kennedy heard what he thought was Frankie Lymon and the Teenagers singing *I'm not a Juvenile Delinquent*. A song not heard on any radio station for at least three decades, that seemed bizarre and downright impossible, and indeed it turned out to be Cyndi Lauper with her *Girls Just Want to Have Fu-un*.

Kennedy got more shakes of the head when he tried to buy coffees for Sherlock and himself with his dollars. He tried with some Yugoslav dinars, his change from his Belgrade hotel, and the vendors laughed. Kennedy could honestly not blame them. He had a shitload of dollars, though, had a Visa card, an Amex card, covered in spiderwebs, okay, but still...He could have had the Midas touch, but they were not about to have any of it.

'You got to sub me into town, Sherlock,' he concluded. 'See?'

Sherlock would have done so too, Kennedy was sure, but he had no more Czech money, being a careful traveller all done with Czechoslovakia. Or so he had assumed.

Kennedy renewed the hustle in the station, tried to have people swap him some Czech koruns for dollars, but there was nothing doing. He thought, *This is really not happening.* But it was. Or wasn't. He thought how in any rail station in Europe you stood there with it daygloed on your forehead that you were an American overseas, and guys made a line at you to hiss, *Change money?* Not in Ostrava, though. Kennedy and Sherlock exchanged a look of surrender, then set off through the arched doors of the station and into the crisp air, a fall of snow light and dry as feathers coming down on them.

'What if it's a Polish national holiday?' Kennedy mused to his grave companion. 'Hey? Or the Pope died. Huh? Stuck in this godawful town the rest of the week till they finish mourning and drinking at the consulate?'

But in fact, Ostrava looked okay to Kennedy. He found out later that it was a town raised by dedicated communists, honeycombed by coalmines, foundries and factories. Kennedy kind of liked its brutalist buildings, with their reliefs of working people, the amphetamine eyes, locomotive chins and steroid forearms of socialist art. He had not seriously expected them to show bad-tempered people waiting in line for bread and meat. He liked the look of the stores, and savoured the smell from the coffee shops, even though it was driving him nuts.

In the town centre they found a bank due to open at eight. Kennedy and Sherlock perched on a stone seat and froze, miming only occasionally. Kennedy was first in line for the bank people to do their stuff. There was as always something beautiful about all that cash being changed and handed over, and it being his to go spend like a fool. He saluted the woman behind the grille, and she liked that and grinned, and saluted back. All through this, Sherlock hung back; he was not going to change money, was still on out of Czechoslovakia. The trainfare he paid was maybe ten decimal places the wrong side of a cent, but Kennedy did not care. Without it, he would have been back in the siding right then, panhandling along with the Romanies. 'We breakfast,' he reminded Sherlock, and led him down the marble stair.

Outside, they were approached by a guy in an orange leather jacket that clashed with the red jeans that led down to his blue cowboy boots. He cut a way through the grey winter people, and blew air through a lopsided moustache. He said – and Kennedy was reluctant to believe it, and decided even as it happened not to even try to pass it off as a traveller's tale – 'Change money?'

'Where were you,' he heard himself inquire, 'when we needed you, you doofus?'

'You will now change money.' The man bowed his head in a curt nod, and patted a pocket. He was formal as a lawyer, and Kennedy had to laugh. Even Sherlock, belly begging for his breakfast, laughed. Hell, the guy even joined in himself, and that made it grotesque, made it three guys on a cold street, laughing at nothing.

'How much?' The man's smile disappeared, and he was all business.

Kennedy bade him, 'Guess,' and the man looked puzzled. He told him, '*Nada*,' and the man made an impatient face and fanned his hand.

Monkey spanker, Kennedy thought, as he latched on to Sherlock's arm and barked, 'We're outside the bank and walking away. Work it out for yourself, Einstein.'

They found a food joint, brown and dark and busy but peaceful too, radio way down in the mix, classy but at the same time down-to-earth. Outside, Ostrava's people went about their business, and Kennedy and Sherlock felt glad to be on vacation as they watched people get off buses and slush along the streets, cross square-cut thresholds into offices and stores, ghost figures as the snow came down and hid them.

There was something about breakfast, especially on vacation, that made Kennedy think all was good with the world: no wars, no famine, no home shopping channels on TV, no people playing Lionel Ritchie songs, no orange leather jackets for guys to put on and approach you in.

'This is the life, Sherl.' Kennedy waved a hand over their spread. 'Right?'

Sherlock said, '*Si.*'

'Fucking A.'

Sherlock liked that, repeated it with a smile, and Kennedy put that smile on too, abandoning it only for more drinking of the best coffee he had ever had.

The Polish consulate

Legendary black-and-white big screen actor Sydney Greenstreet was alive and giant as ever and settled behind the consul's desk in the Polish consulate. Despite the PC monitor to one side of him, he had brought his office intact from the nineteen forties, had an astrakhan hat hung on a peg over a big dark coat, surely had a revolver in his desk drawer. He greeted Kennedy and Sherlock happily, and Kennedy assumed that the sum of everything that ever happened in a town like Ostrava had to be close to zilch. The consul spoke English like an Englishman, and confirmed that he had done a stretch in the London consulate. Kennedy assumed that he had to have screwed up monumentally to have wound up in Ostrava, maybe mistook the English queen's daughter, Kennedy could not recall her name, for a horse, and tried to mount her.

As the consul spoke into a phone to summon their paperwork, and to rustle up yet more coffee, Kennedy winked at Sherlock, and promised, 'Poland will be cool.'

'My observations inform me,' Sherlock declared, 'that, with the outside temperature at minus fifteen, Poland will not be merely cool, but rather, cold enough to freeze the nuts off of a Good Humour man.' At least, Kennedy thought he had to be saying something like that.

The consul asked them as a matter of form the purposes of their visits. He did not speak Spanish. Who did, Kennedy wondered, apart from Spaniards, and a lot of central and South Americans, and the harassed, hairy-legged woman who used to try to teach the language to Kennedy in high school? The consul had neat, effortless French, though, and he and Sherlock rapped away in that for a while.

'My friend's book,' Kennedy began to tell the consul. He saw clear as gin Don Darius's sun-flooded apartment in Bakirköy, could not associate that light with anything real anymore. 'I made a copy, see, but I'm bringing him the original, and when it gets published it'll rescue him from the...stew he lives his life in.'

'Stew.' A true linguist, Mister Greenstreetski was considering, Kennedy could tell, the use of the word in its improper place. 'Interesting.'

'Booze.' Kennedy did a drinking hand. 'Disillusion. Being disgusted with the world and...afraid of it, I think. But also...' A conversation snatched once with Don came back to him. 'You know, a kind of deep kind of...*anguish* about how literature is refusing to reflect real life these days. You know? Not just literature, though. Culture in general. American culture in particular,' he had to admit. 'Gone conservative, and obsessed with the family, and American guilt, and the past, and...well. You know.'

There was a silence, in which both the consul and Sherlock stared at Kennedy, and Kennedy abandoned his babble with an attempt at a goofy self-deprecating face.

'No,' the consul admitted, 'I don't know at all.' And Kennedy, impressed by the consul's frankness, only just had time to register that it was not a statement that required an answer. 'But why did your friend leave this typescript behind him?' Kennedy's host scratched the corner of his mouth with a paper knife.

'I don't know.' Good question, though, Kennedy had to agree. Don Darius winged him a postcard once in a while, a few lines making a tired joke, or surreal observations that mostly made him go, *What the fuck?*, or went over his head. He did not write Kennedy letters about literature; genuine men and women of letters belonged to a different age, he had decided. 'I didn't even know his book existed,' Kennedy told Mister SG. 'Then it kind of turned into one of those mysteries that gets you out of your armchair and onto trains, investigating. But, uh, I always wanted to visit Poland,' he thought it diplomatic to add, though tell the truth Poland had never been first on his list, or even tenth. 'And – sorry – but I forgot to check out the visa situation in my haste to get there.' The consul waved the explanation graciously away.

The coffee came, and they all sipped. Kennedy thought how downright odd it was to be in a room with two guys who were dead ringers for other guys. *Wild*, he chuckled to himself, *Wait'll I tell Don.*

'What is your friend's book about?' The consul asked Kennedy the inevitable question after a little more exercise of his French. That was so neat, Kennedy felt, how the man just skipped in and out of languages; he was an accomplished man, with a real agility of the mind that made that bulk of his perform leaps. That was the way to go: make the inside of your head light up and come alive with the power of the word.

He said, 'My friend's book is about Americans in Saudi Arabia, see, who are like slaves, but slaves of a higher caste than all the other slaves, the Filipinos, the Palestinians, the Yemenis, the Indians, right, and all this is set against flashbacks to slaves from, like, everywhere in the Ottoman Empire.'

'Mm-hm.' Kennedy's audience did not seem too impressed, and even Sherlock had an incredulous face on. 'I see.'

'You know, but it's more than that.' Kennedy hung on in. 'It's lyrical and beautiful, and the thing that shines out is the spirit of people and what they do to keep their identities and their humour and their humanity once they get to rise above stuff like nationality and religion and their places in the food chain. And it shows that, bottom line, it doesn't matter if you're a higher-class slave, because you're still a slave, and you still got to do something about it, and…Well, hey, you'll read it one day.' Kennedy knew right then that Don Darius's book would come out in a classy imprint. 'I'll send you a copy as soon as it comes out,' he promised, and amended, 'well…when it hits paperback, anyhow. And you'll know then what I'm talking about.'

'You are a friend indeed,' the consul concluded.

Kennedy moved shoulders modestly, and mumbled a corny, 'Well…What are friends for, after all…' but thought, *No, I'm just a fool, and I had to make some distance between me and Istanbul, and this is about me, and here I am, and I'm no longer sure why that should be.*

They went through the business of the visas, and Kennedy and Sherlock got stamps in their passports, parted with money, and then with their kind host. He went to the door with the two men, shook their hands gently, and sent them on their way.

Is that service, or what, Kennedy thought, *if Poland is going to be like that, point me there*, even though he was headed that way anyhow.

Ostrava

Outside the consulate Kennedy and Sherlock had to make their own parting of the ways. Sherlock was aching to get along to Poland, it became clear, but it had just hit Kennedy that he had never visited Czechoslovakia, and that he really ought to, and he heard himself say, 'I'm going to check things out here. See?'

'Fucking A,' Sherlock agreed, but a little dumb-show had to follow till at last his face, on the verge of an understanding *oh*, was crossed by a touch of disappointment. Truth be told, Kennedy too was a little heart-ached not to be sharing the rest of the journey with his impromptu friend. That was the way it had to be though, sometimes, when you upped and ran errands across continents. As they shook hands, Kennedy swore he would remember Sherlock, and Ostrava, and the consul, and the siding in the ass-end of no place at all, forever. Then, with a final wave, Sherlock was gone, disappearing into the snow like the prototype Holmes off into the spray of the Reichenbach Falls. Kennedy thought what an *hombre* he was, and wished him the most well in the world.

One thing Kennedy wanted in Ostrava was not to see any more people who looked like somebody else, for a start. Whatever else he wanted, he guessed he would find it as he moved through town.

He was walking along singing to himself that nonsense song about how a girl in Constantinople turned into a girl in Istanbul, could not get it off the playlist in his mind. He went into a store and bought three painted eggs for Ling, his own Istanbul girl. From a kiosk on the street he bought a postcard and a stamp. Then he stopped in a place and drank even more coffee and wrote on the card: *Ling I miss you and need you and wish you were here with me right now as I sit here czeching out Ostrava, January ninety two, Year of the Friend Indeed. Think of me and I'll think of you and our thoughts will surely fly the continent and hook up.* That was all there was room for, but it seemed complete. He appended the Chinese characters that spelled out *seeya later*, and felt kind of good as he read through the words. Then he thought how Ling was not there, and felt so sad that, just for a second or two, he could have hanged himself from one of the wooden beams above him.

Instead, he reached into a pocket and pulled out a scrap of yellow silk. It was all that was left of a hanky Ling had left at his place after he had unwisely chucked it into the seam-tearing button-pulling sock-munching washing machine in his apartment. He stretched it between his fingers and let the light through it, saw the suggestion of blossoms etched into it, then put it away carefully – too late for care, of course. She had never asked him about it, and at times he wondered if she had left it with him as a token of her expectations, like women did in medieval times…or was it Victorian?

It was amazing to Kennedy that he had a girl at all, never mind the only Chinese girl in Istanbul. When he was a teen, he had seen himself at this moment, a guy out in the world someplace, alone and thinking about a girl and feeling shot to pieces. At least, he thought he had. There he was, in any case.

Kennedy had first seen Ling when he was eighteen. She would have been twelve at the time, but that did not matter; she was fully-formed and perfect. Her hair was cut short, and she was wearing what she wore when Kennedy finally met her, a skirtsuit in green heather mix, green ankle socks and chunky brown shoes with a buttoned strap across. She had a blue jewel on a gold chain at her throat. She was shockingly and heart-shakingly beautiful. She had put a warning finger to her lips, stopped Kennedy asking her name. She had risen out of a field in Kennedy's head across which he had scattered heroin for the first time. When he saw Ling, he understood what heroin was, and why he was messing with his yin and yang by doing what he was doing. He had set about finding the figments that refused to populate the world around him, convinced that America was nothing more than an unreal state of mind, and that the real world lay in those fields, waiting to be sown and grown. He was bitten by the cruelty and sadness in that world, saw the fields grow streets of steps, towers and spires and domes and arches and blind niches and doorways, all hiding his good Chinese lady.

In Ostrava, he wanted to buy a fistful of *jetons*, call Ling and find out what she was doing right then. She would be sat in front of her terminal, maybe, writing Kennedy one of the letters she sent across Istanbul once a week or more, writing him how she felt about a whole bunch of things because, she claimed, she could not trap words in English long enough to say them. Another missive, he guessed, on the grand theme of Istanbul itself, and what they thought they were going to do without its crowds to hide in. Kennedy would add it to the stack of correspondence from her, to be pondered on late nights without her.

We are people overseas, she had embedded in her last, the ten-page beast Kennedy had in his bag. *If we are not overseas we have no voice, and without our foreignness we have no reason to exist.* Did that mean anything? He was not sure.

Outside lay a white afternoon scattered with the hurrying shapes of people not knowing they were in a very strange town. Kennedy saw that it stopped short of beauty if you could not show it to somebody you loved. He resisted the impulse to head back to Istanbul right then; he was on vacation, he reminded himself, and he could not spend it hurting at the absence of Ling. Could things really be that bad? He thought about his hard-won Polish visa too, the cold of the railroad night still in his bones. He thought about Don Darius's book. He took it out and began reading parts of it, and let the time drift.

'I'm in Ostrava,' he was telling Don, hours – he did not know how many – later.

'You are?' Don bellowed. 'Oh. Okay. And where is that?'

'Spent the night with Sherlock Holmes.' That sounded so weird that Kennedy had to check whether he had imagined it or not.

'He have a dawg?'

'Listen.'

'He have his doctor friend with him, Doctor McCoy?'

'Spent the morning with him and Sydney Greenstreet. You know Sydney Greenstreet, the big fat wiseguy in all those old Humphrey Bogart movies?'

'Well, who doesn't?'

Kennedy thought he knew the tones in Don's voice well. Don was on the early laps of the race that led to *drunk*. Having not eaten, he was empty, troubled by things he could not name with the spoken word. He asked Kennedy in a burst of enthusiasm, 'Hey, you know the difference between a laxative and an emetic?' Kennedy said he did, thanks, and Don said, 'Oh, well, that's okay, then, just thought I ought to –'

'Your book.' That drew only a weary *oh right* out of Don. 'It's a beauty, man. It's got to get into print.'

'Oh. Okay, Kennedy. But – '

'Now, listen. Here's the thing.'

'What thing?'

'Tell me you did another draft,' Kennedy said.

'Why?'

'Why?' Kennedy tried to sound speechless and, after a second of pointless silence, gave up. 'Because I don't want to hear that you just wrote it, right, and left it behind you in Istanbul, is why. Tell me you got it there, right, and you're, you know, revising it, whatever. Right?'

'Okay.' Don suddenly sounded infuriatingly bright. 'Whatever you say. But listen.'

'No. *You* listen. I'm on the way.' Kennedy looked at his watch. 'I'm just missing the Warsaw train. I'll get the midday one tomorrow, okay? Be in Warsaw late tomorrow afternoon. Right? You'll come and meet me at the station?'

'I'll be there,' Don shoved in at the end of a pause.

'Listen, then. Tomorrow, Warsaw. Right?'

'I'll *be* there.'

'*Watson*,' Kennedy said, but Don had gone, and he was talking to the airwaves. 'Doctor *Watson*, you moron.'

Kennedy found a hotel down whose corridors he had to walk for ten minutes to his room, even though he seemed to be the only guest. He thought how only a few years before they probably packed it with tour groups from other Soviet Bloc countries. There would also have been bus trips of westerners in socks and sandals who were able to admire the mindfuck that was Eastern Bloc communism precisely because they did not have it at home; they were surely brought on tours of Ostrava to be shown a jewel in socialism's crown – well, a gleaming rivet in its hammer, anyhow.

The place was as silent and eerie as the hotel in *The Shining*. Quite honestly, on this day of what the Germans called *doppelgängers*, Kennedy would not have been surprised to see Jack Nicholson gone ape and coming at him down the corridor with an axe. He would certainly have been alarmed, though, would have shat his pants and run.

He could have used some sleep, but then remembered all the coffee he had drunk, and decided that, as he was there, he should seek out what there might be of Ostrava's night scene. Soon he was watching himself in mirror windows, tramping the streets and turning corners. He saw a friendly-looking bar and went in, had a beer in a huge glass that had on it the crossed hammers motif of the east European miner. As he lifted it, he realised how they had worked those forearms. Then he hit a restaurant, scarfed down a serving of a local dish that turned out to be fillet of jokestore rubber chicken, drank a little more beer.

In a corner sprawled a group of American college kids; sounded to Kennedy a lot like freshman year. He was just thinking of getting up and going over to them, then caught a girl complaining tinnily about her pizza, picking bits out of it and holding them up, going, 'What *is* this?' Kennedy got real close to yelling over, *It's a frigging olive, what do you think...* One of the guys was talking about how they rilly *rilly* had to meet this *dude* he knew in some *town* someplace in *wherever*, because he was so, like, *cool?* Kennedy finished up and got out of there, and away from the calamity to which eavesdropping could sometimes lead.

In the street, he felt totally wiped. Trudging through the snow became tiring then, that and the burden of being a friend indeed. Kennedy's thoughts careered in and out, fonts changing, going big and small and plain and fancy, and he let them write themselves onto the snow so that he could follow the trail of them back to the hotel.

The train

The next day brought another seat on another of those trains that all looked the same; more dealings with those border people who all said the same goddam thing. This time Kennedy was able to show the visa for which he had paid good money to a man from the black-and-white past.

Soon he had crossed into Poland, which seemed as grey as people said it was when they could not think of anything intelligent to say about it.

He talked to a kid of maybe sixteen who boarded at Katowice. The kid's English was slow and elegant, and he asked Kennedy questions about use of English, which filled the time. When he asked Kennedy what he was doing in his country, Kennedy started to tell the kid about Don's book. The kid did not seem too interested, and Kennedy guessed that he would have been the same at the kid's age.

Not true, though, he reflected later. When Kennedy was fourteen or so he had gone to the town library and asked if they had any books by Rimbaud. He remembered the librarian going, 'I think you mean *Rambo*,' and Kennedy bleating authoritatively, 'That's *Rim-baud*, lady,' and her laughing, and summoning her pal over to *get this from this wacko kid.* The old stick insect.

'You remember communism?' Kennedy asked the kid on the train. The kid remembered it all right, but had nothing to say about it that Kennedy did not already know. The brutality of the system never seemed to be at the forefront of people's minds, Kennedy had noticed; it was the skull-numbing boredom that stayed with them, all those times they waited in line for essentials, knowing there had to be another way.

The train shuffled them through Silesia, Poland's industrial heartland. The place looked like it could use a facelift. Kennedy saw a lot of churches; some were old baroque and gothic, steeples and towers dwarfed among the chimneys of heavy industry, but some were enormous post-modern hulks that looked like stricken spaceships. Kennedy thought the Poles should have worked crosses and chimneys into their flag, though he did not mention that to the kid. Being American, and living in Turkey, he had come to learn how seriously people took their flags.

He asked the kid if he had ever read Joseph Conrad, and he said yes. They talked for a while about how weird it was that for Poles to read the work of this Polish genius it had to be translated from the eloquent English in which he had written it. The kid also liked Agatha Christie. Kennedy thought that a little sad, though he was not sure why. The kid redeemed himself a minute later, when he said he liked Pearl Jam, and Sonic Youth, Nirvana, and REM, and they talked music for some time. Kennedy had to remind the kid that there was not much to be gained from finding out the lyrics to songs – they meant nothing much, and you just had to get off on the poetry and the sound of them, or not at all. If the kid liked that line about being in the corner and losing your religion that REM were right then whining out of radios all over Christian eastern Europe and Islamic Turkey, then liking it was as far as thinking ought to stray.

'My whole country is losing its religion,' the kid told Kennedy.

Kennedy said, 'You just got it back,' but no: the church was for old people, the kid claimed, who needed another institution in their lives to beef about. It was not for the kid, and his generation would find something else. And no, he did not know what it was – nobody did; a lot of the fun would be in finding out. 'You're cool,' Kennedy concluded.

Driven by the demands of the moment, and in return for a tape the kid gave him of some Polish band, Kennedy gave him the copy of Bret Easton Ellis's *Less Than Zero* he had been going to pass on to Don. It made him happy to see the kid get absorbed in the first few pages as they tracked along. Kennedy put on the music the kid gave him, and let its urgency rock him through the country that, even as it invited him in, zipped itself up in the garb of its impossible weather and let him know that it was going to freeze his ass off.

Two

Warsaw

The fields glowed pale in the dark afternoon, then shaded and faded. The factories got denser, and joined up with apartment buildings that forced the houses and stores to drop out of sight. Warsaw made itself up out the window until its Palace of Culture showed as a tower of lights, sprung up in the way to stop travellers.

They were dumped in what looked to Kennedy like a New York subway station. He stood among a crowd of people wrapped in their winter wear, weighed down by bags, fixed on the antics of travel. He bid the kid goodbye, and the kid wished him a good time. Kennedy stood and searched faces.

He wondered if Don was bombed, laid out on a floor someplace and watching the ceiling doing its comic spinning stuff. He let out long breaths and said *fuck* a few times, which did not help.

An escalator led him up into the fluxing madness of Warsaw Central station's main hall, which was part-mall and part-cathedral. He was waiting in line at a booth to change some money when he spied the slowly-moving back of a guy who looked a lot like Don Darius, and turned out to be him.

The man who joined Kennedy in response to his yell was thinner than Kennedy remembered, a little more pinched in the cheeks, he thought, a little more washed-out around the eyes. Under the harsh lights, his skin looked like a patchwork of shades between ivory and cabbage. Kennedy saw that under his beanie hat Don had shaved his head, which had to mean, with no religion to lose, he was losing his hair.

'Hey.'

'How *are* you?'

'Yeah, good. And good to see you, man.'

'But without a doubt.'

Once Kennedy had handed over dollars at the booth and received in return a wheelbarrow full of Polish zlotys, Don guided him through the people and round the kiosks and concrete piers, past windows and through doors and out of the station. Kennedy caught a kaleidoscope of frowning buildings, quick-moving hordes, and little cars chugging along like they smoked two packs of Marlboro a day. He said, 'So, Warsaw, man,' and Don Darius whooped, and beckoned, and promised to show it to him.

They started with Don leading Kennedy in and out of a leaden ballet of traffic, across streetcar lines and into a crowd at a bus stop. They fought their way onto a bus, and Don breathed wariness into Kennedy's ear; buses were favourite haunts for Warsaw's rip-off artists to strut their repugnant stuff. Kennedy could have guessed that, but appreciated the advice anyhow, and kept a tight hold of his bag.

What Don had forgotten to warn Kennedy was that Warsaw buses were also a good spot for Warsaw Corporation bus ticket inspectors to strut their particular stuff. The bus had crawled only a hundred yards when a guy was in Kennedy's face with a badge, unravelling his ticket-inspecting spiel. Kennedy took a look at Don, who was gazing pointedly at the route map. Kennedy had to stall the guy by turning his back on him, which was hardly the most cunning move he could have made. An inspecting hand was on Kennedy's shoulder by then, so Kennedy turned and let the inspector know that he did not speak Polish. He did not know how he was going to do it, but he wanted to put over too that he was not the kind of guy who avoided paying his bus-fare, especially when it probably worked out at under a nickel. The man was getting very pissed at him by then, going *bilet, bilet*. And because Kennedy was obviously too dense to know this international word, the inspector had taken a ticket out and was showing it to him. Kennedy looked at it like it was a fish caught the week before, and refreshed the man's memory on his lack of Polish.

The bus burped and strained, and concertinaed passengers into one another for an undignified second, suggesting an imminent stop. Don winked over the inspector's shoulder, said, 'We're off at this one, Mister President.' Kennedy started to move with the other bodies, his new pal with him all the way. The inspector was in *excited* mode by then, and from his intonation Kennedy could work out that he was not inviting him to go home and eat dinner with himself and Mrs Inspector and the little Inspectors.

The inspector did not seem to be intimidated by Don looming over him; it had to be Don's inane grin alone that disarmed the man into taking his hand off Kennedy's shoulder. He was glad of the chance to take five from his dumbo tourist part and let Don take a turn.

'We are unversed in your fine language, sir,' Don was claiming, 'although, you know, I wish we knew it. And then we could all, like, communicate, and maybe smoke a little Gunter Grass together. What say, sir?'

The guy did not seem to be grabbed by this idea. He had a little book out, not literature of any kind, had to be a book of penalty tickets. He was growling by then at Don, who had started on a tetchy litany of *Hey, come on, sir*.

To hell with it, Kennedy was waiting for a good moment to say, *let's pay up and be done with the thing*. It was getting nasty, and all over a few lousy dollars. The inspector was just a working stiff doing his job, and it was Don's fault for not reminding Kennedy he needed a ticket in advance – in fact, the fault lay entirely with Kennedy, he anticipated, for not reminding Don to remind him.

Farce stepped in to save the comedy from becoming drama, in the form of a gangly guy in a leather coat and with a head of tight curls like in German porn movies from the seventies… not that Kennedy had ever seen any of them, he had to remind himself later. The guy had the pubic moustache to go with the hairdo, and he shoved this ensemble into the triangle of heads to make a square. Gladly diverted, Kennedy was about to quiz the new arrival about his bad hair day when he shook Don warmly by the glove, saying in nice clear English, 'I say, here, Don, can I help you, please?' This inquiry got Don doing little-boy shakes of the head, big round eyes, a show of teeth. The guy then bent his head to the inspector's, and he listened, and nodded, his face full of *language*, then began to tell Don earnestly that Kennedy's ticket was in sore need of inspection and, if he was not in fact in legal possession of one, then, regretfully, the usual ticketless traveller procedure was about to occur. 'You're being really helpful,' Don assured the guy, who processed the words in a terrible solemnity, and pronounced it to be nothing. 'Thanks a whole bunch.'

The Samaritan was one of Don's students, it turned out. Nice guy, they had to conclude later, because as the conversation took this new turn they were doing Charlie Chaplin little tramp jaywalks, the inspector doing Ben Turpin as he crossed his eyes and shook a fist at them. They wibble-wobbled across the road, dodging its cars and the looming, lit-up faces of its streetcars, their bells ringing like it was Christmas still, and got out of there.

That led them into a street bright with little stores in which, bizarrely, it *was* Christmas still. Kennedy, wondering how to thank Don for his baptism in cheapskate embarrassment, could not help but stop to check out the phenomenon. 'It's January twenty second,' he observed.

'Twenty third.'

'Well.' When Don pointed that out, Kennedy remembered his accidental night on the border, and felt a chill swoop over his bones. 'Whatever. But – '

'The Christmas decorations stay up here till February first.'

'Jesus.'

'That's the guy. Day they take them down they hold what they call Carnival. I looked forward to that a lot when people talked it up. Rio in Warsaw, in February, I thought, had to be a must-see. But you know what they do?'

'Would I?'

'What they do is visit each other, and stuff their faces with jelly doughnuts.'

'Jelly doughnuts? That's it?'

'That's it. I tried to find the, ah, the sub-text of the thing, but that's about it.'

'They ought to call it Dentists' Day,' Kennedy thought out loud.

'That's the next day.'

Kennedy told Don about a kid who was at junior high with him. He was a wan, mousy-looking kid called Theo Krashen, and his clothes never looked exactly right. He had a weird laugh and his own secret smile, and most of the other kids disdained him, but Kennedy saw that he was junior Beat. Like Kennedy, he took time out of school to go hang out in town and play pool and pinball and smoke weed. Anyhow, the only time

Kennedy had gone to Theo's place, first off Theo's mom removed a shoe and started bashing Theo over the head with it as soon as he got in the door; Kennedy never did find out why. With her free hand, she showed Kennedy into the lounge. The room was decked out with cards, paper chains and a baubled tree surrounded by brown pine needles: it was Santa's grotto in there. It was also the middle of June.

'Vermont.' Don shook his head. 'Insane, crazy people.'

'Yeah.' Kennedy snorted. 'Unlike the…*balanced* people of *Texas*.'

Kennedy did not want to talk about Vermont, or Texas, about crazy people or Christmas. He wanted to talk about Don's book. But then the etiquette of the thing kicked in. Some writers were precious individuals who, if you tried to talk about their work, protested with a show of modesty that they did not want to cheapen their *oeuvre* with crass discussion; if you did not try, though, they would get sore at you, and soon start telling you about it. Kennedy fell to thinking that he might go for option two.

In the meantime, he was enjoying stretching his legs after all that time on the train, and enjoying the look of the city around him. He watched it out the corner of his eye as Don splashed daubs on his big picture since leaving Istanbul.

Don was teaching at a couple of places, he said, and liked it, kind of, as much as anybody ever could ever like teaching English. He was also doing some private lessons. 'Hey, I do other stuff, too,' he mentioned, and that was Kennedy's cue to ask him what the hell he had meant by leaving the script of his book behind him in the trash.

Don just held a hand up and asked, 'Well, how *is* It's Damn Bull?'

He had always called it that. Kennedy knew Don did not give a shit how the place was: Don had done Istanbul, and if the people he had known there wanted to stay in such a place, ran his view, then they were all slaves mesmerised by the ghost of the Ottoman Empire. Don had often said that when he was there, and Kennedy had seen the words given more eloquent life in the Saudi novel.

'Same as it ever was,' Kennedy told him. 'Everybody leaving, everybody staying. Nobody knowing why the bejesus they're there. As always.'

'Except you.'

'Except me.' Kennedy put on a weary smile. He knew what was coming.

'How's Flat Face?'

'Don't call her that.'

Kennedy's girl Ling did indeed have a flat face; it was a characteristic of some Chinese people. She had a permanent look of quiet astonishment. One of her black irises turned a little outward; sometimes she looked as if about to burst into tears. Her mouth was small and undoubtedly petulant – imperious, Kennedy sometimes thought. She had sturdy legs, slender hands and feet, and a body that looked shapeless in clothes. And Kennedy loved all of her: from her flat feet to her flat chest to her neat, flat face.

Ling's old man, big cheese on the staff of the Chinese consulate, kind of liked Kennedy, Ling had said. And so far as that went, he had been cordial to Kennedy on the two occasions on which they had met, but had managed to make it plain that, whatever happened, Ling would go back to China to start at business school and meet a well-heeled Chinese capitalist to marry; Kennedy was not going to stand in the way of that, was he, the path planned out for Ling by those gods they held dear? Having chipped away at his impossible chore as ambassador's man for a truly alien nation, Ling's dad knew that his own culture, no matter its shortcomings, was the only one for his only darling daughter.

'Well,' Kennedy said to Don, 'if you're really…concerned, it's going nowhere with Ling.'

From an archive of his nightmares he caught a scene showing Ling disappearing into an industrial centre in some treeless Chinese province, and a pain striped him all the way down through his insides. He got a premonition of what would happen to him once she was gone, saw himself on his own by the Marmara Sea, crying the corny old tears of those who carry torches.

Maybe Don caught the scene in Kennedy's face. Kennedy saw some cheap crack form and swallow itself all in one breath. Don said softly, 'Listen. You got to get out of there.'

'I'm going to.'

'When?'

Kennedy saw Milton flicker across Don's face, declaiming *Eyeless in Gaza, at the mill with slaves.*

'When Ling leaves.' The idea revealed itself to Kennedy right at that moment, but in truth there had never been a different plan.

'Jesus.'

Plenty of people said they would leave Istanbul someday, when this happened or that came to pass. A lot of them never did, and some said they would stay there till the end of their days, then were suddenly gone.

Kennedy guessed that Don saw him there with Ling forever, doing an endless odd couple walk under minarets and city walls. The idea of Don's being so vexed at the notion drew a surprised laugh out of Kennedy, which got Don going, *what, what*, in the voice of a little boy.

The vision of Istanbul faded. Ahead of Kennedy stretched the same narrow, busy street, lined with imposing buildings fronted incongruously by those little lit-up stores with their twinklers and Santas, their signs in a language that was recognizable, yet possibly put together under candlelight. Little cars honked squeaky horns, and people kept up a continual criss-cross on the sidewalks.

'So, hey, listen.' Kennedy decided he might as well take some advantage of Don's consternation. 'Your book.'

'My book?'

Kennedy stared, said nothing.

'Oh, okay,' Don decided to say. 'Well, what about it?'

'What…*about* it?'

'Yes. What *about* it?'

'Uh, well.' Kennedy felt blackmailed into feeling foolish. '*Tell* me about it.'

'I don't know,' Don began, and he stopped, as if the effort of thinking precluded walking. 'I guess I just wanted to tell about what they got there, over there, in Saudi. I thought maybe if I kept it to myself it might…poison me. You know what I mean?'

'*Poison* you?'

'Yes.'

'*What?*' Kennedy thought about the claim with some suspicion. He took a look at Don's face, but it told him nothing. He saw the first scene out of the book: a guy wakes up under the burning horror of a noonday sun and wanders on black sand between Saudi and Iraq, watching, and watched by, little specks that turn out to be border guards with guns and no English and not much patience. 'Well, you *do* tell it, man. And people have got to read it.'

They set off on walking again, but it was Kennedy who set off on the talking. And Don neither agreed nor disagreed, made most of his responses with shoulders and hands. Kennedy asked questions about this part and that, and finally trailed the questions away.

'Had to get it all out of me.' Don's eyes looked odd; closed when they were open, kind of scary. 'You know what I'm telling you here?'

'Hey.' Kennedy thought he did. 'Ah, come *on.*'

'I did it for me.' Don nodded.

'Yeah, right.' Kennedy made his lips purse to say, *Per-lease, with this* artiste *crap.* 'You left it behind in the apartment. Why didn't you just destroy it, if it was so…so – what? So *personal?*'

'I put it in the trash. I left you the key to the apartment so you could pick up…a food mixer gizmo, hah? And that little heater that'll fry your liver at ten paces? What were you doing going through my trash? Did you bring the fishbones and coffee grounds and empty cans?'

'Got them right here in my bag for you.'

'What?' Don laughed. 'Listen.'

'What?'

'How *is* that heater doing? Does it… you know – *heat* and all?'

'You written anything else?'

'What's it to you?'

Good question, maybe, but Kennedy overrode it with the words, 'Junk this shit, man, and tell me.'

'Okay, okay. But let's get out of this…*weather*, and get someplace and get warm.'

He led Kennedy on a line up that street, flanked by municipal signs displaying mermaids. Distracted by them, Kennedy asked Don what the deal was with mermaids.

'The *syrenka*,' Don said. 'Symbol of Warsaw.'

'Mermaids are cool.' Kennedy had always kind of liked the image of them, for some reason. All little boys started out liking mermaids, he reflected, probably to do with the fact that they were a dead cert for being topless.

'Certainly.' Don laughed. 'When you're fed up with them, you can eat them in a fish soup.' It seemed to Kennedy that Don was looking around him to make sure that neither citizens nor mermaids were party to this unseemly gag. Then he said, 'She protects the city.'

'Oh yeah?' Kennedy had seen plenty of pictures of Warsaw in ruins.

'She was on vacation during the Second World War,' Don anticipated.

Then he was suddenly the writer, back to his book. As he mentioned that he had been working on a new draft, something changed. Don's casual tone, Kennedy thought, could not mask something more than an eagerness to be read: it was a longing.

Kennedy reminded himself of Don's question: what *was* it to him, exactly? Part of the answer was in the sound of Don's voice; unable even to imagine the same longing for his own work to be out there, Kennedy guessed he just wanted a piece of the feeling Don had. He found himself telling Don exactly what he had come all that way to tell him: he would help Don edit it, would do a shit-hot synopsis, then the donkey work of writing the spiels and making the calls that would hook Don a decent agent. He ran out of things to offer to do, then thought of them all over again, and was still saying them as they sat down in a steaming, crowded bar on the edge of Warsaw's Old Town.

As Don went off to order food, Kennedy found a table. He sat down and pulled off his overcoat, jacket, sweater and shirt, got down to his t-shirt. 'Getting fat,' Don observed when he came back.

'No I'm not.' Despite the protest, Kennedy patted the evidence. 'I'm just buying smaller clothes.'

'It's...*description*,' Don assured Kennedy. 'Not criticism. But, hey, Kennedy, now you've had a chance to cross-examine me, you tell *me* something, about this...*literature* thing.'

'Tell you what?' Kennedy heard *literature* as a dirty word, and marvelled, and was quietly outraged, at Don's power of transforming it.

'Yes.' Don pointed at his pal. 'I haven't forgotten that you're one of these writer types.'

'Hey, come on, man – '

'*Yes* you are. Tell me about the writing you do.'

'I don't do any,' Kennedy had to confess, and he couldn't help it, but somehow enjoyed the discipline of remembering his empty nights evidenced by blank pages, and kept up a low-key desperation as he ate, realising that he was famished, and cared about nothing but filling his face. 'None at all.' He talked instead about all that kept him from writing, his wanders through the impossible beauty of Istanbul, his life with Ling, his contentment, failing to mention that it was edged with a fear of sudden loss and abandonment, that he would wind up as the wreck of the SS Kennedy, rusting on the shores of the Sea of Marmara. Once they had eaten, and with Kennedy happy to play the game, they skirted Don's book carefully, and talked then about other books, letting words strike them with their influences, in the way that bookish people did. There was an insular, nerdy wonder to it which, Kennedy remembered, he had been missing sorely.

Maybe the wonder had something to do with the vodka Don had kept calling for. 'I love that.' Don held his little glass up. 'Vodka when it's still almost frozen in slivers, and you see them for a second just before they react to the heat in your hand, right there before your eyes.' Kennedy was unable to argue with him – it did look beautiful – and he decided to love it too, with predictable results.

'You know where we're going to wake up?' Don asked, many shots of the stuff later.

'Sure I do.' It was one of Don's well-worn Istanbul gags, but Kennedy still had to laugh. 'In that little German town.'

'Bad Hangover.' Don clapped Kennedy on the shoulder, stupidly pleased that his friend had remembered, forgetting that Kennedy had to have heard it maybe a hundred times. 'That's the place.'

But really, Istanbul was the place. It was still on Don's mind, Kennedy could tell, because Don started asking him then in detail about people on the Istanbul scene. 'Tell me,' he commanded, 'about the people I knew and loved and avoided and forgot, and about that damn town that still catches me out in my bad dreams.' Kennedy ran through people's faces and fates and fortunes and foibles and follies. 'I hated that place,' Don reminded him for no good reason. Kennedy in turn reminded him of their first conversation, in which Don accused him of being possessed of some kind of madman's genius for having learned enough Turkish to go straight-faced through the social rituals of a country and people Don would never want to understand. 'Good people there,' it occurred to Don, but he meant lonesome world-weary loafers like Kennedy and himself, overseas and out of place, not the millions of decent Turks. It was during conversations like this that Kennedy had to part ways with Don, because nothing Kennedy had seen of the Turks told him that they were anything other than the best kind of people to be among; quirky, okay, but he had known quirkier people back home. He was looking distractedly around the little bar they were in, and he saw at least one guy quirkier than any Turk he had ever met.

In Kennedy's first year in Istanbul he had known a Brit who was assistant director at some crappy private school. People who worked for him said that the first three letters of his job title were very apt. But small world: there the guy was, sat in that bar in Warsaw, his arm around a girl who looked like she was fresh out of high school. Kennedy said, 'Hey, Don, see that skinny guy there? Stan Laurel hair? Dark suit and tie? Draped around the jailbait?'

'Guy name of Monchateau,' Don said.

38

'I know him,' Kennedy said.

'An asshole.'

'I know that.'

'Not French, despite the name.' In reply to that, Kennedy sent Don his tight-lipped pissed look, and Don said hurriedly, 'But – oh yes. You know him from Turkey, right? Wasn't he there the year before I got there?'

Kennedy remembered that Alan Monchateau doctored his voice because he had some hick Brit accent. He spoke like he had a razorblade-stuck Halloween apple in his mouth. Obviously a result of the classless society Brits were always thumping their chests about.

'We say hallo.' Don made a dismissive gesture. 'Not my first choice of a guy to go for a night on the town with, but he's... *bearable.*'

And that was kind of what working overseas was sometimes like; even a self-styled sapient dude like Kennedy, for example, had to be careful not to wind up working for people who had no talent at all for anything at all. Other Brits in Istanbul had said that Monchateau was a throwback to the twilight years of the British Empire. This was back when the upper classes ran the runts of their litters through those big deal private schools, and if they were too clueless to put into banking, or too chickenshit for the army, what they did was send them out to some corner of the empire where, it was reasoned, the natives were even more clueless and spineless. Bad call: those natives ran rings around them, and maybe one of the reasons the Brits' empire folded was because there were too many runts sent to staff it. In the same way, people like Monchateau wormed their way into management positions in language schools in places like Turkey and Poland, and got away with all kinds of crap until they came up against the wily old native.

It was hard to say whether Monchateau had spotted them or not, but the place was hardly Madison Square Garden, so Kennedy had to guess so. He was really too weary to pretend to want to chew the fat with the man. He looked over, and Monchateau seemed intent anyhow in chewing the ear of the bimbo he was with and, glad about that, Kennedy proposed that he and Don take the air.

It was only hazily that Kennedy remembered that he had at one time had the idea that he should get to Don's place straight off the train, dump his bag, take a shower and sleep for ten hours before he did another thing. The last part of it still had great appeal, and he assumed that Don was leading him home to his gaff, and followed trustingly. But what Don did was walk him back through Warsaw's Old Town and out onto a terrace with a vista of a lit-up bridge over dark water. Then, in the shadow of a large white church, they were crunching their way down an icy hill. They passed through a square made of pastel palaces, then were level, on a fringe of crunchy, frosted grass. Don led Kennedy across a quiet main road that formed a bank of the river.

'I got to confess,' Don began.

'What?'

'That I can't believe you came all this way here just to…talk to me about my book.'

'And yet,' Kennedy said carefully, 'here I am.' For a moment, he thought Don's statement was a prelude to an interrogation, and he was unsure what he would say, if he were feeling particularly truthful. He was wary of the honesty that alcohol sometimes brought. It certainly was true that he wanted to help shove Don's book through its next phase – of course it was. But past this top layer of truth there were some deeper ones that rose as he stood there by the river. He saw a picture of himself kicking his heels in a version of Istanbul that had suddenly taken on a truly foreign dimension, not the tourist panorama of minarets and moonlight, just narrow dark suburban streets in the rain, closed in by dimly-lit blocks. Ling was lost to him for the ten days of the vacation, studying, apparently, some tests coming up, apparently, yadda yadda. He may have been paranoid – he often was – but he suspected that the whole thing had been engineered by Ling's dad as a kind of trial separation. He saw that the old fellow was being kind in his own way, both to him and to Ling, but that was hardly going to make Kennedy feel any better about it. At other times, he thought it was all just a screen to hide the fact that, when he got back to Istanbul, Ling would already be gone. And his pals there were away for the break. Well, not all of them, but he had begun to realise that he was growing apart from them, alienated from them even, would be no company for them anyhow. 'I craved a little distraction, man,' he confessed. 'But, hey, the book's the thing, right?'

'It is, hah?'

'Sure.'

'Really?'

'The book's the thing, man.'

No interrogation developed, of course not. Don had no side to him, as Kennedy's dad might have said; you saw all he had to offer, no two-faced stuff, no guile, no agenda.

'Well, that's...' Don raised a hand to dismiss the conversation, and aimed a thumb over the embankment wall. 'The river Wisla. But what you and I call the Vistula.'

'Neat,' Kennedy said, though in fact the river did not exactly make him draw in a breath he had not already planned on drawing in. He saw trees on the other side of the stretch of water, but that seemed to be it: there was nothing monumental about it.

'Undoubtedly one of history's great rivers.' People who did not know Don put his way of talking down to southern gent pomposity, but it was not that. It was just regular pomposity.

'Well, at least,' Kennedy compromised, 'one of geography's.'

'We're here in Warsaw.' Don's voice boomed. 'And here's the Wisla, but, well, you go to Krakow, and what do you see?'

'Uh, chimneys?'

'What?'

'Churches?' Kennedy gestured surrender.

'Eh? You see the Wisla, again. Go to Gdansk, you see the same river. Just follows you around the great parts of this country.'

'Neat.' Kennedy had to ask, though, 'What are we doing here?' meaning, in the night time, in sub-zero January.

'Wanted to show it to you.' Don clapped Kennedy on the back. 'That's all.' Then he was at the side of the road, waving for a cab like a man touched by the moon.

Kennedy woke on Don's couch next morning, and at once heard Don shuffling and snuffling around the apartment. Don chirped out that he would go get breakfast, so Kennedy rose and showered and shaved, and marvelled that he could ever have turned so...*rancid* just from sitting on trains and in sidings and in bars. After a search for the makings of it all, he got coffee brewing, and lounged at the table in the kitchen. His bare feet elicited a cold clink from a bunch of empty bottles, and Kennedy shoved his chair back and leaned down to take a look: mainly beer, and the local hooch. He thought he ought to be worried about them, but then forgot it and busied himself with giving his contact lenses an overdue wash and shine. By the time he was test-running them Don slammed back in, bringing a cloud of cold air in with him.

'These are *croissants*.' Don dumped them out onto a plate.

Kennedy seemed to be expected to say something, so he took a look at them, and commented, 'No kidding.'

'But here they call them *rogalki*.'

'Uh.' Maybe Kennedy just looked like the kind of guy who gave a shit what *croissants* were called in Poland. They were a square yard of fat with a spoonful of flour, and, okay, the French invented them, so they were stuck with them, and had to eat them, but why would anybody else in their right mind want them? 'Right.'

'Say, you know what I miss?' Kennedy felt Don's eyes drilling into his face: this was important. 'Frosted cornflakes.'

'Uh-huh.' Cornflakes, Kennedy thought he ought to get it straight, for people too freaking lazy to put their own sugar on. 'Very interesting.' This was just breakfast talk with Don, though, and he mm-hmmed and yessed and noed and filled his face with the dreaded *croissants*, which were really not so bad, and got on with the breakfast side of things.

'Breakfast sure is a great idea.' Even as Don said the words, he seemed a little down, and Kennedy knew why when he drained his coffee and exited the kitchen only to reappear in his peacoat, scarf and hat, a daypack clutched in a gloved hand. 'I'm off away out along into the gloom to teach some American. Listen.' Don threw his keys across to Kennedy. 'I'll be back about three thirty, but if you need to be out in this merciless weather, leave the keys under the rug outside.'

'Right.' Kennedy stopped his complacent, post-prandial nod. 'Hey. Hey, wait a second.' He followed Don into the hallway. 'Where's the book?'

He saw Don about to wonder what book that could be, but there was nothing in that for him, and he tossed off a file name and made his exit.

Muttering the name of the file to himself in case he forgot it, Kennedy souped himself up with more coffee. He booted up Don's computer, which took its time to open the latest draft of the Saudi book. Kennedy watched it appear in some trepidation, then got lost in the hours as he skimmed all twenty thousand words of the first section. It was slimmed down from the script Kennedy knew. Though he felt sad not to see some parts there, it was way better. He made notes that ran to pages, and as he typed got a sense all over again that what he was doing in his own writing was garbage.

He tried not to dwell on the thought. He walked to the window. The snow had stopped, more or less, and he got an impression from a peculiar mixture of light and silence out there of a pause in the weather, a threat maybe of worse to come. He looked out on a narrow street that seemed to be at cross-purposes with itself: though buses growled along, and the occasional truck, it did not seem to be a main street at all; stores broke the monotony of the apartment blocks, and sometimes people appeared, but then there would be nobody for minutes at a stretch. It looked more like anybody's clichéd idea of an east European city than the part he had seen the night before.

When Don got back he was red in the face and cold as a witch's tit. Kennedy let him get half his coat off before regaling him with some of his comments on the new draft. Don held hands in the air, whether in protest at what Kennedy was saying, or in agreement, it was not very clear. 'Ah-hah, right,' was the most Don got to say as Kennedy ran through the marketing gameplan.

They settled in the lounge. Don put on a tape of some ancient jazz, stuff played by hip orchestras in the twenties and thirties, though it reminded Kennedy mainly of the background music in Laurel and Hardy movies. It brought a serene smile to rest on Don's face, as Kennedy sketched out what he thought could advance the book.

'Success, hah?' Don's smile disappeared. 'Is that what we're talking about? Well, okay, good. Success is…ah, a great idea.' He took what seemed like a long, resentful look at Kennedy, and Kennedy was about to ask him what was up, and then Don kind of answered him, saying, 'But in the meantime today, I teach again at six thirty. That's here and now. Now listen. What have you got in mind for this afternoon?'

'I don't know.' Kennedy had thought nothing further than that he might go take a look at the city, and that was about it. There he was, though, dressed only in t-shirt and boxers, comfortable in a chair, a considerable chunk of the afternoon gone.

'How about a bit of a walk?' Don suggested. 'I can show you stuff. We can stop for a drink someplace.'

'Sure,' Kennedy could not help but agree. 'Say.' Maybe it was the mention of a drink, or the memory of the empties under the kitchen table, of the melancholy street out the window, or maybe just the general impression of Don that Kennedy had accumulated, that prompted him to ask, 'Are you happy here?'

'Well, I like the apartment.' Don took it in with a spread of fingers. 'It's central. Got a minimart on the corner. The mail office is right underneath. My dentist is right there.' He pointed. Kennedy stared at him through this. 'Sure I'm happy.' Don ran a hand over the stubble on his head. 'I got to be happy, don't I? Surrounded by all these happy people? Come on, Kennedy. Get your pants on, and your coat and whatever else, and we'll go out and…observe people going about their happy business, hah?'

The afternoon light in Warsaw looked to Kennedy like dawn in Istanbul, and that set him thinking about the Turks and their optimism about life, and the first line in their national song about not being afraid if dawn failed to show. He thought how in Poland it must often seem like it had been cancelled.

'See,' Don began as they trudged up the hill from his place, 'I left Texas.'

'Right.' Kennedy stifled the words, *Well, you're here, aren't you?*

'Grew up wanting to leave Texas.' At that, Kennedy looked up at their route, apartment blocks making the high sides of a rising street carpeted wall-to-wall in dirty ice and slush, and he doubted if anybody could dream up such a view down in Texas. 'Wasn't just Texas I wanted to leave. It was America.'

'Uh-huh. Right.'

All Americans who lived in Europe had undergone the need to leave America, though. Sure, Kennedy had met the ones who whined that they missed all things American as soon as they had left, or did not know until some revealing moment in a foreign store that they loved America and had never really wanted to leave in the first place. But they were more like long-stay tourists.

'I knew I'd be a slave before I went to Saudi,' Don said. 'Knew they were all slaves there. I went there to make that.' He made a money gesture.

'Well, everybody does, I guess.'

So far from America, Kennedy thought, as he looked around him, *so far*; and a long way too from Saudi. Why did Don have all this on his mind? And he realised then one thing that defined Don Darius for him: a guy who was always unhappy in the place he was in.

'No. Not true. I knew Americans in Saudi who thought it was good for their souls, too,' Don went on. 'They live there and do the same things they do back home, you know, have their barbecues and their bridge evenings and their pot-luck parties. Only they aren't the things they'd do back home. They're the things their parents would've done, or their grandparents. It's the nineteen fifties down there, people living that dream we stopped hearing about after Vietnam. You know how much of a damn...*fool* I felt sometimes? I left America because I hated living in a small American town where everybody knew everybody else's business, and I wound up in a compound in Dhahran, living in a small American town where everybody knew everybody else's business.'

'Women with Mary Tyler Moore hairdos,' Kennedy remembered from Don's book.

'For instance.' Don stared. 'I jumped ship and went to Turkey to make a...an adjustment in my life.'

'Uh-huh.'

Kennedy saw Don at parties in Istanbul, hanging with other Americans, with the Istanbul Brits, bopping in bars with the city's outcast Africans who were cooler than polar bears. There he was, drunk and sad, getting Kennedy thinking at times that he was the sorriest creature he had ever seen. He saw the two of them in a late-night cab on the road along the Marmara Sea, and Don knowing what kind of day was coming at him, and thinking that the best thing he could do right then was stop the cab and get out, and dive through the scum of oil and fish-guts into the water till his hot air gave out.

'I came close in that damn town.' Don stuck finger and thumb together. Maybe he and Kennedy were thinking about the same thing. 'Had to get someplace better.'

'Well, you're here, man.' *See*, Kennedy was thinking, *so far, and yet still so fucking*...damaged *by the idea of it.* 'You're a long way from Istanbul.'

'I am.' Don's face brightened, as if he had just remembered. 'I am, too.'

Don signalled Kennedy off the street and up steep steps cut into a section of seriously high wall, and then they were in the spread of a white park with black trees scratched out of it. It was school home-time, with mothers herding children along the paths, trying to distract them from the sheer fun of the snow. They passed a woman leading a sick dachshund, its wurst belly scraping the ice, its head stuck inside a post-surgery lampshade collar.

'Hey. Fred Flintstone's vacuum cleaner.'

That was classic Don Darius, and Kennedy roared laughing. He was glad of the interlude, but it was just that. Don paused, as if he might laugh too, but then he didn't. They flattened frozen grass with a clink-clink as if walking on shards of glass, and left a trail as they set off across the park.

'See,' Don resumed, 'that society they got in Saudi made me laugh fit to bust. Not at the Arabs. There is absolutely nothing to laugh at about them. One thing I guess I like about the Arabs, in fact, maybe the only thing, is the way they make it clear how they hold non-Muslims in total contempt. They don't pussyfoot around pretending they want into our culture. It's just, *We hate your guts, and in recognition of that, here's a shitload of dollars you can't get in places where they like you, just for teaching us your horrible language.* I have no problem with that.'

'Well I do.' Kennedy's hackles rose. 'They liked us well enough when they wanted us to go kick Saddam Hussein's sorry butt out of Kuwait last year.'

'No. Listen. That was business. *You do the job*, they said, *and we will continue to be the mother of all esteemed customers to American companies.* No law says you have to like the people you do business with. That's the scenario.'

Purposely or not, Don had said it like *see-now-rio*, and Kennedy's first reaction was the need to quip, *Still reading your James Joyce, I see.* But the play on the word disarmed him, and made him muse on it, and believe that he did indeed see it now, and he nodded.

'No,' Don said. 'I didn't laugh at the Arabs – it's their place, and they can be how they want there, and they're welcome to it. I laughed at the Americans, and the Brits, mainly. Laughed for a year like a clown, and that's okay for a year, but how long can you spend laughing at tragedies? In Turkey I laughed for a month is all. And then, you know what, I ran out of laughs. You know what I'd do if I went back to the States right now? Hah? I'd laugh. And you know what they do back home to people who just sit in corners and laugh.'

'Well.' There was nothing for Kennedy but to say, 'But you're here, man, right? Oh, hey. Listen to that.'

They had come through the park gates into a street that was quiet and classy-looking, and somehow pleased with itself; it was mainly apartments, could have been Paris, or Budapest, New York, even, though still like something out of the Cold War. From above came the sound of a soprano. It was no stereo system: it was a real woman, with a real piano behind her.

'That's neat,' Kennedy said.

'That's why I brought you this way.' Don called to mind for a second certain guys who worked in the Turkish baths Kennedy frequented: *I did good, now gimme a tip.* 'This is a music school.' He pointed out a set of windows above them. 'They learn music here.'

'No shit. Well, that's music, all right. Hey, ever go to the opera here?'

'Not much.' Don seemed to want to justify that. 'Fine opera house they got here, despite being an ugly thing that looks like a giant, mean kid made it from outsize Lego. But no. I just don't have the stomach for the length of the thing anymore. I don't have the ass for it, maybe, sit there all night waiting for the fat lady to sing. I just want to fast-forward through, or rewind to the bits I liked. But I saw…let me see now…*Rigoletto.*' Don authenticated the statement with a snatch of *La Donna e Mobile.* Kennedy ouched it to a close as quickly as he could.

'The lady with the cellphone.'

'Right. But hey, we can go if you want. There's one on this week.'

Kennedy waited, then asked, 'Has it got a name?'

'Well, sure it does.' Don thought about it. 'Mozart thing.'

'Right.'

'Roman thing? Got a fellow in a toga on the poster, anyhow.'

'Oh yeah. That's…*Tito.*' Kennedy tried to conjure up the title. 'Uh…*La Clemenza di Tito.*' Or maybe, he had the idea, it was an opera of the National Lampoon movie *Animal House.*

'That's the boy. Want to go see it?'

'No.' If Kennedy was remembering rightly, *La Clemenza di Tito* was one of those operas that, as far as a schleb like he was concerned, got opera a bad name. It featured a few *bona fide* arias, but it was mostly just people warbling phrases over an annoying keyboard. Kennedy did not mention this to Don; a harpsichord was tinkling an alarm to remind him that in Istanbul Don was always dragging people off to the opera, then grizzling the whole time about it boring him shitless. Kennedy lied, and said, 'I saw that one already.'

'You did?' Don did not look too disappointed. 'Does it work?'

'I hesitate to recommend it, man. A good tune or two, but…' It bugged Kennedy, just in passing, that he could not remember any of the arias from *Tito.* 'You know, it's like eating a seafood salad, see, and you only got one mussel in it.'

'Oh. Right.' Don looked wistful, and pained at the same time. 'I ate that salad. Spare me another. No. Listen. Tell you what I like. Where I go to hear music is there's this little palace in the grounds of a park, okay, and it belongs to Warsaw's music academy, and every Sunday morning they throw the doors open and have recitals. Kids from the academy do their stuff, and it costs maybe twenty cents. Okay, so you get the false starts and the bum notes, but not often. But what I like is you're right in on the process, and, well, that takes my breath away. You know, no props, or anything. You see a soprano singing a few feet away, and she isn't all dressed up in costume, and you see the muscles moving in her face, and in her stomach, her chest, see her ribs contract and her tonsils vibrating…What you get is a look at the mechanics of her art. Excellent.'

Kennedy laughed. 'Do they sing naked?'

'Not in this weather.' Don put on what could have been an *I-wish* face. 'Excellent, though, I tell you. In fact, it's a pity you're not going to be here on a Sunday, or you could've come along.'

'I am so.' Kennedy put a question mark into his face. 'Today's Friday.'

'Oh. Yes, you're right.'

'So?'

'I lose track of time here,' Don claimed.

'You're in Warsaw.'

'Right.'

'Not, like, hovering around International Dateline.'

'Ah, yes.' Don seemed keen suddenly to move on. 'Anyhow, it's only music.'

'But, well, it shows people are cultured here,' Kennedy decided.

'Cultured.' Don absent-mindedly kicked at a lump of ice, sent it spinning over the road to clatter against the base of a streetlight. 'Cultured, right,' he repeated, looked amused, and looked up. 'There ought to be something good in that, I guess, but…I don't know.' He seemed troubled. 'I…question the idea of culture sometimes. People read the books here, though, do the research, present the papers, talk the talk, but…it doesn't seem to teach them much.'

'No?' Kennedy remembered the kid on the train, and his Agatha Goddam Christie.

'Read all they like,' Don said. 'But learn nothing. Know why?'

'Why?'

'Gold in their eyes. Look at that, will you? Magpie contemplating turd.' There was one too, the size of a small turkey, which was indeed moving its beak curiously around a neat deposit of dog mess. 'Can't find anything that glitters in this town. But it will. They think capitalism's going to come save them. It isn't, though. I know that.' Don's eyes gleamed a little madly, Kennedy felt. 'I know that, and I tell them that. But are they listening?'

Some people were, it seemed to Kennedy. Don's voice was loud, and the little street had become populated, mainly with student types, judging by all the denim and hair in evidence. Faces turned toward them for seconds, then forgot them. Kennedy wanted to point them out to Don, but instead found himself sliding after his friend, wanting to hear more.

Don led Kennedy around a corner, and they were on Christmas Street again, its stores giving off a red-and-white twinkle. Don pointed a triumphant finger at the passers-by. He made a professorial shake of the head, saying, 'No way is capitalism going to do anything other than enslave these poor bastards all over again.'

Kennedy looked at the people of Warsaw as if seeing them for the first time – what was it, Varsovians? – in garments that looked like elephant-hide, but then, what, coats and hats made of felt, a child's cut-outs in red, blue, green. An old man in a mac and a beret, he saw. An old woman in tweeds. They had lived through oppression and repression, and now they were going to take on capitalism. They deserved Kennedy's respect, and he watched them, and felt at a loss because he was unable to let them know it was theirs. Like they would worry, though.

'Hey.' There was promise in Don's voice. 'Show you something.' They were at a monumental crosswalk, and Don pointed one way. 'Down there is Ulitsa Marshalkovska. Historic street, Avenue of the Marshalls, and that's Poland's military tradition, right? This street here's the Street of the Holy Cross, and that's the religious tradition. Okay? They got scaffolding up on the corner right down there at the end – see it? – where they're building a humungous McDonalds.'

'So?' Kennedy made a face. Don seemed to want him to engage with this, a new undercurrent to his words and tone, but all he could offer was, 'That's just…hamburgers, man.'

'No. Wrong.' Don bit on his lip, and Kennedy got the sense of his friend thinking hard. 'Hamburgers are just the start. Already you can buy pornography here, see fifteen year-old kids out of their minds on smack. What I mean is, this is a Catholic country, okay, with a lot of history and tradition.'

'Well, okay. I know.'

'Hmm.' Don stopped, seemed to be searching the walls along the street. 'Empires worked the place over, and then they had Nazis, came and worked them over like no country ever got worked over before. You know, right where we're standing, the Nazis reduced it to rubble? You know that?'

'Yeah.' Kennedy thought again of that Warsaw mermaid: fine time to take a vacation. 'I know.'

'I mean – Jesus. And then the communists ran the show, and...'

'And what?'

Don put a hand on Kennedy's shoulder and stopped him. 'Know what Stalin said about Poland?' Don seemed to be slipping effortlessly back into a conversation Kennedy was not sure they had ever had. 'Old Uncle Joe the Sheep Killer?'

'No.' Kennedy laughed at the description. 'What?'

'He said bringing communism to Poland was like putting a saddle on a cow. Meaning, he knew it was never going to work, but he still went ahead and thought, *Well, let's work Poland over again anyhow.*'

'Yeah.' *That was dictators for ya though*, Kennedy thought. 'Well.'

'Interesting times,' Don said, 'it seems to me, come almost solely out of the whims of big-time killers like Stalin.' He halted, and turned to Kennedy. 'You know that old Yiddish curse?' he asked. '*May you live in interesting times.*'

'Not Yiddish.' Ling had told Kennedy that. 'It's Chinese.'

'No way.'

'It is – it's Chinese.'

'Yiddish.'

'*No.* It's Chinese, from Confucius.'

'*No.*'

'No yourself, as old Confucius himself might've said.'

Don hooded eyes at Kennedy a second, then said, 'Whatever. *Who*ever. But listen. You know what the biggest curse of all is?'

'What?'

'It's us.'

'Us?' Kennedy sounded curious, and dismissive. In fact, he had often thought of himself in this novelty role, imagined seeing himself from outside, tried to imagine what they all looked like to the people who lived there, all the loud, crass foreigners with their stupid ways and obsessions.

'Americans.' Don searched out something American to point at, chose Kennedy. 'Brits, Germans, the French, whoever. I told you before, how the Arabs get us over to hellholes like Saudi and pour loot into our pockets to give them the language, and nothing more. Here, when they let foreigners in, what they get is the language, but also all the worthless crud that comes with it. What I mean, I guess, is that capitalism is going to finish off all these countries out here with their fragile economies, in a way communism never could. Capital is going to kill their spirit for keeps, and bury it. Difference is they think they're having a time while it happens. Hey. You hear that song?'

Out of some store blared a song about living in a happy nation. Kennedy could not remember who it was by. They were treated to a chorus, drifted away from the verse. It was annoyingly infectious.

'Hah?' Don was pleased at this little finger of coincidence. 'Happy nation – right, in their dreams. But forget about capital a second, and think about that other old demon you always rap on about, Kennedy, culture. What was all that we were talking about back there, the opera? Verdi, we mentioned, right? Mozart. They weren't Polish. Ask any kid here about Polish composers, and they can't name a single piece by them. Mention Kurt Cobain, and they'll stand there and sing you all of that *Team Spirit* song.'

'I think you'll find that's *Teen* Spirit.' Kennedy laughed, and thought of the kid on the train: he was hip, he was finding out stuff about the world, he was happy enough, it seemed to Kennedy. And he was not so sure he was prepared to take Don's word; people were sometimes cagey about their own culture, protected it by keeping it to themselves. 'Well, okay. But what's so wrong with that?'

'What's wrong with it?' Don walked on. 'Hmm. Well, see, the state they had here before, it seems to me, filled in all the spaces for people. And when the state does that, there's no place for the intellect to go. I look at this stuff around me, right, and sometimes I think the same mess is going down: communist space-fillers gone, we come along and fill the cracks with our own...*crap*. Picture of despair for you – forget that magpie contemplating a turd. Think about a whole nation waiting for its first McDonalds.'

'Hey.' Kennedy may not have been very convinced by the truth of what Don was saying, but was impressed all the same; anything had to be better than the apathetic slob Don Darius had become in Istanbul. Kennedy was excited, suddenly, at the potential of this preacher-man strain in his friend, and asked him, 'You're writing all this down?'

'What?' Don was suddenly far away. The preacher was gone. 'I bought a Snickers bar in Auschwitz,' he said.

'What?' Kennedy thought he might have misheard, but knew he hadn't.

'Auschwitz.' Don stared past Kennedy, was looking at the place on a slideshow in his head, Kennedy could have sworn later. 'You know? The big concentration camp?'

'Yeah – I *know*.'

'Where my mom's family were murdered.' Don conjured up another image. 'And I go there fifty years later and I buy a Snickers bar?'

'Jesus.' Kennedy had a flash out the window of the siding near Ostrava, of freight cars rattling past in the night. 'Your mom's family?'

'My mom's family.' Don bowed his head a second. '*My* family.'

'Jesus. Don – '

'But a Snickers. What is *that* about?'

'Yeah. Well, it's – '

'What that is badly screwed up.'

'It is.' Kennedy tried to picture Auschwitz; it was a museum, he knew, had a visitors' centre, he supposed, like George Washington's house or Niagara Falls. The idea of Don buying a candy bar there was funny more than tragic though: crass, okay, but in comparison to all the other stuff that had gone down there, it really wasn't the thing Don was making it out to be. Was it? 'But tell me…'

'What?'

Kennedy got stuck over saying how he simply wanted to hear more about Don's mom and her family and their time in Auschwitz. It was just history, he thought, but ugly, on the point of a rant, stood challengingly in their way on the street. He looked again at the wrapped-up passers-by. Only the survivors could use the respect, he reflected. What good was it ever going to do the dead and the disappeared? Kennedy had read someplace that anybody who walked over Warsaw was walking on a monument to the dead, and he slowed his steps, looked down at the stones and, when he looked up, Don was waiting, and waving, urgency in his eyes.

'Say, Kennedy.' Don seemed to have forgotten about his candy bar purchase among the memories of the dead. 'When you were little,' he pre-ambled, 'did you have dreams of going overseas to check out Europe one day, when you were big?'

'Sure I did.' *Who didn't*, Kennedy wondered, *except Europeans?* He realised he was in the flow of Don's thinking, and decided he might as well paddle.

'So tell me.' Kennedy had the feeling that Don was probing back into his psychology major for the right tone of voice to adopt. 'What did you think about when you dreamed of hitting Europe? The exact thing, I mean.'

'Windows,' Kennedy said, with no hesitation.

'Windows?' That spluttered Don out of the Viennese shrink shtick. 'Eh?'

'The exact thing, you said.' Kennedy thought about Neal Cassady asking, *Have you ever dug windows?* Cassady didn't ask Kennedy's dad that, he asked Kerouac, though he was Sal Paradise at the time, and Cassady was Dean Moriarty, and it was in *On the Road*. But, come to think of it, he probably asked Kennedy's dad the same thing, had begun to recycle his wiseguy asides by the time Kennedy senior had run into him. 'Glass, in frames,' he teased, then spelled out, 'Like, tall, narrow apartment buildings with tall, narrow windows that led onto tall, narrow balconies with iron rails.'

'Oh. But...' Don seemed mightily perplexed. 'That's all?'

'With the sun on them,' Kennedy remembered.

'That's all? Windows? But...I mean...Where were they, these windows?'

'Paris, France.' Again, no hesitation from Kennedy. They could only have been there, in a city lost in time and place to Americans, embedded in Hemingway and Scott Fitzgerald. 'But no, not only windows. Other stuff.'

'Right.' Don looked relieved. 'Like what?'

'Bookstores.' Kennedy tried to see them again, the ones he had imagined before he finally saw them. 'Real little ones.'

'You didn't have bookstores in Vermont?'

'Sure we did. But the ones I thought about were different. They had, like, Sam Beckett coming in to browse.' Kennedy's old man had once told him that, being mostly Irish, they were allowed to call the great man Sam. 'And Jean Genet. Or you saw them out the window with, like, Sartre and Simone de Beauvoir, on their way to that café they all hung out at. In back of the store,' Kennedy remembered, and was enjoying himself by then, 'in a little glass case, there were first editions of stuff, by Verlaine, and Baudelaire, you know, bound in leather with gold leaf. Had one of the first run of *Ulysses*. Had petite girls with small tits who wore tight black sweaters and glasses.'

'Okay – right.' Don started to look happy. 'But tell me, what did they do, these girls, when they finished work at the bookstore? Where did they go?'

'Why, they, see, they met a boyfriend, right, dude in a long coat and with a day's beard, and he comes along a – an avenue, and he's carrying a stick of bread. Then they take a stroll up a boulevard, and they go to a café on a sidewalk, and…Why?'

'And what do they drink in the café?'

'I don't know, man, but see – '

'But not rootbeer, right?'

'No, they'd drink, like, red wine, or maybe Pernod.'

'Would they eat a hamburger?'

'No, they'd – '

'Would they eat a Snickers bar?'

'No way.'

'You get me, then?' Don blinked at his pal in a kind of triumph. 'You see my point?'

'Yeah,' Kennedy said, then amended it at once to, 'that is, no. What are you talking about?'

'Aw, come on.' Don threw hands up.

'Come on…what?' Kennedy thought how a guy could easily waste his whole life away in this conversation: no job, no apartment, no marriage, no kids, just this damn conversation.

'Listen. I had those dreams, too.' Don shut his eyes and took a brief look inside his head. 'Sat there dreaming of the same places – Paris, Rome, Vienna, Berlin, wherever, all those big cities with a vibe of their own. Last thing I figured on was coming here and seeing all the same stuff we got back home. I don't want to come to Europe and eat Snickers bars. I don't want to eat McDonalds. I don't want to watch Larry King on TV, see, and I don't want to read the *Herald Tribune*.'

'Then – '

'I know. Then don't do those things. It's more than that, though. I don't even want to know all that stuff is around. I want to think of it as being back in America. And before you ask, no, I don't want to see *any*body doing them. Listen. I left the States to see other people's cultures, right, and I come here, and what do I see?'

'Well, what?'

'Cargo cults.'

Kennedy could have sworn later that the little corner of Warsaw they were on had conspired to eavesdrop on them. Cars and trams calmed their engines for a stop light, and yet the people around them had not yet started to walk, and had reached a lull in their talk. Music blaring out of a place near them came to a between-cuts silence. Had there been a dog barking, even it would have stopped too, to listen to Don bellowing the two words. From every direction, heads turned. Kennedy felt as if he and Don were on a stage.

'Hey.' Don spread hands, and grinned. The heads turned away, and people crossed the road, vehicles coughed into life and were on their way.

'Cargo cults?'

Kennedy had heard the term, he was sure. Don told him then about the cargo cults that had sprung up in the Pacific islands after the Second World War, once all the colonialists had been kicked out. He did not understand the phenomenon completely, he had to admit, but, as he saw it, some of the islanders believed that, if they observed certain rituals to qualify them to deserve it, a bunch of freighters would make a line for them from the horizon and, basically, dump stuff: food, whiskey, rifles, cars – he didn't know – Barbie dolls, cloth of gold, Siegfried and Roy videos, for all he knew, Snickers bars – whatever. Where beliefs like that had arisen, Don had not been able to work out though, there in Warsaw, he thought he was beginning to. 'It's the same thing here,' he elaborated. 'They think all these things are going to come to them, just like that, and that they're never going to have to pay for them. And, in a way, right now, it's kind of true.'

'How come?' Kennedy was intrigued.

'Well, independence – they got that here – it was the Poles started it, way back with the Solidarity workers. Right? And now? Well, dollars and Deutschmarks and sterling are pouring in, going to build factories, take businesses and stores over, build apartments, fix new telecom deals – the whole capitalist thing. The connection they don't want to make is that foreign money comes from foreign investors who are sooner or later going to want their returns. One day they're going to wake up and realise the Soviets were right about one thing, at least. All those silk-hatted fat bastard capitalists really are going to bleed the country dry. But right now it's cargo cults, and, for a time, anyhow, the cargo is arriving.'

'Uh-huh.' Kennedy was taken up in Don's unravelling spiel. 'And so? You're writing all this down?'

'Sure I am.' Don did not at all look as if he were sure, then made a commitment. 'Sit up nights here, nothing to do but drink, nobody to talk to, look out the window at the snow coming down…Because…'

'Because what?'

'Because, well, I…I *know* people here. In Saudi, the people I met – Arabs I met, I mean – didn't have a life. Came and did their lessons and went home, stayed with mom and dad in the little house on the Camel cigarette pack, and that was it. In Turkey, okay, I turned the pages and taught little kids who mouthed the words I asked them to mouth, went home and forgot it. Okay, I didn't blame them. Here, I teach people who do have lives to live, and not one of them, that I know, has taken a look at all this, and said, *Do we really need all this?* Not one has said to me, *This is bad*, or even, *This has the potential to go bad*, and that…really pisses me off.' For a moment, Don looked to Kennedy as if he were about to cry. 'You know, I got a private student, a businessman, pays me about half the weekly salary of a girl who works in a store. For three two-hour lessons a week? What kind of…*nonsense* is that? But they don't stop for a minute to think where all this is leading. Too busy dreaming of that cargo.'

'Yeah, well.' Kennedy was trying to work out if it could be as grim as Don was making it sound. 'But, you know, maybe they feel they got to go through it before they can come out of it.'

'What?'

'Or something.' Kennedy tried a laugh.

'Just like Karl Marx said?' Don joined in with his own snort of a laugh. 'Well, maybe.' But Kennedy had to admit that Don was making a good case. The way Don saw it was that the people of the east of Europe were on the verge of a chance to cut through the bullshit of the times – bullshit foisted on them by the west, and for which they were paying – and forge a new system, and that they were flushing that chance down the can. 'Tell you what I see ten years down the tube,' Don stated, calm now. 'Unemployment, and no welfare system to handle it, the place full of heroin and porn, and a big mafia running the whole show. I see a dog-ugly society just like the one we got back home, based on greed for the holy dollar. And you know what ugly societies do?'

'Yeah,' Kennedy said. Don looked at him sharply. 'No,' he admitted. 'What?'

'They find somebody to blame when it all goes out of whack.' Don pulled up pistol fingers, sighted at a nearby statue, squeezed off a shot. 'Start killing each other. Even in the happiest of nations. But, you know, I mean, why did we leave America? Huh? We wanted something different, okay, and what do we find? We find it right here, wherever you look across this whole damn continent. America.'

'God bless it,' Kennedy offered.

'Hey.' Don showed a palm. 'Don't get me wrong. Me, I'd rather be raised in America than in some goddam banana republic someplace. But I think we made a lot of mistakes in America, that can't be unmade now, and…we just got to bite the bullet and live with them, get on with stuff in spite of them and be the best citizens we can, you know? Other people don't have to go through all that, though. They got the choice to make a new start, and what makes me mad is they don't want to take it.'

Kennedy was impressed into silence: the grouch next to him was an all-new-formula Don Darius. He had a picture of Don then, up nights, writing, and knew in his bones that it was going to be good. Don spilled the seeds of his ideas along the street, and Kennedy gathered them, promised himself that he would help them to sprout.

Up along the end of the street a square was revealed, guarded by a stone king on top of a column, his sword drawn. Don commented that Poland's kings had only ever stuck their swords right up the country's ass, and this take on Polish history amused Kennedy, and depressed him at the same time.

'Royal castle.' Don pointed across the square. He pre-empted Kennedy by stating, 'Looks like a bunch of municipal offices to me, but a royal castle is what it is. Hey, listen. I'll show you a real castle. I'll show you the biggest ever castle you ever saw.'

'Okay.' That sounded fine to Kennedy. 'Where?'

'Ah.' Don looked lost. He stopped, and half-raised a hand. 'Oh, right. This way.'

'Where?' Kennedy asked again.

'Where?' Don frowned, and pointed. 'To the town, the town that lives again.'

'Well, okay.' Kennedy was only slightly puzzled at the cross-conversation; he would hardly be likely to miss the biggest ever castle he ever saw when he saw it.

And Don doubled them back on their route of the night before, down a street of churches nestling among stores vending souvenir crap, and then the main square opened out with its pastel-faced buildings. 'They're called tenements,' Don declared. Kennedy thought briefly of movies set in the Bronx; they were not those kinds of tenements. 'Old Town square,' Don explained. 'Raised in the fifties over the rubble the Nazis left. That's why it all looks so new, see?'

'Looks like a movie set,' Kennedy commented.

'Well, hmm, it does, a little.'

They took a narrow street that led to the city's defensive walls, put up in the sixties, and then were through the Barbican tower and into another street of churches. Then there was another square, the New Town square, more of the Walt Disney historical. Kennedy could not deny that he was enjoying it all, but already felt a little sightseed-out.

He also had scenes from Don's book fragmenting in his mind. Change a word here, delete a sentence there, expand one here; beautify this paragraph, chop that one dead short, cut that whole page out: he was Mister Editor, his nitpicking just for once a valued skill. He wanted to get back to Don's, spread a hard copy out in front of him, wield a pen, get Don banging keys.

All this kind of thing seemed to be furthest from Don's mind. Each time Kennedy mentioned anything to do with the book, Don grizzled, acted like it was nothing to do with him.

Finally Don stopped, let out a weary breath, and asked Kennedy, 'What does it matter?'

'What does…*what* matter?'

'My book.' Don looked away. 'Or your book. Or *any*body's book. Hah? What makes it important? To *any*body? Listen. Come with me, and I'll show you something.'

'What?'

'Just come with me.'

'Well, okay. I'm coming, aren't I?' Books mattered, Kennedy wanted to say, because…they just fucking *did*, but he was silent as Don walked him on some, then halted them in front of a stone plaque on a wall. It was in the shape of a cross, and it was engraved with a list of names.

'These guys died right here.' Don shoved his back against the wall. 'Shot by the Nazis in the process of working Poland over. These things are all over the city. You know Hitler had a thing about Warsaw? Even the very idea of the place made him mad – I forget just why. I guess if a guy is crazy as a camel with a rocket up his ass to start with, there's nothing in it for anybody to start asking questions like that. Anyhow, he just got fixed on blowing it right off the face of the earth.'

'He did?' Kennedy knew that, though – anybody, he guessed, knew that.

'Yup. Oh, hey, and he did it, incidentally, with Uncle Joe Stalin's Red Army sitting right across the river smoking their black cigarettes and playing their balalaikas. Could've driven over in their tanks and kicked the Nazis' asses real good, but no order came to do that, and so they just sat there, armed to the teeth, and watched.'

'I didn't know that.'

'No. But the Poles remember. And, you know, after the war they were going to leave Warsaw as a ruin, just the way it was, to testify to the achievements of Nazis, and the…*machinations* of Russians, build a new capital, or maybe let Krakow be the capital. But once they got to thinking they'd rebuild it, they got a lot of the people who'd lived here back.' Kennedy let Don lead his eyes to the names inscribed in the stone. 'And those people started remembering, first about where all the buildings were, and the roads. But then about all the things that went down, not just that a bunch of Nazis shot a bunch of people here, and there, and wherever. They remembered just who exactly got shot, and then, of course, just who exactly shot them. Those Nazis all had names. See, even under the most extreme conditions, and the most extreme…heartbreak, people remember. You can't rub out a whole people. You always leave survivors. So screw books.'

'What?'

'That is my point. No poetry after Auschwitz. Wasn't that what the fellow said?'

'Well, yeah, he *did*, but…'

'But what? What's to say, after that?'

'Uh.' Kennedy tried to think of the context of Theodore Adorno's famous statement, but couldn't remember it. He grinned, stated, 'He was in a bad mood that day. He didn't mean it. And nor do you.'

'Well…'

'Do you?'

'I don't know.'

'The book's the thing. I told you that. You just have to believe me.'

'But…Okay.' Don gave up, but wagged a finger promising more another time, and let out a bright laugh. 'Right. But listen. All I'm saying is, look around you when you're here. See all these…monuments to ordinary little people who otherwise would've been forgotten. Don't just – you know – don't just walk them on by.'

'I won't.' Kennedy meant it.

'Don't just be thinking of books.'

'No. I won't.'

Don laughed again, and the sound banished the sombre mood he had drawn over, it seemed to Kennedy, the whole damn street. 'Right now,' Don said, pointing, 'we're going to take that street, and I'm going to show you the humungous monument to the Warsaw Uprising. Okay?'

'Okay.'

'Then I'll show you where we eat tonight, so you can meet me later. You understand?'

'I think I can grasp that.'

'Good. And then I'll get off and teach my class. I'll impart some crucial knowledge to them, I'm certain.' He laughed loudly again. 'Why, I'll change their lives, surely. I'll get that out of the way, and then we'll meet, and eat, and…ah…'

'Drink.' Kennedy found himself thinking of how Jack Kerouac died, his liver so pickled it could no longer process the railroad of impurities coursing through him; with no place to go, his blood backed up on itself and busted the veins all around his orifices and sprinkled itself all over his bathroom. No way to go. That was not going to happen to Don, was it? But as Kennedy had uttered the word *drink*, Don had chimed in with *talk books*. Kennedy took a long look at his friend, made Don say *what?* No, it seemed to Kennedy that there was an aura of good around Don Darius, and he felt reassured. Despite what he had perceived as Don's attack of gloom, his friend's walk was sure, and there was an air of contentment about him. As they got to a corner and stopped by the Uprising monument, Kennedy felt reassured by almost everything around him: he was glad that Don was not as broken as he remembered him, and glad the Poles had reached for a limelight preserved in plaques and statues and memory.

Don brought him down another long street along which tiny automobiles whizzed like toys, not seeming dangerous until they brushed pedestrians with the wind they made. Don led Kennedy past big churches flying the Pope's standard of yellow and white, and past little ones set in niches in walls, past palaces owned at one time by Poland's biggest cheeses, and all, Don reminded Kennedy, recreated from heaps of dust with the aid of Canaletto's paintings.

One of those palaces had an amazing triumphal arch set in its walls; classic imperial Roman style in the middle of northern Europe. 'See that?' Don enthused. 'Now that's what I call a gate. No messing around, no *Is this a gate or not? I'm not sure. Help me out here.*'

Kennedy said, 'Those big-shots sure knew how to make an entrance.'

He got the confession from Don at last that he would not want to be anyplace else in the world right then doing anything else. 'Nothing?' Kennedy checked with wide eyes, and Don said then how the only thing he would rather be doing was having a brew for the road before he got off to his students and that, hell, he was going to make that little wish come true. Kennedy followed him down narrow streets again, crowded with people hurrying home from work. They walked with no comment over the grid of a city that had died and come back to life, and that was an awesome thing that came close to humbling Kennedy as he took his place in the crowds.

Kennedy thought they had to be near the Old Town square again, but it was dark by then, and there was snow spitting, and the place was a warren. He and Don weaved in and out of groups of tourists thumbing noses at the bite of the cold to see Poland anyhow. Kennedy thought it was a bunch of priests he heard behind him, leaking holophrastic Latin, but Don revealed them as Romanians; traders, Kennedy saw plainly then, weighed down by striped nylon bags. A little crowd ahead parted respectfully. This time Kennedy guessed it had to be Lech Walesa on his way home, but instead it was a titanic pregnant woman doing her best to full steam ahead, and he and Don got out of her way very sharply. Then they were among a gaggle of nuns done up in brown. They reminded Kennedy of veiled Muslim women, with faces glowing pale as the flesh of veal calves.

They went into a tiny bar and slipped into seats with a window onto all the wrapped-up people with homes and churches to go to. Don persuaded Kennedy to order a warm beer. Kennedy had heard of this: Polish hot beer, which had in fact made it into his top ten of things not to ever get talked-into, but his wavering left him open to it, as it so often had; he would never have tried heroin, he remembered painfully, had he not wavered, one day in back of a pool-hall in downtown Montpelier, when he was supposed to be in class. At least, he reflected, having warm beer in Poland saved him the hassle of going to England to drink the notorious brews complained of worldwide. He sipped it. Honey, he tasted, and herbs. And maybe aspirin. It was on the verge of drinkable but – call him fussy – he really would have preferred a cold one. He eyed Don's with envy, which did not stop him doing cheers with him.

Out the window, a guy made a Quasimodo face in at them, and formed signs with his hands that they chose to ignore. That did not stop the man finding his way in and panhandling them. He was not exactly a midget, just little, and drink-wizened. Don lifted his ass to fish in pockets for bills, straightened some out and handed them over. The guy said something solemn that made Don answer him with a sweep of the head and a handshake.

'Guy says I'm a true Pole,' Don explained.

'He does?' Kennedy thought Don probably drank enough to be any number of national stereotypes. 'I guess you *are*, too.'

Don's new pal went off to rattle his chains around the other drinkers, drawing, far as Kennedy could see, only grimaces, curses and indignant silences. The woman who ran the place lifted her head and shoulders out of a conversation to yell at the little man, pointing imperiously to the door. Then she turned to Don and made her displeasure with his magnanimity known. Don made noises of apology, hands held up.

'Now *she* begs to differ, and says I'm a true *ass*hole,' he confessed, but in truth it did not seem to bother him. 'And maybe I am.'

'Well.' Kennedy thought of himself again, in a men's room in that Vermont pool-hall, wavering, and next thing a guy was shooting a very weak and very free sample of the local crazy horse into his arm for him. He said, 'I guess we're all assholes, sometimes.'

'Are we?' Don eyed him. 'Even you?' Then he looked down. 'Kennedy,' he said. 'I think of you as one of those guys who…'

'Who what?'

'Who gets stuff…*right*.'

'You do?' Kennedy did not know what to feel about that. Was that a compliment, exactly? It was not true, in any case – of course not, not all the time – but he did not want to go into that at all. 'Well…'

'Who, for example, will help a guy *out*. You understand?'

'Sure I do.' Kennedy wondered if Don was about to touch him for a loan. If that was the case, it would have to be mainly in Turkish lira that would not make too healthy a transition into dollars. He was about to say this, but held onto it. 'Well, I guess I'll try,' he promised, and to his surprise Don said only that he would drink to that, and followed a link broken some time before, and then they were back talking about writing, about literature, about the ghost of some American tradition, and about Don's book in particular.

'It's there,' Don kept confiding to Kennedy, 'all this stuff we've been talking up, all there, the things we both know. But sometimes I wake in the afternoons.' He paused and grinned uncertainly at the laugh Kennedy let out at this, joined in a little. 'And I think it's all just drink-thoughts.' He looked at his drained glass, held it out as if in proof.

'It's not.'

'No?'

'No.' As Don busied himself in calling for more drinks, Kennedy leaned over to make sure he was getting a proper, cold beer. He was diverted then by the sight of two outrageously pregnant women squeezing side-by-side through the doorway, and the complicated operation that got them seated, with two men, the perpetrators of the outrages, presumably, giving up their places. There was another pregnant woman ensconced in a corner, he had already half-noticed and, just as he was about to comment on this to Don, another came in. 'Hey, see that?' He nudged Don. 'And, come to think of it, I keep seeing them out the window, too. What's going on?'

All at the same time, Don accepted the drinks, smiled charmingly at the owner of the place, who was still a little pissed at him, it seemed, paid, and squinted out the window, read out, 'Pre-natal clinic. Right across the street.'

'Oh. That explains it. So Poland is fucking,' Kennedy gathered.

'It is,' Don confirmed. 'It's fucking cold, dark, fucking big, full of trains.'

'Full of churches,' Kennedy laughed out. 'And chimneys.'

'Sure thing. It's fucking a lot of things. But it's also just fucking. Well, look around you. What better way to spend a winter night? Snow out, crap on TV. Why not conjure up a few new Poles?'

'Why not indeed. And so how about you?' Kennedy took the opportunity to put it to Don, better than thinking about all the fucking he himself was definitely not doing, nor, probably, going to be doing anytime soon. 'You managing any of that in between writing great books?'

'Well,' Don came clean, 'not as much as I'd probably like to.'

Kennedy's dad had been the MacKennedy in that old blues about the Saint James Infirmary, who wanted crap-shooters, a jazz band and painted

63

whores to liven up his funeral. Apart from his old man, Don Darius was the only guy Kennedy had ever known who, as they say, consorted with prostitutes on a regular basis. Don's girls in Istanbul were Bulgarian and Romanian women who commuted over on Black Sea ferries, fucked like bunnies for a week or two then went back to being mothers, big and little sisters, sweethearts, wives, government ministers, for all anybody knew. Rob, the guy Don had roomed with in Bakirköy, had told Kennedy how he had gotten sick of waking up for school and seeing these women eating his muesli and drinking his coffee, looking sheepish and, often, very much aware of the scary lives they were leading.

Don had told Kennedy one night that he was not in a millennium going to stick around Istanbul all his days, and how he did not want any attachments. Kennedy had cracked, *What, not even herpes?* But it had been the same with his dad: no woman was going to take the place of his wife, so he was not going to try for some corny old second marriage shit, blah blah. Like a real gentleman, Kennedy had refrained from reminding his dad that it had been one whore too many that had driven his mom away in the first place. He had not wanted to see his dad squirm around trying to find a beat answer to that.

'But attachment is…*good*,' Kennedy had said to both his dad and Don. He had meant: *keeps you washed and brushed and shaved and clothes pressed and shoes shined, and all that stuff, if not for yourself, and not for your lousy job, then at least for the woman in your life.* Kennedy's dad had known better, had been there and done all that, gotten the t-shirt, the divorce decree and the clinic appointments.

In the little bar near Warsaw's Old Town square, Don began telling Kennedy how he had started a thing with a one-on-one student of his, which had developed into a literal one-on-one. Don was vague, but Kennedy gathered that it had come to Don having to punch his student's husband on the snout in a bedroom scene out of an English farce. That had sent Don's romance down the pan, where it belonged. But, Don was saying, and so carefully that Kennedy did not at first notice the shift in emphasis, there was a much bigger prospect of Romeo-and-Juliet-type proportions in his stars. Kennedy was just about to dig out more about this when Don turned the tables, wanting to know, 'How about you, though? Is old Flat Face putting out these days?'

'Hey,' Kennedy said sharply, 'I told you, already. How about not calling her that?'

Kennedy was not as mad as he sounded. He got to thinking again how Ling was the best thing that had happened to him, possibly ever. For all that, though, it did not matter a lick: thanks to Ling's dad, it was going to join Don's sordid liaisons in the dumpster. He gave Don a look that said to sit on his finger, and kept his nose in his beer.

'I didn't mean anything,' Don said.

Kennedy didn't utter a syllable.

'Hey. Hah?' Don nudged Kennedy. 'Say what?'

Kennedy said, 'She's great.'

'I know that.'

Kennedy narrowed his eyes, looked at Don sideways, and pursed his lips in answer.

'No,' Don protested. 'Listen. I know.'

Kennedy had met Ling at some crappy party in Istanbul. There she stood in her green heather mix and her button shoes with her short hair and skew-whiff eye. For a second Kennedy had gone back years to his first sight of Ling; he was lying on his bed having just shot Chinese heroin into his arm, listening to David Bowie's *Sound and Vision* over and over, the record player arm fixed back to let the stylus hiss up then drop down again. At the party he had had to resist the urge to cross the room breathing out, *I met you in a dream and I love you.* All the same, just a little later he was next to her suggesting they meet up the next day. And maybe get married. She had laughed out gold and silver, said, 'But I'm going to the dentist tomorrow. The day after would be better.'

'I know it,' Don said again.

He did not, Kennedy thought, and you had to forgive a guy that. 'Your green-eyed shit has no effect on me,' he informed Don. 'I love her.'

And a little voice inside him asked, *So why aren't you with her right now?*

'I guess you do, too. Hey, listen. I…respect your choice, Kennedy.'

'Sure you do.' Kennedy nudged Don back at last. 'But let's forget true romance. I thought we were talking about you?'

'We were?'

'Yeah. I guess the whores are busy in Warsaw, then, finding a sucker like you?'

'No.' Don shook his head vigorously, like a little boy accused of something. 'It's not like that.' Kennedy caught a hint from Don of some deep embarrassment. He started to think of a smart reply, but then saw that an odd kind of seriousness had overtaken Don's demeanour. 'Not like that at all for this boy, at all.'

'Well.' That boy did indeed have romance, Kennedy saw suddenly, was sick with it. 'So.' He saw then that Don had been busting to tell him about it ever since they had met at the station. 'Tell.'

Don had met a woman, he began to relate to Kennedy. 'Not a girl,' he digressed, presumably to make sure that Kennedy was able to make out the difference. Kennedy persuaded him that he could. Don had met her on a train; he had boarded at Gdansk and settled opposite her in a car on the express that ran from Gdynia to Krakow, and got talking on the corny subject of the *Teach Yourself Polish* book he had open on his lap. They had soon junked that and had hit it off to rattle on about other things, real things, ordinary stuff, big stuff, small stuff, funny stuff. Then the lights of Warsaw had startled their faces, and next thing the train was pulling into Warsaw Central. She had already told Don that she was going on down to Krakow to spend time with friends, but would in a day or two be back home. Was Don going to see her again? That was the only question left. She took Don's number, and gave him her word that she would call, and maybe make things happen.

'Ola,' Don said.

'What?' Kennedy wondered, 'We're going to practise our Spanish?'

Don explained, 'Her *name* is Ola.'

'Well, that's kind of a nice name, man.'

'It is. It has…music.'

'It does?'

'Yes, it does.'

'You're right.' Kennedy didn't think any kind of music could be achieved in two measly syllables, but thought he might as well agree. 'So what happened?'

To cut a short story dead, Ola had not called Don. He seemed convinced that this was because she had lost the number he had written down for her.

'Hmm.' In the interests of…balance, Kennedy brought up, 'Maybe she just thought you were a jerk.'

Don managed to remain modest while having none of that.

'Well, okay.' Kennedy did not really want to shake Don from his conviction. 'You were there, man.'

'I was there.' Don said it with an air of finality. Or so Kennedy thought.

'Not a lot you can do about it.'

'Well.' Don brightened a little. 'That's where I thought you might be able to help me.'

'Me?'

'Yass.'

'Uh…' Kennedy's caution was abandoned for a passing cloud of amusement. 'Well, okay.' Curiosity, he realised with a slight sinking feeling, was taking a steer, too. 'How?'

There was no way Kennedy was going to drag up to Gdansk to help Don look for some girl, or even some woman, he had met on a train. And that was just as well, because it did not involve going to Gdansk; it involved going north past Gdansk and on to Gdynia on the Baltic and then further along the coast to a town called Abel. 'A small town.' Don was zinging on the high point of his spin. 'We'll find her easy.'

'How small?' Kennedy pressed, but showed a hand in case Don mistook the question for assent to such a crazy idea. Don did not know how small, exactly, it was clear. 'And, small or not, what are we going to do? Knock on every frigging door in town?'

'Not at all.' Don put an *I-got-the-trump* look on. 'Listen. She goes to church.'

'Good.' Kennedy was happy that she would be able to save her soul. 'But so what?'

'So we get there for Sunday. Then we got it.'

'We do?'

'Yes.'

'No way.'

'Oh, come *on*, Kennedy.'

'No *way*. Include me out.'

Kennedy changed the subject and at the same time injected a little excitement into the proceedings by asking Don exactly what time he was supposed to be teaching his class. The question got Don spluttering graphically into his beer and up to the phone, leaving a trail of *oh Lords*. He came back to the table looking chastened, but clutching more beers, from which Kennedy gathered that his friend was not about to go declaiming and declining for the edification of students with nothing better to do on a Friday evening and no friends to see nor lives to lead. Kennedy asked him what had happened but, keen to get back to the thing that was foremost in his mind, Don waved it away, saying, 'I handled it. But listen, Kennedy, serious now. What do you say to a rail-trip, hah? Think about it, now. I mean...'

Kennedy told Don in user-friendly terms that he was rail-tripped-out, having schlepped up already from one European coast. He knew that he really ought to put his feet up for a day and chill. He was beginning to like the idea, also, of Don getting out of the apartment for a day, which would give him a chance to settle down and read through Don's other work, check what needed to be done with it, and to think about who he could call, people he thought might look at the Saudi book and even publish some of it, maybe as a work-in-prog. 'But you should certainly go find her,' he advised, not very artfully.

Don ignored the suggestion, saying, 'Come *on*, hah?' into Kennedy's face.

'No hope.'

'Bit of immoral support?'

'No.'

'Listen.'

'*No*. Not a hope in *hell*.'

'But *listen*.'

'I listened, already. It's not going to happen, man.'

'Come *on*, Kennedy.' Don dug an elbow hard into Kennedy's ribs, and Kennedy dug him back.

'Well.' Don gave Kennedy a long, studied look. Not exactly disappointed; Kennedy thought that maybe the craziness of the idea was permeating through to Don, now that they had talked it out. Good ideas needed to be talked out, he reasoned. And so did bad ones. 'Hmm. Okay.' Don raised hands. 'Okay,' he admitted. 'I was out of line to ask you. Listen.' Kennedy was listening. When Don asked him again to listen, Kennedy felt moved to point to his ear to convince Don. 'Make you a deal,' Don began.

'No deals,' Kennedy stated.

'You're not listening.' Don put on a face. 'I asked you to listen. I craved your indulgence in this. And you told me that was exactly what you were doing. Turns out now you were deceiving me.' The wounded face Don put on was so funny that Kennedy almost broke a rib, one of Don's. 'But listen now. This is what I say. Forget I ever mentioned it. That's the deal.'

'That's it?' Kennedy made suspicion show in his brows.

'That's it.'

'But?'

'But what?'

'Well...*is* there a but?'

'No buts.' Kennedy's mind was not exactly put at ease by Don's words alone. 'No howevers or neverthelesses.'

'Well.' But Kennedy wanted to know suddenly what the woman-not-girl was like and how she looked and what she wore and how she smelled and if she had good teeth and no moustache and all. 'Good. But – '

'No buts. That's it. That's an end to my great lost romance that never was nor ever will be.'

'Hmm.' Kennedy could read nothing on his friend's face. He was about to waver, he feared, and then saw all over again what an *idiot* scheme it was. 'Okay. Good.'

For a little while it did not look like the two were ever going to talk about anything again. They sat and sipped. Kennedy felt a wave of weariness break over him, and at the same time sensed his brain's resistance to it. He did indeed want to talk about the woman Don had met – he had sensed her importance before she had even been mentioned – but found himself talking about the beer there in Warsaw, and how it seemed to be good. Don said, 'They sure do know how to make beer here,' and that was it, the beer conversation they had had so many times before. Kennedy said how the vodka had been good, too, and Don told him how he had to try green vodka, green because it had a stick of fragrant grass in it from the east of Poland where the buffalo roam, or, maybe, roams, and how it was called bison vodka because of that. Kennedy knew that, though, as they had suffered that same conversation only the night before.

'Okay, okay, listen,' Kennedy said. Don cupped an ear, and Kennedy told him to cut the crap. 'Just listen. If you really want to hare up to wherever in search of this woman, then maybe we ought to – '

'Ah-ah.' More theatrics, this time with Don blocking his ears. 'We'll forget it. It's crazy. Right?'

'Yeah. It is.' That was good, Kennedy thought: it had to come from Don. 'It actually is.'

'*Actually* is not a word I like to use.' Don's confession managed to embody the wordsmith's scorn. 'It's too...*British*. But it's the correct one here. It'd involve heading up to the Baltic Sea, which would freeze our butts big time and send us back home with triple pneumonia of the ass.'

'Right.'

'And we really don't want that.'

But Kennedy began to wonder again what was quite so important about whatever-her-name-was in wherever-town. What could ever have been so important about anybody you met on some train? The thought idled and fizzled away. He found himself thinking of Bruno and Haines in Patricia Highsmith's S*trangers on a Train*, given flesh by the actors in the Hitchcock movie…Maybe the woman on the train had swapped a murder with Don. Maybe she had been drunk enough for Don to think of her as a true soul-mate…

'Forget it, then.' Don examined the dregs of his beer briefly, then drained them. He gave his drinking an air of completion by putting his glass down. All the same, Kennedy thought, he looked as though he wished it were full again. 'And listen. And tell me what you've got in mind for this evening here in this burg.' Before Kennedy could answer, Don went on, 'Because it's not worth for you to go back to the apartment, really. I thought maybe you could come along to my class.'

'Your class? But I thought your class was right at the bottom of that glass.'

'No. I relocated it.'

'Relocated it?'

'And, ah, re-timed it.'

'What?' To Kennedy, ruled by a draconian school timetable that only the heirs of Byzantium could have dreamed up, this was something he had to see.

They paid their tab, then made more circles in the snow around Warsaw's old quarter. The first thing Kennedy did as they turned a corner was tread on a slide of glacial ice and fall on his rump. It was shocking and sobering. 'I do that a lot.' Don seemed cheerful to get that off his chest as he helped Kennedy up. He told Kennedy how he was real careful each time he approached a spot where it had happened before; he made a magic lantern comedy for Kennedy, of a man making careful strides only to get safely past the spot and then, when he was least expecting it, to tumble a little further on. 'You really cannot trust the snow.' When Don said that, Kennedy was reminded of his old man, who had gone on a lot about the treacherous weather, like the weather owed you. To Kennedy, if you could not even trust your family, or your friends, or your police force, or president, or the things your own mind sent your way, it was a mark of insane optimism to feel that the elements should be your friends.

They resumed careful steps. They were close behind a middle-aged tourist couple. The guy let out a series of farts Kennedy could hear plainly, even though Don was talking his ear off about ass-prints he had left all over the snow of Warsaw. Kennedy was about to draw Don's attention to the man's comic breach of street etiquette when he recalled Don saying *I do that a lot*, and refrained. It was because, a few years before, Kennedy had rushed into an empty classroom in the crappy private school in Boston where he had been filling in time before heading overseas, and had let rip with a perfect trail-bike burner of a fart. Perfect relief for him until the cloud cleared and he saw that the room was not in fact empty. A woman with whom Kennedy had so far exchanged only teacherly talk, but who he thought was kind of cute and kind of liked, was bent down by a cabinet gathering a brace of dictionaries. She had of course been diverted by his *petomaine* performance, but as he caught sight of her she put her nose back into the cabinet. Probably the safest place for it. 'Uh, sorry,' he had called to her. 'I...uh...didn't mean to...uh...offend you. Or anything.' She had just mirrored his wishes and acted like he was not there, but the thing was, it was a teacher thing: all teachers had to stick a cork up their asses till the end of a class if they had been foolish enough to eat the wrong thing for breakfast or lunch, and the woman must have gone through that a thousand times, but there was no fellow-feeling there. She could have just lied, and said, *Hey, I do that a lot, too.* Kennedy never had asked her out on a date, like: *Hey, you want to go someplace nice and die of embarrassment when I fart?* In any case, then, though Kennedy did not for a second believe Don's story about slipping and sliding all around town, he appreciated it, and wanted to run on ahead and tell the farting tourist, *Hey buddy, I do that a lot – burn on, man, and warm up the street ahead of us with that methane.*

Don stopped at a door, pushed it and led Kennedy through a crowd around a bar to a back room. Cheers went up from a table when Don appeared, room was made for him and his pal, and then Don was introducing Kennedy to his get-a-life Friday evening class. 'He's a Kennedy,' Don declaimed. 'Note the name, and the toothy grin and the leonine hair and say nothing more, and let's hope nothing unlucky happens to him in our care, hah?'

Nobody, not even a lion, would willingly think of their hair as leonine, and Kennedy had no habitual grin of any kind, he liked to think, but even as he smiled Don's comment aside he tried not to show any teeth. He did not get all the names: there was a guy there who had liberated himself from his tongue-twister Polish name to reinvent himself as Larry, another who called himself Peter, a woman who said Kennedy could call her Aggie, and a frothy girl whose name was pronounced as *you'd-eat-her*. 'Because she's that good,' Don guffawed, an old gag, Kennedy assumed, that got her slapping Don on the arm, and got the others laughing indulgently. There was a doctorly oldish guy who was indeed a doctor, and a girl with huge glasses, who looked all of fifteen. They were Don's proficiency exam class, and they looked to Kennedy like a good crowd.

It was not the first time Don had left a message at the school for them to meet him in that bar; they wound up there often, junking grammar and structure to discuss stuff – movies, the government, hamburgers, Chomsky, whatever. Kennedy instantly liked the rapport Don had built up with them, and saw at once that they had become friends in the course of their classes. He was envious for a time, thinking of his baby eleven-year-olds, and his hormone-haunted fifteen-year-olds, and how to them he was just this remote teacher figure, some guy in an Ivy League sports coat and necktie who made their lives that little bit worse by being one of its agents of burden.

'So.' The doctor character was in Kennedy's face almost as soon as he had sat down. 'What do you think about JFK?'

'The movie?' Kennedy checked.

'No no.' The doc did a smile that looked as if a slice of lemon had been forced into it. 'I refer to your president.'

'What about him?'

'I ask who assassinated him, of course.' The doc made a gesture to suggest that this was the most natural question in the world. 'Do you know?'

'Me?' Kennedy thought of Howard Markevitz, a guy with whom he had studied at college, whose whole life was taken up with rooting out conspiracy theories. *And practices*, Howard was forever reminding people. He had written a book called *American Kafka* which had sold to all the other conspiracy-fixated geeks. Kennedy kept a photo of Ling in his billfold; Howard Markevitz, people assumed, carried one of John F Kennedy on a slab, his eyes open, his head all exploded and broken but, somehow, the part in his hair intact. If Howard had been present

Kennedy could have bowed out of the conversation and left the doc to him. 'I wasn't there.' Kennedy's protest merely made the doc look very puzzled. His smile hung inviting, then limply, for a second on his face, so he added quickly, 'So I don't know who shot JFK. But I know a guy who does.'

'Who?' the doc demanded.

'Lee Harvey Oswald.' When a round of laughter hit him, Kennedy became aware that the eyes of all Don's group were on him. 'He shot JFK,' *with his bow and arrow*, he thought. *Poor old Cock Robin, the big patsy.*

'That is the simple answer.' The doc seemed as unhappy with it as Mrs Oswaldski and Oliver Stone.

'But how do you know that?' Peter put in, reasonably enough. 'Nobody can know it now, for certain.'

'Well, think about it this way.' Kennedy leaned forward and, maybe because of the subject matter, they made a circle of conspirators. 'Everybody in the world who was alive at the time remembers where they were when JFK got shot, right? The only person said he didn't, was Lee Harvey Oswald.'

That broke the huddle. Kennedy's crack had gone down a storm with everybody except the doc, who gaped at him, genuinely pissed off. But who really wanted to have a serious conversation about the JFK murder? Apart from Howard Markevitz, one-time English major at Syracuse University?

'Listen.' Kennedy thought it might be time to build a bridge with the old sawbones. He remembered one of Don's tales and, inspired, pointed to Don. 'He's the man to ask about this.' He was sorry he could not say, like one of Agatha Christie's genteel gumshoes, *It was him did it. Take him away, constable.* What he did say was, 'Don Darius *was* there.'

That day in November sixty-three, Don's mom and pop packed the kids and the picnic lunch into the Buick, festooned it with Democrat pennants and hit the road for Dallas. They rubbernecked in the crowd – and were captured fleetingly, in fact, in Benjamin Zapruder's movie of the shooting – and of course heard those shots whiplash through the day into the schizoid dreams of a whole generation. They felt the wild will of somebody's agenda make a frenzy that played out in every face around them before it rippled into the rest of the world. Don started to recount all this, though in truth there was little to tell; he was six at the time, after all. So did he look up at the windows of the book depository, he was asked, and said, 'No. Nobody told little old me the shots were supposed to have come from there. Now, next question from the floor.' Did Don's dad take any photos that day? 'Nope,' he said. But why not? 'Didn't have a camera.' But it was an historic occasion – did it not feel like one? '*A* historic occasion,' teacher Don corrected. 'Not to me. I was hungry. And we ate right after the killing.'

'Even Lee Harvey Oswald went to see a movie right after,' Kennedy remembered, and that got the doc glaring again, and got Peter banging Kennedy's shoulder in appreciation. 'No, but it's true,' Kennedy insisted.

'What was the movie?' Aggie asked. Kennedy did not know. First time in his life he had ever needed Howard Markevitz around to answer a JFK question. And where was he? He had surely been killed in a bizarre accident. Or was selling insurance to farmers in Wyoming.

'Will there be a future president Kennedy?' That was the doc, back on course.

How the hell would Kennedy know? He and Don talked about it later. Don said the Poles were grabbed by the idea of a Catholic being in charge of the good old US of A. Why, though? The only people in the world who were religious, as far as Kennedy could see, were Muslims: religion mattered so little to the people of the western world. And he had never been able to grasp the Catholic slant on politics. All the same, neither did he get non-Catholics rustling up such hostility at the idea of a Catholic president.

'There might be a future president Kennedy,' Kennedy said to the doc, though it seemed to him that any Kennedy may as well paint a target on his back and stroll around a rifle range as run for presidential office. 'Not going to be me, though,' he laughed.

As if he were a real clan Kennedy, and this conversation were taking place in a study in one of the Kennedy mansions with uncle Ted, the doc asked Kennedy, 'What, then, are you going to do with your life?' His tone sounded critical, kind of: *Okay, so you don't want to run for president, but you do know how teaching English in a school overseas isn't a real job, son…*Maybe the doc had missed the comic thrust of Don's introduction, thought the object of his advice truly was one of those real-live Kennedys wafted magically to Warsaw to drink a beer with him. Kennedy looked at the doc, thinking, *And just exactly what business is it of yours, pal?*

What Kennedy said was, 'Hell, if I knew that, I guess I'd be someplace doing it. Right?'

Because you could not tell people that all you really ever wanted to do was write, and edit, and publish – you just could not tell them that. Unless you were already a fuck-off big writer, people just went into sneering overdrive. Tough, really, it seemed to Kennedy; nobody dissed bank clerks because they had not yet made bank president.

'I will tell you what I think.' Kennedy had been afraid the doc might do that. He was back in conspiracy mode, gave Kennedy's arm a squeeze. 'You should enjoy your life. I think your responses in our conversation reveal you to be a rather bitter young man.'

'Right.' Kennedy had begun to nod. 'Huh?'

'Rather yes. I think your humour, whilst being funny, is derivated from bitterness.'

'What?' Kennedy was irritated; he knew the doc was partly right.

'You have the possibility to enjoy your life.' The doc did not blink. He believed everything he was saying. 'You seem to me like a sensualist.'

He waited for an answer, but it was only Kennedy saying, 'Uh…right.'

The doctor explained kindly, 'A man who seeks only to enjoy what he can enjoy from the things which have been placed within his reach,' which had to have been learned word-for-word from the nineteen fifteen edition of *Webster's Pocket Pedants' Dictionary.* 'All men who are young in these times have a potential for a good life. I do not mean a lazy one, of course.'

'Of course.' The doc caught that, and waggled a finger at Kennedy, like: *See what I mean? Bitter.* 'Uh, well, what kind of life, then?'

'An interesting one,' he said, then confessed, 'I do not enjoy my life at all.'

Kennedy really did not want to hear about the doc's unenjoyable life. He also, most emphatically, did not want to live in times that were too interesting, it struck him. His thoughts drifted unwillingly to a short movie of Ling being taken away from him forever to the ass-end of Asia, the two of them cursed by Confucius. That was *interesting*, wasn't it?

The doc went on to tell Kennedy that he had done everything right by his mom and his dad, by the priests in his life, by the communist assholes in it, and now he was doing right by the great book of capitalism; he had junked doctoring, worked now for a German pharmaceutical company and got paid shitloads, but what did it all mean? Kennedy did not have even a rhetorical clue. A look up showed him that the others were all talking and giggling; he got the feeling then that the party was going on all around him, pricked by a memory of a freshman bash when he got stuck in the corner with the suicidal nerd from his dorm.

'You tell him, doc.' Don leaned over.

'I did.' The doc giggled, and turned back to Kennedy. 'I enjoy my English lessons very much, in any case.'

'Well, that's got to be good.' Kennedy's few words did not put over how impressed he really felt. He was almost as cheered by the doc's statement, and the scene around him, as he was by Don's writing, because it was another sign that Don had happened on some good stuff as he ambled through his drinking days. Kennedy scanned the faces around him, saw for a second the faces of his little Istanbul gremlins, willing only very reluctantly to be enthused and entertained and to put a little of themselves into it. Sometimes. Even if the teaching of English did not have a lot to do with real life, Kennedy set a lot of store on the value of these moments of communication, which kept a guy from giving it all up and going to farm sheep in North Dakota.

Don butted into Kennedy's moment and winked him to his feet, asking him quietly, 'Hey, listen. Are you holding any of the old magic baccy there?'

'Are you crazy?' Don had to be joking: you did not carry stuff like that around Europe on trains, not if you wanted to cross borders controlled by a whole lot of bad-tempered people in uniforms.

'Well,' Don said. 'Ah, you want to smoke something?'

Kennedy did not really know, in fact, but said he might, if the price was right, and Don beckoned him into the front bar, going, 'Well, like the fellow says, come on down.' He brought Kennedy to face a guy he signalled out of a little group, introduced each of them simply as a pal. Kennedy sure was glad not to have to go through the whole *President Kennedy* rigmarole again.

The guy reached out a paw, pulled on Kennedy's hand, said, 'Pleased,' and Kennedy decided he might as well be pleased, too. 'We speak English,' he informed Kennedy as he made them a path to the swirl of cigarette smoke that indicated the door. 'It is cool.' Kennedy was happy to take the guy's word on that as a blast of icy air hit him hard in the face.

Kennedy did not speak any language at all as Don and the other guy small-talked the short way along the street to an abrupt, dimly-lit turn into a building, and up a flight of echoing stairs. They went into an apartment, and the guy shchushed a greeting out to somebody in a room. An open door revealed a glimpse of an attentive middle-aged woman poised, halfway out of an armchair, and then Kennedy and Don were led into a room. It was their host's room, surely, but it seemed to Kennedy to be a child's room, had lots of record albums and books and ugly stereo equipment, a battered Spanish guitar in a corner, posters on the walls. Kennedy looked up and saw the child-bearing lips of Aerosmith's Steve Tyler. There was a big poster too for *Apocalypse Now*, all orange carnage, and another featuring an ad for Nike. These had no doubt replaced the ones of Rosa Luxemburg and Felix Dzerzhinsky he had been forced to paste up there when he was a hideous child communist, or so Kennedy guessed.

Their host was all in mismatched shades of black, and had shaved his head. The thick lenses of his glasses pushed his eyes startlingly out of his face, and added to Kennedy's overall impression of a guy who had recently done his own lobotomy.

'You want to turn on?' he barked at Kennedy.

Kennedy felt startled by the age-old junky-talk, meaning only smack in his days of dead time. This echo of his vein-abusing was more uncomfortable to him than he might have expected.

'I want to get high,' he said carefully, 'if that's where you're at.'

'At?' The guy looked puzzled for a second, a doubtful smile on his face before he decided, 'Yes, I am there.' Then he trapped his tongue between his teeth and nodded, excited. One of those guys, Kennedy saw, who was into the ritual of the thing as much as any of its other benefits. He began to rummage among things in a closet, and Kennedy could smell musty old clothes.

'From Lebanon.' It was obviously a capitalist habit of Don's pal, for he had a deal wrapped and ready. He part-unwrapped it and handed it over. Kennedy gave it a token sniff, and made a show of looking appreciative. If it was the real Lebanese deal, then Kennedy was a geisha girl. But it looked okay, and smelt okay.

'Cool?' he was asked.

Kennedy looked from the guy to Don. He wondered if it would piss either or both of them off if he asked if there was any coke going, or any means of getting hold of some. He looked from Don to the guy. It was an etiquette gap he couldn't bridge.

'Cool,' he echoed. 'Sure.'

The guy's eyes looked about to bounce happily out on springs. Kennedy started to pull money out.

'Hey hey, now.' Don put a hand up. 'Listen. My party.'

'Hey, come on, man.'

'No no.'

Kennedy thought he kind of knew what was occurring; Don's loony find-the-lady trip to the sea came back to him. And if Don thought Kennedy could be bought off with a deal of cheap blow, then he was out of his fuzzy mind. Kennedy sheeshed up at his new friend's lampshade as Don went through with the deed that sealed the deal even tighter than a wrap of tinfoil, and sent Kennedy the aside, *hey, later.*

Like in a movie running backward, the three men reversed their steps, walked again into the cold, and the guy was back with his cronies at the bar, and Don and Kennedy were back among Don's class. The group was barely holding together now, and people left one-by-one until they were left with Peter. He was a stocky, relaxed-looking dude of maybe thirty, in check shirt and black Levis, dark hair in a ponytail, and very black eyes. He worked as an engineer at some institute, and accordingly had an air of blue-collar-going-white about him. Kennedy, who had heard only snatches of his conversation when ensconced with the doc, found him instantly likeable. They quickly decided they were hungry. Don scooped up the huge pile of banknotes left by the others, and he, Kennedy and Peter threw some more onto it. They paid the check and left. The three of them walked along that same street again, through the barbican tower and the city walls and toward the Old Town square.

'Old market place,' Peter called it, as he did his host part. 'Every north European town has one. It used to be a town's…focus, you know? This one was destroyed, of course, by the Germans.' He said the building on the corner near them was the only remaining part of the original square, impervious to dynamite. 'It's a real triumph of the will,' he said, without, as far as Kennedy could tell, any irony in using the Nietzsche phrase, 'to have built Warsaw how it was.' Kennedy's thoughts of how the city centre looked like a movie set resounded in his head, ignoble and petty. He regretted them, and resolved to give the place a little more respect when he thought about it in future.

They were not going much further. As Don led them up steps to a restaurant, Peter warned Kennedy, 'You're getting the real tourist Warsaw now.' They were going into *the* Fukier's restaurant, Kennedy gathered quickly as they got their overcoats off and dumped them on the checkroom babooshka. Kennedy had never heard of the place, but then who was he?

A waiter in a bright red vest came up and asked in English if they had a reservation. Kennedy had a few, as the place looked horribly expensive, but he did not think it seemly to mention them.

One time in Paris, Kennedy had gone with a pal into a restaurant that had been recommended by some guy they had talked to in some bar. They had sat down, scoped the menu, then worked out quickly that if they ate there they would blow all the money they had been intending to jive on for the two-day remainder of their stay. Nothing to do on that occasion but to apologise to the waiter for having fooled him into lighting the candles at their table; he had been no way near as snooty as he looked, and in fact had been a real *mensch* about it as he let them skulk out with no drama.

Kennedy saw then that the waiter in Fukier's had dropped the oily demeanour and was bantering with Peter, who had been delayed doing the same thing with the check-room lady. They were led to a table off to one side, not one of the best ones, Peter said solemnly. The concept usually went over Kennedy's head – if they had it in restaurants, though, then again, who was he to kick up a fuss? It had legs, and was flat, and covered with a white cloth that dared you to put elbows on it, had candles, napkins and enough silver to upset the commodities market, had all that was needed for a guy to make a meal of things, so it was fine by Kennedy.

He was handed a menu, all hand-tooled leather and gold leaf, looked like a first edition Walter Scott. He felt a little silly just trying to hold the thing up. Peter was telling Don and Kennedy how he had wanted to go to Fukier's all his life until he got to age twenty five. Once he had reached the status of big-shot engineer, though, and had to keep bringing clients there, the experience had become run-of-the-mill.

That rang a bell in Kennedy's mind: why was he being entertained like one of Peter's clients? Its chimes faded, but it tinkled all the same.

Peter told Kennedy what was good eating and what was not. Both Peter and Don advised a dish called bigos, all meat and cabbage and apparently very Polish, and very good for hitting the spot before, during or after a shitload of beer.

Peter might have been a little jaded with Fukier's, but Kennedy fancied he saw a look on the guy's face that reminded him of Don's dealer pal; he too was caught up in the paces of the thing, and he was loving it.

As they sipped their beers, and as Peter and Don digressed into some serious talk about the use of the past perfect progressive mode in English, Kennedy took a look around the place. It was a genteel kind of scene, with elegant couples candle-lit at their chow, though two pairs of businessmen had slipped from small-talk to big talk, of trade, and were fencing with calculators. Other than that, there was what looked like an extended family group having a hushed good time at a table in the centre of the room.

The food arrived. It did indeed go down a treat with that pale yellow beer, filled them up and, as they snorfed it down, shut them up.

The silence was filled by a couple at a nearby table, a wizened guy of maybe seventy, in a suit way too big for him, and a blonde dame in her spreading fifties. She had pink cleavage, all pumped-up and in-your-face, and seemed to think it was one of her positive attributes. Her audience learned that she got an alpha-gamma, whatever that was, at Oxford, presumably the one in England; she was a Russian, and not just any old broken-backed Soviet prole but a countess; she was staying at a hotel in Warsaw in which the towels were not changed regularly enough. She spoke a weird kind of American-accented English peppered with puzzling oddities such as, *I make a protestation* – she made a lot of those – and *Pray continue*, that nobody would have noticed except that she had to say everything she said ear-crunchingly loud and at least three times. She did her countess part well by talking a lot about common people, whoever they might have been. Kennedy would not have blamed anybody for getting up and going over and sticking a tablecloth down her throat.

'Great,' Don said, 'how in this day and age we finally found a good reason for Uncle Joe the Sheep-Killer.'

'He means old Joe Stalin,' Kennedy had to explain for Peter.

Peter laughed his good loud laugh, and confessed, 'In fact, you can't quote me, but many of us in Poland used to feel that the Russians were indeed in fact rather like sheep.'

'*Baa*,' Don offered.

'Used to?' Kennedy grinned.

'If you can find somebody like this anywhere in Poland, however,' Peter said, 'it's here in Fukier's.'

'Maybe they're why this isn't one of the best tables,' Kennedy suggested.

'If she's a countess,' Don said, 'then I guess the guy's got to be a count.'

Kennedy beat him to suggesting the removal of one vowel.

With the countess's racket in the background, Peter started telling Don how he was not being a great host, meaning that Warsaw was okay, but why would Kennedy come all the way to Poland to see only Warsaw?

Good question, Kennedy thought. He had a vision of himself, on trains, burdened by literature in the concrete and abstract and some way in between. *Here comes the friend in need*, he teased himself.

'Ah now, Kennedy's all travelled-out.' Don dismissed the idea of more travel with just a little too much verve, it seemed to Kennedy. 'He did Belgrade on the way, and some town in Czechoslovakia – Olomoutz?'

'Ostrava.' Kennedy talked about his brush with bad-tempered railway officialdom, and then about the kindly consul in Ostrava, and his day of doppelgängers. Behind it, though, he could see the way the conversation could be leading. Peter said Don should be dragging Kennedy down to Krakow, and on from there to the mountains, maybe. The Baltic was not mentioned.

'Up to Gdansk, maybe?' Kennedy could not remember the name of the little town around which Don wanted to do his find-the-lady.

He got to thinking that maybe he was getting just a little paranoid when Peter rolled his shoulders and said, 'Gdansk is interesting, okay, but, compared to Krakow, not what you can call a beautiful city. So, Don,' he finished, 'get your act together,' going a little shy despite his confidence in using the idiom he had recovered, 'and show President Kennedy a good time. Hey.' He indicated the big family group at the centre table. 'You know who is that, that guy there?'

'No.' Kennedy and Don did not need the description Peter began to supply: at the heart of the group was a guy who could have been any age between twenty and forty, gaunt and blond, features cut with diamonds, a mouthful of big, bright teeth.

'Is he a count?' Don laughed.

Kennedy laughed too, but in fact he was just thinking that the man really did look like what you might imagine to be a count, one from Dostoevsky, maybe: very spare and aristocratic. He asked, 'So who is he?'

'He is Zenon Yaskula.' Kennedy and Don were disappointed. They made blank faces. 'He is a famous bicycle rider.'

Just to make certain, Kennedy guessed, Don asked, 'He rides bikes?'

'Yes.'

'Oh,' Kennedy put in. 'Bikes.' He glanced over at the countess's wobbling décolletage. 'I know a great place he could park his bike.'

'What?' they said, but then Kennedy wanted to leave those forgotten aristos forgotten; he also felt slightly ashamed of his crude joke.

'Not one bike,' Don wanted to get clear, 'but bikes? I'd pay to see that.'

'He will race in the Tour of France this year,' said Peter. 'You know, this important bicycle race?'

'Ah *yes.*' Don was impressed, at last. 'Those guys are just the most amazing athletes.'

'They sure are,' Kennedy had to agree. In truth, though, he had never been able to get too excited about bike racing. He had gone to see a varsity race one time, guys blasting x-number of times around a track, and the first guy home won, and that he could understand. The pro stuff was not so straightforward, though, he remembered, when the guy who rolled first over the line got to hold up a bunch of flowers, but did not necessarily get to be champion. The thought of going around a country the size of France on a bike was pretty awesome, though, and he said, 'Well, here's to him.'

They all drank to Zenon Yaskula, rider of bikes, and at that the man himself looked up and over at their table, and bowed his pedigree head a little. That got them pleased to the point of no betterment. And then Peter said he had to get home, faced an early start the next day.

Kennedy had the feeling that he and Don would be doing the same.

It was no surprise to Kennedy that they had a paperless meal; no check changed hands, no cash. 'A little business.' Peter's eyes shone with that *it's-my-party* thing and, when he went to the bathroom, Don told Kennedy that he guessed their humble little meal was nickels and dimes in the entertainment budget of Peter's Deutschmark-driven company.

They all shook hands outside. Kennedy thought Peter was a great guy, and was drunk enough to say so, and said how they should all try to hook up again. 'When we get back,' he said.

Peter said, 'Sure.'

Don said in the background, 'Back from where?'

'Don't dumb up, man.' Kennedy sent him a wink. 'Dumb down if you really have to, but don't dumb up.'

Don put himself in the frame for disingenuous asshole of the year, in Kennedy's opinion, when he claimed not to know what that meant but that, hell, it seemed a lot like useful advice…Waving to Peter, they walked on along the edge of the Old Town square.

'Hey.' Don leaned into Kennedy in the square and said with some enthusiasm, 'I saw David Bowie here.' Diverted, he pointed at the snow swirling busily in the glow of a streetlight and said, 'Now doesn't that make you want to get your hands wet with some snowballs?'

'No,' Kennedy did not take long to decide.

'Me either.'

Kennedy saw little Don Darius dreaming of snow at a window in Texas for a second. And then sensibly, it being a fool thing to dream of in Texas, he was gone. Kennedy felt his feet want to slide under him, and was brought back to the horrible reality of the stuff.

'You saw David Bowie?' Kennedy did not want to be drawn from the subject of their doings next day, if he could help it, but he was intrigued. 'You mean, like, doing a gig?'

'*No.*' Don's frown gave it some emphasis, and Kennedy could not in truth see Don wanting to watch David Bowie, not even if he were performing in Don's kitchen. 'Just saw him walking along the sidewalk, like I see you right now.'

'Just…walking?' Kennedy could not imagine David Bowie just walking along the sidewalk, pictured him travelling only by limo.

'Just one foot in front of the other.'

'What did he look like?'

'Eh?' Don combined a smile with a frown. 'Looked exactly like that David Bowie cat.' He helpfully did Bowie for a second, guy with a microphone.

'Maybe it was just a guy looked like him.' Kennedy was thinking again about those Ostrava look-alikes.

'Well.' Don seemed to consider. 'That's one explanation. No,' he established happily, 'it was the bard himself. Trust me.'

Kennedy stared. He would like to have trusted Don; specifically, not to talk him into anything that would take the form of trains and coastal towns and churches and stray women. He was about to say this, but then all he said was, 'I used to think the best song ever in the world was *Sound and Vision.*' He did not know why he was telling Don that; heroin had spoiled the song for him.

'Oh. How does that one go?'

Kennedy treated Don to a line of the song, which got Don smiling, saying, 'Oh, okay. Best song in the world, says you, is about a guy's *wallpaper?*'

'*Used* to think so,' Kennedy reminded him. He thought of his room way back home in Harrington, Vermont, and how at times it had seemed like it would be the last thing he ever saw.

It was not so late, but the square was empty, which showed Kennedy that most people in Warsaw had more sense than Don and him, even David Bowie, if he was still around. That new snow kept falling, looking big as banknotes in the lights of the lamps. The square in front of the royal castle was deserted too, and when they reached the road it was a quick and easy thing to hail a cab and sink into it all the way along the street and past its phoenix buildings and statues, and down the hill to Don's.

Kennedy was bombed. He sat on the couch and listened to Don clink and clank in the kitchen. He heard beers being poured, felt comforted by that and fell asleep for a few seconds. The TV woke him up, some of that corny Hollywood jazz Don liked. His attention hovered around it, and he was just about to close his eyes again when Ginger Rogers' face filled the screen, big-eyed, mouth full of teeth, lips full and fat, singing, *We're in the Money*, in Polish, he thought at first.

He said, 'Jesus.'

'No.' Don was standing there. 'Ginger Rogers. *Gold Diggers of Nineteen Thirty-Something.* Runs maybe once a week on satellite. I never get sick of this opening part. We're in the money, hah?'

'Pig Latin,' Kennedy worked out. 'She's singing it in Pig Latin.'

'She sure is.' Don knelt down to watch. 'I mean, isn't that just genius?'

'No,' Kennedy sang out. 'Just a dream.' He remembered his dream of Ginger Rogers in the siding near Ostrava, but could not be bothered to explain it to Don, so just peeled off, 'Getting in the money, that is.'

'Surely. Right.' Kennedy wondered if Don was thinking of all the petrodollars the Saudis had showered on him. He roused himself and slugged down some beer. On the screen, cops were breaking up Ginger and her supporting cast of Busby Berkeley babes, and Kennedy could not help but sit there wanting to go, *attaboy you cops*. 'But listen,' Don was saying. 'We going to smoke some of that good old natural produce from the good old Middle East?'

'Yeah.' Kennedy made his mind up even as he spoke. 'That is, no. Not me.' He was too full of beer, too full of his long day. It was a sign of getting older, maybe, but for some time he had begun to enjoy his ability to discern the road-signs to Bad Hangover. 'Uh, but you go right on ahead, man.'

'No,' Don said. 'I won't if you won't. In fact, let me congratulate you, sir, on the sterling choice you just made.'

'Uh, right.'

'And anyhow, I don't want to be stoned alone,' Don said, which was kind of considerate of him, Kennedy felt, as Don was wacko enough when he was not stoned.

'And hey,' Kennedy prompted, 'might have an early start in the morning, right?'

'The morning?' Don paused in his task of pulling bedding out of a closet and held up a finger, as if he had never considered the morning. 'Kennedy, let me tell you about the morning…in the morning. How does that sound?'

'What?'

'Let's you and me wait and see, hah?'

'See what?' Kennedy wanted to lose his rag with this waiting-and-seeing crap. Then, without a pause, he was on the verge of sleep, and could say only, 'So we'll sleep on it, huh?'

'That's the idea.' Don nodded like a pleased little child, and Kennedy saw an odd gleam in his eye as he bent over him and waved, and he wanted to protest, but found that he was looking again at those streets covered in snow, leading to blind halts without features.

Three

The Laikonik

Around six next morning, Kennedy was not entirely surprised to find himself and Don mooching around Warsaw Central station before boarding the Laikonik express for Gdynia. 'Hey, lucky Gdynia's there,' Don said, several times. When Kennedy had to give in and ask why, he got, 'Or the train'd go right on into the sea.' Kennedy thought he knew then what kind of trip it was going to be.

His first-thing-in-the-morning thoughts had been of Ling, the way she woke in afternoons darkened with drapes and pressed her body into his and reminded him that they ought to go at things like it was their last-ever time, just in case something terrible happened, and it turned out to be true. That scared and saved him all at once. He wanted to call her right then, but they had never been good on the phone, at any hour of the day. Maybe that was why they had disdained it for cumbersome letters.

Maybe that last time *was* truly going to be the last ever time, he was thinking as he hoisted himself up the steps of the train. And what in all the world could he do about it?

On the train, a morose-looking old fellow stood in the corridor and looked in at Kennedy and Don for what seemed like a very long while. His red eyes swam in stale beer and ran the trailer of that old movie *The Lost Weekend*. He ventured into the compartment and made a solemn greeting. He sat down laboriously, and fell asleep inside a minute. Don launched into a disquisition about how the Poles always said their *good days*

89

in this sombre manner. 'Greetings of people who just know they are about to get run over by a big truck,' he finished.

'English.' The old man was awake, a finger that had seen cleaner times pointed at Kennedy's face.

Kennedy's *no* got him thinking. Five minutes' rumination got him deciding *English* again. Kennedy raised hands and told him, 'You got me, Sherlock,' which got a gappy leer out of the man.

'Margarette Thaycher.' The man looked pleased to have named the wicked witch. 'Very nice lady.' Then he was silent, and Kennedy was glad.

'The Wisla river.' That was Don doing his guide part as the train clanked over the water. 'That is, the Vistula.' Maybe he was concerned that Kennedy might not be good at remembering the multilingual names of bodies of water. Kennedy was looking instead at the riverside trees all frosted white, like they had been sculpted overnight out of ice by somebody with artistic flair and time to kill and no sleep to get. He also looked down at a soccer stadium that made the centre of a street market, and at throngs of market people setting up, who obviously just couldn't lie in bed after five in the morning.

At Warsaw East station, the train was invaded by a whole Barnum and Baileys troupe. People put their heads into the compartment to say those grim *good days*, then brought in a whole mess of baggage revealing them as merchants. They also brought a whiff of salami, cheese, bitter coffee and what smelt like rubbing alcohol. A big blond guy looked to Kennedy like a Scandinavian pirate out of Eugene O'Neill, and Kennedy for one would have let the man steal his goods and chattels, no question. He and his woman companion were in big padded jackets, bluejeans, and boots that took up most of the floor space. Another guy leaked vodka out of his pores, had Apache Indian hair braided at the back, brown and green teeth melded into green and brown gums, eyes haunted by nothing Kennedy wanted to guess at. A woman and her daughter looked to Kennedy like trailer park trash, though he meant that not in a derogatory way; it was more by way of general description: grubby white leather jacket, denim skirt, scuffed blue suede boots with fringes missing, and the child in denim and mangy felt coat, big wild eyes, fruit-juiced teeth an alarming orange. The kid's name was Angelika. Everybody worked that out because right away her mom started to say, *Angelika, do this*, or, mostly, *stop doing that*.

'We're travelling fools.' That was Don, being real Texas.

'Well,' Kennedy answered, 'one of us is.'

90

Don nodded very pleasantly.

Kennedy asked, 'How long to…Where is it we're going?'

'Gdynia?' Don said. 'Where? Why, right where it was this morning, I hope,' and he roared.

Everybody there stopped whatever it was they were at and took a frank look at Don and Kennedy. The big blond fellow let out a snort that said, *I eat pussies like you for breakfast.* Don did not seem to notice, just leaned across and tapped Kennedy on the knee, put a finger up, said confidentially, 'You know Thomas Pynchon?'

'Well?' Kennedy said it as quietly as he could.

'He's J D Salinger,' Don confided.

Kennedy said, 'Oh. Right.'

The red-eyed old fellow leaned over one more time and once again claimed Kennedy for the English, a note of triumph in his voice. Kennedy was not sure he would be able to stand such sparkling repartee all the way to Gdynia, wherever and however far away it was. He resolved, like the people around him, to settle down and fade. He thought Don was still in the mood for the loud imparting of platitudes, so he avoided looking at him. Old red eyes slipped into a coma in his corner, his breathing sounding like an iron lung that needed bleeding like a radiator. The blond dude got out a paperback all folded back on itself, held it up to his face. Kennedy, rather snobbishly, did not have him down as a reader, wondered if he was just one of those people who needed a real big chunk of paper when he blew his nose. His lady friend looked like she was meditating. The Apache might have been daydreaming about scalping somebody. Him and Don, probably. Instead, he kept going out to the corridor passageway to smoke cigarettes that stank of backyard garbage fires.

Kennedy only smoked cigarettes if he hung out with smokers. He kind of liked smokers' panache, an increasingly rare breed of people who said to themselves, *I'll probably catch cancer and have a miserable death at a young age, but…uh, have you got a match?* Something crazy to admire in that. They also fulfilled an economic role with all the tax they paid. They had a social role too, in letting everybody else feel superior. Kennedy watched the Apache smoke, and wished for a while that he could walk out there and smoke with him.

Angelika might have been five, six, seven. She pissed the Apache off by stomping on his leg each time she moved in her seat, knelt up, bounced down, put feet up, down, driving him out each time for another session of garbage combustion. Then, with some song she went into *fortissimo*, she woke up both the old red-eyed geezer and the pirate's companion. *Don't catch her eye*, Kennedy told himself. As far as he knew, it was against the law to throw kids out of train windows, even with everybody's approval. He shut his eyes.

'That's the Bug.' That was talking guidebook Don Darius a little later, as the train crossed Poland's other great river. It was beautiful, Kennedy thought hazily, seeing the land split up to reveal a great sheet of ice, translucent patches showing holes in the skin of the earth.

'Neat.' Kennedy sat back in his seat. 'Great place, man – majestic.' He had the fleeting idea that maybe he was beginning to enjoy the trip at last. Then he shut his eyes again.

People woke, pulled out stuff and ate it, Angelika standing in front of them with big eyes on each piece of bread or cheese, big mouth open in hope of a reward. That trick drew a very sharp exchange of views between the pirate's lady and Angelika's mom, who dealt with it with weary, practised ease. Kennedy thought she could have saved it by bringing along something for the kid to eat, though. He learned a little Polish on that leg of the journey, due to suggestopedic drilling from Angelika's mom. The two words *nye volno* stuck with him, meaning, *You can't do that*. It hit Kennedy that they must have been heard a lot in communist Poland.

This was their soundtrack as they passed up through the country, saw flat fields of snow, uprooted trees, little houses seemingly sculpted out of ice, churches rising from the land like giant Stop-and-Shops. They made a halt, and the red-eyed guy got off with a sweeter *good day* to everybody. Don did his gentleman overseas part, and made the man a gracious return. Kennedy thought how that was good, the way Don could pick through that scratchy language and be cool with people.

He was just about to breathe out and spread a little on the seat when a tubby guy in leather coat and sweatpants tucked into moonboots came in. His hair was cropped on top and sides but left long at the back, classic trailer park mullet. He smelt of vodka, mostly, and immediately struck up a conversation with the Apache. They grunted in the corner as the train got under way again, talked maybe about the best way to disembowel sheep, Kennedy guessed. They went out to smoke together, double garbage.

The train carried on northward, seeking the edge of the continent. 'Beautiful country under that snow,' Don commented, and Kennedy said it was beautiful over it, too. 'You ever see snow like that?'

'I'm from Vermont,' Kennedy reminded him.

'We don't get snow in Texas.'

'No.' Kennedy tried to imagine snow covering Texas, and had to laugh. 'Well, we don't get…*armadillos* in Vermont.'

'No? Listen. Watch the houses,' Don warned.

'Why? What are they going to do?'

Kennedy watched them for a little while just the same. They were the colour of babies' diarrhoea. He tried to imagine the people who lived in them and what they thought and did and whether they ever had the wish to get on the trains that passed them and never come back. He watched little towns build up, church spires emerging to mark them, saw them spin past under pylons, saw them fade to fields again.

He was struck as he often was on trains that he was the only one looking out the window. He wished for a minute or so at a time that he could go to the john and snort some speed. Or some coke, but speed would do; it was such a suitable narcotic for travelling, like setting the world on *blur*, and yet the magic was that you could still see it.

One thing he had liked when he was into smack had been riding on trains, or planes, or in the backs of cars, seeing the spin of the world. When he had come off the stuff he had not clucked like a lot of junkies, just had mind-crushing headaches using up all his memory, for days on end. He had not been able to dream, could barely remember the last thought he had, so was often never sure whether he ever had any. One of the worst things had been that, after smack, he had not been able to handle the motion of travel, not for a long time. He had had to learn how to travel all over again, and in the meantime had learned to appreciate his room.

Angelika made the noises of kids in yards out back of Kennedy's old room, or out front, playing in the road. That made him remember that he had stood at his window full of the empty space left by heroin, and watched them play, sometimes wished he could shrink in size and go join them, wished sometimes though that he could go get his dad's revolver and take potshots at them.

He looked at houses on a roadside, saw himself standing there beside places just like them back home in the snow, winter of…eighty one, eighty two. Eighty three, maybe…but in any case wondering where on earth he had been for the past three years. The melancholy of it got to him; Jesus, was that really him? Some people liked playing with fire, he often thought. Some did not, but went ahead and did it anyhow. He could never work out which was more stupid.

'Watch the houses.' Don nudged him.

'I *am* watching them.' Kennedy nudged him back.

'Oh. Okay.'

'Hey.' *Watch the houses*: that was such a…*junky* thing to say, and that, it had just hit Kennedy, was why he was fixed on those lousy times of his.

One time Kennedy had lived among junkies, in Philadelphia, and they had pissed him off by having the TV on the whole time. He had hit on a simple, junky solution: he waited till everybody in the house was out or crashed, then took the TV set and hocked it. He had scored some stuff with the money he raised. He had been going to come home, he deluded himself, cook them all a teaspoon treat – yeah, and then things would be wonderful. He took a hit himself, and first off it gave him the clarity to know that they would have beaten the shit out of him, because they could not live without their old TV. The next thing the clarity brought was the certainty that he had just committed a junky act, a genuine no-fucking-doubt-a-fucking-bout-it-you-are-a-fucking-junky act. That had been the first time he knew for sure what he had turned into. He had cried electric blue tears. Until then, Kennedy had been the kind of junky who said things like, *Oh sure, I do stuff, but no way am I a junky*. Sticking a needle into his veins had not told him what he was, for some reason, but hocking the TV had. The next time he ran into his cathode-deprived pals, the good news was that they had forgotten all about the TV; the bad news was that he was unable to look at them and think, *You junky losers*, the way he used to.

He watched the houses anyhow, and they changed.

Don told Kennedy that they were by then in the part of Poland that had once been Germany, one of the parts that got handed to the Poles after the Nazis' worthless *Reich* collapsed round their ankles.

'The houses,' Don said. 'Did you see them change? Not Polish houses at all, now, this red brick stuff – see it? – but nineteenth-century German public housing. This town, right.' He pointed out the window at the town that was making itself frantically around them. 'Used to be called Soldau. Now called Dzialdowo.'

It was market day out the window, and they were making a stop there, Kennedy could tell from the way their fellow-travellers were grabbing bags and putting on hats and gloves, and the way Angelika was struggling as her mom stuffed her into her coat and placed a scarf around her neck. *A little tighter*, Kennedy urged Angelika's mom silently, *Go on, just a click*.

But Angelika kept her tongue in her head, used it to give voice to her song again as she was dragged out into the corridor to the rest of her life, still hungry. Mullet-head and the Apache bade everybody manic-depressed goodbyes, and the blond guy and his lady made similarly grave tones of farewell as they hefted their bags out, like Kennedy and Don would never see them again; the good news was that they ninety-nine-point-nine-percent certainly would not.

Dzialdowo

'Place to ourselves.' Even as Don said it, though, a grey little gent came in and settled by the window with a satisfied breath. It came out like a slow sneeze and let Kennedy and Don know that he had breakfasted on something with onions in it. They managed both to greet and ignore him.

'Back that way,' Don indicated. 'Little town name of Mlava. My mom came from there.'

'She did?'

'I missed it,' Don was realising. 'Couldn't see the town for looking at the houses. Just passed on through. Damn. But never mind.' He smiled brightly. 'I'll be through again. Mom was from there. She had a brother, right?'

'Right.'

'He would've been my uncle, I guess, only he stole medical supplies from the Germans and sold them. He wound up hanging for a week from a gallows in the market square, sign around his neck to show he was a wise guy, but that the Nazis were wiser.'

'Uh, right. That's – '

'Mom had a friend who got out of Poland before the war happened. She settled in Paris. Finally the Germans nabbed her when they got to Paris for their piece of the old *vie Parisienne*. She got sent back to Poland with her Polish beau and, when they got back, the Germans wanted him for slave labour. But she was a skinny little thing, and she was sick, and didn't look like she could work. She looked kind of Jewish, too, though far as I know she wasn't. She'd been a schoolteacher, though, I believe, and this put her into the category of the...*intelligentsia*, the way the Germans saw it. And one thing they hated, and were scared of, were Poles who were smarter than them. So a German soldier shoved her to one side and cocked his gun and she said to him, *Listen: I'm twenty two years old, and I'm in love*. Know what he told her? He told her, *Even people in love get smashed by bullets*. Then he shot her in the head.'

95

'Jesus. That's…*horrible*. But listen.' Kennedy was not sure why, but he had to ask, 'How do you know that? I mean, with quotes and all?'

'Good question. And I got a good answer. Eyewitnesses. A lot of it got written down and preserved, you know, on scraps of paper and matchbooks, got hidden in people's shoes, or behind farmhouse bricks, or, hell, you know, just…*remembered*. Wound up in a book about survivors someplace.'

'The names make it real,' Kennedy thought of those Warsaw plaques. 'The Nazis didn't take that into account, right? Thought there'd be no people left to tell it like it happened, huh? Audacious, man. They tried to murder the whole world.'

'Ambitious, certainly. I'm not crazy about people who count ambition as one of their virtues. Forests all around this town.' Don was almost down to a whisper. 'Full of dead German boys, doing their stuff for the festering fatherland, fourteen years old, some of them. Jesus.'

'Christ.'

'They were victims, too, I guess. History, it's…*sad*. Mom, right, she wound up in Oswiecim, which is Auschwitz to you and me and the world. She made it through, though, somehow, saw this Chinaman poke his face into the hut she was in. He was a Russian soldier, though, a Kazak, an Uzbek, maybe. He signalled to her that outside there was a big pot of porridge, and some of it was hers if she could just walk out and get some. He wasn't going to help her any – they just didn't have enough men for that. That was it, her last test. If people got out to the porridge, then maybe there was a chance they'd live. So there she was, crazy but alive.' He looked up, fancied maybe that he saw a question in Kennedy's eyes. 'Yes, crazy, certainly. Who wouldn't be? She stumbled out that door, and ate so much she thought she was going to die all over again, but in one way she never made it through that doorway. There's a part of her stayed in there to this day. But hey, listen.'

'What?'

'I got another story for you.'

'It's nineteen thirty eight, okay. There's a guy.' Don had hardly paused. Kennedy knew that feeling, wanting to get the story out into the light. 'Just an ordinary German guy. Got a little farm outside Soldau, right here where we are now. He gets called up by the fatherland. He's a farmer, right – he doesn't think, *Hey, this is propaganda* – he's never heard the word in his life. He's no Nazi, but he's bought the line that this is bigger than some political party. It's the fatherland. You got to imagine what that word means. It's, like, your father, right, tapping you on the shoulder and saying he's sired and raised you, clothed and fed and protected you.'

And Kennedy thought of his dad, of course, and the many taps he had given him, on the shoulder, on the back, on the chin sometimes, and he bowed his head and, for a second or two, felt bad, felt like he had never done enough that was good, nor enough that was bad, nor anything to be commented about at all. Thought mainly of the times he could just have humoured the old man, said, *Yeah yeah, Dad, that is so cool,* times when he didn't, just turned a disdainful adolescent nose up at his dad's endeavours.

'But now he needs your help,' Don continued. 'He's your *father,* remember, even though, really, it's only that squeaky-voiced charlatan Hitler. This guy, then, he goes to fight over the border in Poland. Then he goes to Holland, Belgium, kicks some butt. What he finds, first, is that it's all kind of...easy – they all just run away. He's not sure he *likes* it, right, but it's just not as...*difficult* as he might have thought at one time. He stormtroops into France. He's there when Hitler does his drive around the pissed-off city of Paris to do an inventory of all this amazing stuff. He's got the Eiffel Tower, got Montmartre, he's got the Louvre, got the fanciest restaurants and classiest joints on the continent, and if you land on one of his squares you got to pay Monopoly dollars through the nose, right? And this guy, he's a part of it. He takes a shower once a day, his uniform is always nice and clean, his jackboots squeak and shine. Life is *good.* But he sees the way the Parisians look at him. Some of them nod and smile, but most of them, he can see, hate his guts. Then he sees that, in this Monopoly game, a lot of them don't collect two hundred dollars, just go to jail, and never come back. He starts to realise that he has a choice. Does he think, *Wow, this is great,* or does he think, *Jesus, this is wrong?* We see him standing on a street corner, wondering about that. Cut to two years on. He's in the mud and shit at Stalingrad. His uniform's in rags, he's got lice and rats running through everything he owns, got tenacious old Ivan shooting at him every time he puts his head up. He's lucky enough to get shot in the shoulder, and he hobbles onto the last transport out before the Nazis get surrounded, then get what's coming to them. Ah, Kennedy, you got all that?'

'Yeah, I think so.'

'At the moment, it's called *Kurt Vogel's Song to His Father,*' Don said. 'Now, you got all that, you say? So, he's a survivor, which kind of seems good, for a while, just like shooting at runaway armies seemed good, and just like swaggering around Paris did too. He finally gets nabbed by the

97

western allies. He does some time in jail, but, really, they didn't know what to do with them, the millions of soldiers, just kicked them out into the pig's ear the Nazis made out of Germany.'

'Is that it?'

'No. This guy, he tries to go back to Soldau, finds it's now Dzialdowo. The Poles tell him to get his ass out of there or they'll kick it. What about his farm? Well, what *about* it? And his wife? And his little daughter? What *about* them? Nobody knows or cares. He sets off back into Germany to find them, and that's where we learn that he wasn't as white as he seemed all through the war. Paris whores come to him in his sleep to torment his soul now, and not to fortify it. He sees again the eyes of the little Ukrainian kid he shot because, basically, he'd just shot the kid's parents, and didn't know what else to do with him. And every night he sees the look on the face of the girl partisan he hung from a frame in a village square, when she said to him, *You can't kill all of us, you Nazi bastard, and if my friends don't get you I'll come haunt you in your sleep.* He realises one thing. That wasn't real anguish, back on the Russian front – none of it was real. The real pain, it lives in your head when you make the wrong choices, and it'll live with you forever. He might never find his wife and daughter, but he'll never be without company.'

'Wow.'

'Hmm.' Don looked pleased. 'Yes.' Kennedy had watched him pull out a notebook and add some details; he knew it was like when a writer started writing a synopsis, and found things that were not in the actual work, but should have been.

'Listen,' Kennedy said. 'Did you write this yet?'

'Hundred thousand words.'

'Jesus.'

'There it is.' Don waved out at Dzialdowo as the train started to pull out of the station. 'Glad you came now?'

'Uh, well.' Kennedy was about to point out that Don could have told him Kurt Vogel's story in a bar in Warsaw, or on his couch, could have let him at the files on his computer. But at the same time he knew that Don had had to be there, in Dzialdowo, for the story to complete itself, and what was more, Kennedy had to be there too, for Don to tell it to. 'Yeah, I am,' he had to decide, but added cautiously, 'kind of.'

'Scene of Kurt,' Don thought out, still scribing, 'at the Paris opera. He's in his shiny boots. And his collar is so starched it starts to irritate him. And there's a pretty French girl next to him. And she grabs his arm, and says she'll love him forever. And they're listening to *La Clemenza di Tito*, right – Mozart, right? The place full of Nazis. And it's about the mercy of an emperor, and none of them get it. But they ought to. Right? Is that good? Kennedy, does that work, or what?'

'It works, man.' It did; Kennedy saw it.

Happy with that, Don held a hand up and turned to a fresh page in his notebook, and started to write some more. Kennedy left him to it and started to think.

The Laikonik

'Punishment,' Kennedy was able to say, once Don had put his notebook down. 'You're into punishment, big time.' It had occurred to him the day before, the frightening inevitability that Don's blind optimists and misguided idealists in the Saudi book would be punished for their presumption. 'Your man, the Nazi guy, he seems to get away with the crimes he did, but there's no escaping them. Is there?' he pushed.

'No.' Don's answer was immediate.

'Punishment is important to you. It's a theme that runs through your work.'

'If you say so.'

'Like in the Saudi book.' Kennedy put more pieces together. 'The people who live there just enjoying life, and not thinking about the chain they're a part of, they wind up punished, right?'

'Maybe.'

'Even if they're not particularly...*bad* people.'

'Possibly.'

'Possibly?'

'Probably.' Don came clean with a Roman thumbs-down. 'I'm sick of people who get off on screwing people over for the hell of it. And I believe in a law that says they get screwed in return. Listen. Call me Biblical, an eye for an eye, right, but I just think scumbags have got to...partake in a little of the grief they spread around. Hang on, though. Listen. Don't go assuming from this that I took a turn to the right. Old Uncle Joe Stalin wasn't exactly right wing, was he, and he had a determined policy on scumbags.'

'Hmm, well...yeah,' Kennedy kind of agreed. 'And on a lot of non-scumbags, too.'

'Well, nobody's perfect. And Hitler, was he right wing?'

'Well, uh, he was, in fact.'

'Wrong. He started as a socialist, and bust out of the wings, rewrote the book in his own psycho way. But in the end he was just another scumbag who thought he wouldn't get caught, thought he'd fix it so there was nobody left to remember evil things and write them down and put names and faces in and make it all real, to get through the nightmare version he made of reality. Those who screw get screwed back.' Don looked almost comically stern. 'That's what the justice lady says in my mind. She's blind, right, but she's not stupid. Hey, Malbork.' He pointed.

'Uh…what?'

The bulk of an enormous castle grew out of the snow, and its red-brick walls and turrets began to fill the view. Kennedy kept his eyes fixed on it as it went on, and on, eating away at the pale sky and the iced-up river that halted below it.

'Big castle,' their companion piped up helpfully. Kennedy had almost forgotten the man, and forgotten too about Don's promise to show him the biggest ever castle he ever saw.

'It sure is.' Kennedy tried to sound impressed.

'Prussians.' Both Don and the man were talking at Kennedy, so he got a bilingual spiel about how gargantuan Malbork Castle had been the centre of the Teutonic knights' empire, the hub of the amber trade they controlled as they headed the line of people waiting to work Poland over. This went on until their travelling companion joined yattering tourists in the passageway, all out to spoil the effect of the biggest castle in the world by getting up close to it.

'Place to ourselves.' Don risked the optimism again, and stretched out. 'Excellent. Onward,' he ordered the train, with the aid of stately, plump Buck Mulligan at the opening of *Ulysses*. 'To the scrotumtightening sea.'

'The snotgreen sea,' Kennedy added – Don was not the only one who could rattle off bits from James Joyce. How come Kennedy could remember stuff like that, when he could not remember to pick up a carton of milk on the way home?

'Right.' Don held a hand up, and Kennedy did a perfunctory high five with him, laughed at this meeting of old Dublin and old Harlem.

'I still can't believe we're doing this.' Kennedy had not mentioned Don's crazy idea the whole day, and thought it was about time he did. That took Buck Mulligan's face out of Don's, and brought it to a momentary impasse.

'*You got to try.*' Don borrowed the phrase from Lyle Lovett at the end of one of his big band tunes.

'*You* got to,' Kennedy corrected. He saw the optimist skedaddle out of Don's face for a second, then reassured him, 'Hey, I'm here, man, along for the ride and having a time seeing this beautiful country and its big castles and hearing the stories you plan to racont to the world. I spent worse days. But listen. I got a story for you, too, about a guy gets on a train in search of a girl.'

'Not a woman?'

'Well, okay, a woman.'

'Well.' Don regarded Kennedy a little cautiously. 'Tell.'

'Well, he finds her.' Kennedy let it rest.

'And they what?'

'They live happy ever after. They have kids and a dog and a house and a car, buy kitchen appliances, and printed furnishings, and…what-all.'

'That's…nice,' Don said. 'But it's not exactly a story.'

'Not really.' Kennedy let that sink in for a while. 'And a lot's got to happen,' he resumed, 'before they get to the printed furnishings part. But we're on the way, dude. Where is it we're headed? After Gdynia, I mean?'

Kennedy looked up Abel in his guidebook. 'Place full of sand and water,' he summarised. 'Really shouldn't be too hard to find the lady. We just look behind every dune and rock. So, Don, better describe Ola to me, if I'm going to do my detective part.'

Don had been to Gdansk for the weekend maybe three weeks before. He had woken at four thirty one Saturday morning ready to work on some writing, and had seen Warsaw filling up with distractions. *Out of here*, he had thought, *bring a notebook, write*. That was what he had done, up in the city of historic shipyards.

'So.' Kennedy gave Don a nudge. 'What does she look like?'

Don had taken a room in Gdansk that Saturday, bought a bottle of vodka and packed it in the snow on his window ledge, had taken a walk by the Wisla river, had sat in cafés and, back in his room, had done a *quid pro quo* with the vodka, let it pour into him, to in turn let the words pour out of him. 'About five thousand of them,' he claimed.

'Right. And so how about this Ola, then?'

Don had boarded the Laikonik express to go back to Warsaw, and met her. He was doing this, and she was doing that, and –

'Yeah, but –'

Shortish dark hair – how dark, though, and what shade of dark, and shortish like what? A part on one side, Don thought – but which side? Eyes kind of dark, nice mouth – what? – just *nice*, Don knew what he meant, like her nose, nice, and her ears. 'Nice too,' Kennedy had to guess. 'Not too sticky-outy, huh?' Don ignored the crack and nodded earnestly. Maybe five seven, five eight tall, maybe a hundred and fifteen, a hundred and twenty pounds, kind of fit, looked to Don at first like she worked out, but no: what she did was get into costume and dance in a folkloric troupe. She went all over Poland with it, and to other places too, got as far as the Vatican one time, she told Don, and danced for and audienced with Karol Wojtyla the Bishop of Rome.

Another thing she did was not drink alcohol, not at Christmastime, not for Easter, certainly not at seven in the morning. And what else she did was go to church every Sunday and on weekdays too, sometimes. A thing Don liked was that she was assertive about these things, and not evangelical. He liked too that she was no cargo cultist, and that she had not fallen for the line that the west was coming to save her country from its past and set it up for its future. It also grabbed Don that she liked literature and movies in that order, and was not crazy about TV. She had a nice ass, too, he thought it best to mention, had bright white teeth that were crooked, just a little. He liked her good English, but also her ear for his ponderous Polish, liked that she listened as well as talked.

Don liked her name. For some reason nobody seemed to know, *Ola* was short for *Aleksandra*; maybe people just thought it was big fun to contrast the multi-syllables of the one with the abruptness of the other.

Don could live with that kind of woman, it had come home to him: no booze, no misanthropy, no sadness, except maybe when she had to leave to go dancing for Popes. She could inspire him, he had thought, and he in turn could inspire her, too, surely?

'All in an hour on a train?' Kennedy had to ask. No: two and a half hours.

The woman on the train had looked at Don's face and had spied the vodka in it, maybe, had cut to the chase and said, 'Your life is sad.'

He had appreciated the candour of that, had felt able to say, 'Hey, though, but if a woman like you were around, then maybe it wouldn't be sad at all.' Then he had given her his number. When she called him, he had told her, he would be there. Simple as that.

'Clean living, though?' Kennedy felt he ought to pitch the question. 'God-fearing? Hmm.' Don said he had been thinking about that a lot. 'But aren't clean living and God-fearing for people who, uh, live clean and fear God?'

'I...guess they are.'

'Think you fit the bill?'

'Listen.' Don's eyes seemed to say, *Can I trust you not to hold this against me, should it all go wrong?* 'Clean living? High time I found some room in my life for that. Think I'm happy getting out of my skull on cheap vodka?'

'No.' Kennedy thought, though, *But how about the expensive stuff?* 'No sir.'

'That I can handle.' The evidence of the past day or so did not convince Kennedy any. Maybe Don had just been acting sociable; on his way to Sociables Anonymous. 'No, really – I can. God, though? For me? I really don't know.'

'*You got to try.*' Kennedy quoted Lyle Lovett again, a little cruelly, it seemed to him later. 'Listen, though,' he hurried on. 'Maybe it's time to...get real about a whole lot of things. But I'll tell you now, man. Time for you to get those books out of your system. And, well...Look, don't get me wrong here, but this really might not be the right time in your life to find the companion your...soul craves – no, let me finish – but at the same time this could be it, man, and you got to follow it up, so you're doing it. Right? Am I right?'

'Sure.' Don did not sound so sure, and then Kennedy felt the absurdity of it all walk across his back: there he was persuading Don that it was not a crazy thing to be on that train, when he knew damn well that it was.

'Right?' he persisted anyhow. There was nothing else to say.

'Right.'

'We'll do it – we *are* doing it.'

'Gdansk – we're here,' was all Don said to that, and indeed Kennedy had become aware of the city forming and gliding past. He looked out on towers and churches and tenement houses, fragments of city walls, tall apartment blocks and little stores.

'We'll find her, man.' Kennedy spoke with his optimist-idiot voice. 'We'll find her sitting on a dune by the sea like that kick-ass mermaid, and we'll wait politely for her to finish talking to God, and then we'll talk to her, and...Hey.'

'What?'

'Maybe she'll have a friend. You know, like, for me?'

'Maybe.'

'Flat-faced girl with a cute ass.'

'Right.' Don laughed hesitantly. 'Well…maybe.'

People got on at Gdansk, but more got off. Kennedy and Don were alone still, stretched out on their seats, boots off. They were comfortable and warm, but all travelled-out. Kennedy really could have killed a brew or two, and was cheered already at the sure-fire thought of one up the line someplace, with whatever else waited for them.

Gdansk

Kennedy looked out the window, grabbed by the thought of being in Gdansk, where such monumental things had gone down to lead to the bookmark in time that was and would always be nineteen eighty nine: men with moustaches had imposed their features on the city, and, through it, on the world, making the place a conduit down which history had flowed. 'Cool,' he said, and Don agreed that Gdansk was cool, but would be a lot cooler once it had shaken off its past and grabbed a life of its own; that would come, in the new Poland, he guessed, would be flawed, would be part-made by the German tourists who would swarm back there not daring to call it Danzig out loud. But it would be a life of a kind.

They chugged out of the city, then, through swatches of forest, and past little settlements, people in tin cars, kids on skates and bikes, the wind whipping their clothes around them as they waited at crossings, who then faded like ghosts into the landscape the Laikonik left behind it. Gdynia started abruptly, and made itself up in a hurry as if just for Kennedy's and Don's arrival, and then they were there.

Gdynia

Kennedy and Don got down from the train and into Gdynia's big station. A sign there should have said *Welcome, especially if you're insane enough to come to the sea on a day like this.* Don checked out the schedule of trains for Abel, but Kennedy knew his pal would feel the same as him; they had to take a breath, throw a beer down their necks, and follow it with something to warm their extremities.

When it got to around minus twenty, the only thing you could think of to say first off was how frigging cold it was. You knew it was banal, but had to get it off your chest, along with the green stuff deposited there. 'Oh, man,' Kennedy decided to share with Don. 'Welcome to the coast, huh?'

'Quick drink,' Don said, 'to warm the heart and lungs and lights, I say,' and led Kennedy around a corner, and across a narrow street and through a door flanked by sparkly windows and red lights. They saw a whole lot of shoes all over the place. They made shit-eating grins to the couple in back, and stepped out. They took a closer look again at the front. Don agreed, 'Well, that does say *shoes*, all right,' but could not be shaken from the fact that, with all its razzle-dazzle, it looked exactly like a bar. 'Right, well, what we do now is look for a place that looks like a shoe store – that'll surely be a bar.'

The place they found did not look a lot like a shoe store, but it certainly was a bar. Don opened the proceedings by asking, 'Hey, do you by any chance sell shoes?' The bartender scratched his ear and made the faintest of snarls. He was twenty, maybe, though balding, and had the disturbing face of a spoilt child. His girth distorted the big face of Kurt Cobain on his t-shirt, though nowhere near as hideously as it would get a couple of years later when Kurt blew his head off. 'Just checking,' Don calmed him, and then made their simple order.

They sat, waited for their beers, made travellers' talk about trains and times. Don had a little xeroxed guide listing places in which to stay in Abel, but had the idea that they would not be open at that time of year.

'Isn't that a, kind of, like, major obstacle?' Kennedy put to Don.

Don chucked the question at the bartender. The man smirked, just a little, and said he thought that Kennedy and Don were probably crazy. He said that what they needed to do was stay in Gdynia and do Abel on a daytrip. But another time.

Kennedy could have told him that what they actually needed to do was stay in Don's apartment in Warsaw watching MTV and getting safely drunk.

Don thanked the bartender, who put on a *suit yourselves, assholes* face. He was on his way back to the bar when he turned and told them that serious snow was on its way – did they know that? – and so it would be a good idea to forget going to Abel altogether. 'In summer,' he appealed to Kennedy, 'is good place – great place, seaside.' The man made a bikini girl with his hands. 'But now…' *But now, you're nuts to even think of it*, he was telling them kindly.

'Well, uh, what are we doing?' Kennedy could have meant it in any way. Right then, in respect of their immediate needs, he realised that he was talking about food. Kennedy left the ordering to his friend. Ten minutes later, soup arrived. It looked and smelled good to Kennedy, full of vegetables and the unrecognisable parts of some animal.

He ate. It *was* good, apart from the bread roll that accompanied it. 'Christ.' Kennedy looked at the rock-hard…*boulder* in his hand.

'Jesus.' That was Don's agreement.

'Kill for a bagel right now.'

They tortured themselves by discussing the best bagels they had ever eaten. That killed a minute. The ordering of more of the local loony-juice ate up more time. They missed a train. Kennedy did not care. By then he could have sat in that bar and drunk the afternoon away, watching the snow come down and cover the outside. 'This is cool,' he said cautiously as they worked their way through their beers; cool to stay there, went his subliminal tickertape, not to go to Abel at all, not even if it was, like, Ginger Rogers, dressed in spangles and talking in Pig Latin, waiting there for Don. 'Cool place.'

'It's cool.' Kennedy saw a trace of alarm imprint itself into Don's face. 'It *is* cool.' Don was taking a long look at his nearly empty glass. 'Very cool.' Don drank up and held up the glass, looked deep into it to check whether it was as empty as he feared. 'Hmm. Yes.'

'One more?' Kennedy asked him keenly. 'For the old roadski?'

Kennedy caught Don's eyes in his for a second. He saw the snow falling down into them, saw Don's tongue venture out and collect something at the corner of his mouth. Inside, Kennedy let out a touchdown *ra-ra* as Don summoned the bartender.

The snow became real. A few other people crunched occasionally into the picture: a woman dragging a shivering hound, a slope-shouldered, disgruntled kid on what had to be a reluctant errand, a fellow drunk and on his lone and puzzled way someplace, a teenager with a violin case.

'We only had to have one more,' Kennedy whined. 'Just one more.' And it sounded to Kennedy more like Don talking – Jeez, he was turning into Don Darius.

'Come on.' Don put a hand on Kennedy's shoulder. 'Let's shop.'

'What?'

Soon they started to pass people laden with the stuff of shopping. Women carried bulging bags and bulging kids. Men carried even bigger bags, bigger kids, or six-packs, and bottles of the local firewater. One guy carried a chicken. It was dead, Kennedy guessed.

Suddenly they were among hundreds of people. They were wandering around market stalls, and listening to a band made up of a bunch of old timers; accordion, violin, guitar, and wheezy voices joined in mournful choruses of, Don said, songs old as the world, a soundtrack of the country's woes.

Don hovered around flower stalls. Just a look from Kennedy told him what any flowers he bought would look like by next morning, so Don made a change of plan: no flowers. He paused over fat sausages and waxy cheeses, but gave them a miss too. The trays of broken cookies got a smile out of Kennedy, almost. The paths of bathroom taps laid out on blankets were not without their humour, either. The funniest thing Kennedy saw, he remembered later, was a stall weighed down by bluejeans, Levis look-alikes with the leather patch and the red tab and the pattern stitched on the back pockets and all, and the white paper tag, which announced, *This is a Pair of Lives.* He picked up a pair, said, 'The frontier spirit, huh?'

'I guess it means *caveat emptor.*' Don rested a hand absently on the piles of denim. 'See anything you need, huh?'

'Uh-uh.' Kennedy needed no rusty tractor parts, no lead-painted Korean toys, no bottles of Remy-Martell VOSP brandy. Don led him through a doorway, and then they were in the market hall. It was more of the same, only not quite so cold. Kennedy smelled coffee, though, and it got his nose twitching. 'That is, yeah.'

'Coffee might indeed be of some use,' Don said, and glanced at his watch.

'Hey. Don?'

Kennedy forgot coffee. He grabbed Don's arm, and made a statue of his friend in mid-stride. There was a woman standing in line for a stall, and it was the damnedest thing, because, not wanting to lose her place, she was waving crazily in Don's direction. She was tall and pretty, Kennedy noted. Something inside him did a jig of joy to know that Ola had spotted Don Darius just as if she had been looking out for him, because that surely meant that she had a thing about Don just as big as the thing he had about her. And to be honest, it was mostly to do with he and Don not having to schlep any further across the permafrost.

'Look there, man,' he breathed. 'Look right there. I don't believe it.'

'Ah,' Don said. Kennedy, all ready to cue the music, hearts-and-flowers and barf-bags, knew there was something amiss when Don merely touched his arm, and stepped unhurriedly over to the woman, shook her hand and stood there talking away in his goofy Polish. He was in the conversation and out of it inside a minute, and then was leading Kennedy once more in search of coffee.

'My dentist,' Don explained.

'Oh. Right. But,' it occurred to Kennedy, 'you come all this way to get your teeth fixed?'

'No. That lady pulls teeth right on the street where I live. She comes from here.'

'Oh. Right. But, what?' Kennedy was thinking how the early morning Laikonik express could put any dentist in a very mean mood to start the day. 'She goes to Warsaw every day, just to fix teeth?'

'No,' Don repeated patiently. 'I'm talking origin here. Place of birth. She's here visiting her folks.'

'Oh. Right.' Kennedy guessed it was just his brain being packed in ice that was making it work in slow-mo. 'But...Well, how come she wasn't wearing a white coat? Then I would've known at once it was your dentist.'

'Eh?' Don guffawed. 'Right. Hey, know what the weird thing is here about dentists?'

'Like I would.'

'They don't give you a shot first. Not unless you ask for it.'

'Wow.' Just thinking of that made Kennedy's teeth shrink. 'You're shitting me.'

'No. I mean, before, right, they just didn't have the stuff – the anaesthetic – and so people just adjusted to gritting teeth and taking it like men.'

'Gritting teeth sounds about right.' Kennedy decided he did not want to imagine it.

'I had an appointment one time,' Don continued, 'and I go in, and the receptionist says sorry, I can't have my whatever done right then. Not convenient. I was pissed off, because – okay, I don't mind the dentist, but I still got to psyche myself up for it, you know? And I thought, all that psyching, gone to waste. When the receptionist was looking down at the book to make me another appointment, I looked in the surgery, and there she was, my dentist, sitting on the edge of her dentist chair, and...Know what she was doing?'

Kennedy dreaded to think. 'Her own root canal work?'

'No. She was crying her eyes out. That was...well, very sad. I stopped looking right away then, because it felt wrong. But I learned one thing that day.'

'You did? What?'

'That dentists hurt. Just like you and me.'

'Oh.' Kennedy had never doubted that. The one he had bitten way back when he was a kid had certainly hurt, the yelp the poor man had let out. 'Right. I guess they do. Hey,' Kennedy wondered, as they slipped into a little fenced-off area that made the coffee bar. 'Did your dentist ask you what you were doing here?'

'Ah, yes, she did, in fact.'

Don hallooed the woman behind the coffee counter. She was bald and old, wore orange and brown; she looked like a Buddhist monk. She seemed in no hurry to get off her ass and furnish her customers with the delights of the Oriental coffee trade.

'So,' Kennedy persisted, 'what did you tell her?'

'What do you mean, what did I tell her? I told her…ah…well.'

'I fucking bet you did,' Kennedy spluttered out. Later, not much later, he did not recall what had happened to produce this seam of meanness. Maybe it was his false relief at seeing the woman in the market and believing that it was Ola, and that their search was at an end; maybe a part of him had just not been able to handle the disappointment. 'You're lucky I'm here, man. I'm the only person you know who's dumb enough to come on this trip and not laugh my socks off at you.'

'You *are* laughing, though.' Don turned to Kennedy. 'Aren't you?'

Kennedy did not know what the true answer was. He just gave Don a nudge, because by then the dame behind the counter was saying the Polish for, *Can I help you, you weirdoes?* Don ordered coffees, and they were prepared in front of the customers' eyes: spoonful of coffee stuck in a glass, boiling water sloshed into it, and that was it. The first sip rebooted Kennedy's central nervous system, which was one thing coffee was, after all, supposed to do.

'I'm not laughing at you.' That was the truth, as far as Kennedy was concerned. 'No, man. I'm the laughable one,' he thought out, 'for dragging all this way up here with you. This coffee,' he had to say, 'has got to be the worst coffee in the whole wide coffee-drinking world.'

'Yes.' Don got distracted looking at his own coffee, like maybe if he looked hard at it for long enough, it might turn into a frothy cappuccino. It just sat in his glass and steamed. 'Well, they're still working on coffee here. They call this Turkish coffee.'

'Guess they never went to Turkey.'

'Well,' Don retorted. 'I wish I never went to Turkey, too.'

'Right.' Kennedy had kind of known that Don would say that.

'Don't know what you see in the place.' Kennedy had known that Don would start on that one, too.

Kennedy himself was not sure what he saw in the place. Ling was there. That was about it. Was that not enough?

He saw the Bosphorus full of dead sheep the time a transport ship went down with two hundred thousand of the creatures on board. A hanky to his face, he had looked over the water thinking how you did not see that kind of thing happen in Vermont. Another time, a guy jumped off a motorbike pillion and shot another guy in the face a few yards ahead of Kennedy on a busy main street. It was an American the man shot, some big business cheese in the act of bringing cargo. The clearest scene to Kennedy had been just after, and the killer getting back on the bike and pausing to hitch his pants up a little at the knee for his ride back to whatever killers went home to. *Police are looking for a man who takes care about his appearance*, Kennedy had wanted to crack to the cop who took his witness statement. The cop had suggested that Kennedy get counselling, though he had not been able to suggest where from – the consulate, maybe? – and Kennedy had thought how that was Turkey all over, old and new, street assassination and counselling.

Maybe Kennedy was glad that he had seen these things because they let him know all over again that he was not in a little town in Vermont, reading in a newspaper about events in Istanbul; maybe the witnessing of such events justified his being overseas.

'I can't begin to know what keeps you there,' Don complained.

But Don should have known, Kennedy thought; he had been there, and in that case it was not worth Kennedy's telling him a thing.

Kennedy thought of a respectable Turkish guy he had worked with, a family man totally besotted with an English teacher who, one time, had let him kiss her at a party. He avowed that he would leave his wife for this dull Brit slut who, with the addition of just a trace of alcohol, made a habit of kissing anybody anytime anyplace. Kennedy would have left the guy's wife for a six-pack of beer, personally, but that was not the point. The point was that a kiss given idly at a party meant a whiff of sexual liberation to this guy, and knocked his entire world out of kilter. And why had the man told Kennedy all this? Probably because there had been nobody else to tell. That was one reason why, in Turkey, you could get into conversation with a guy when you were out someplace, and he would tell you about a life lived in a whole different light, not because he wanted to bend your ear in particular, but because he could not tell any of his friends or family; they would have slammed shame on him, or maybe would have confessed to the same thing. To Kennedy, that was one mark of a very unhappy society. What *was* his business there?

'Well, *I* know what keeps me there.' He saw Ling, sitting up against his creased pillows, shaking her fringe out of her eyes, smiling, stretching, noting the darkness outside and trying to catch sight of his alarm clock.

Don etceteraed on.

Kennedy knew though that he was indeed a little sick of Istanbul. He loved it, okay, but had been there too long. When Ling left, that would be him out of there too. He would blow the school out, get a midnight ride, go. Where? That was a question for a different time.

He might have been sick of it, but Jeez, he did not need Don to articulate its shortcomings; only he was allowed to do that, and he wished he was in Istanbul right at that moment.

'Hey, change the tape.' Not begging or urging, he said it dully, in a way that, he knew, would fail to register at once.

'I know what keeps you there.' Don looked at Kennedy over the rim of his coffee glass. 'Got to be old Flat Face.'

'Well, award yourself a cookie, then,' Kennedy answered. After a moment's thought, he added, 'Listen. We're a long way from Istanbul. For Chrissake, Don, you don't ever have to think about the place again. It didn't suit you – fine. You had bad shit, there – okay. Bad shit happens. Life wasn't what you expected it to be there – right, I believe you. But get over it. I'm going back there.' Kennedy poured his coffee out on the ground, mixed it into all the other market detritus. 'Going to go drink some *real* Turkish coffee.'

'What?' Don looked startled.

'With the girl I love.'

'Eh?'

'Right this fucking minute.'

Kennedy had the notion that if he did not hustle, Ling would be gone. He walked fast, in and out of the shoppers and waiters-in-line, gently avoided their bulk and their bags.

Don too seemed to be intent on getting to Istanbul in a rush.

'Get right back to that station.' Kennedy spoke over his shoulder. His voice strained, out in the air, reached the perfect tone of plaint once it competed with the wind and the deadening effect of the snow. 'Get on a train, get back to Warsaw, get back to Belgrade.' He said it like he was talking about hopping on a city bus and changing at the stop near the library. 'And back to Istanbul.'

'Hey, Kennedy.' Kennedy enjoyed the alarm in Don's voice – yeah, that was pure meanness. 'Kennedy, hey, listen.' Kennedy pushed on through the laden shoppers and the weekend drunks and the little kids with blue faces, under the awnings of scowling buildings hung with stalactites, out onto the streets that led back the way they had come. 'Hey, come on back – stop.'

Kennedy stopped. Even as he registered that his feet were not anchored as securely as he might have hoped, a little effigy of Buster Keaton got up off of a stool in Kennedy's head and made an *ah-hah* face, pulled a lever marked *slapstick*. Don bashed squarely into Kennedy, and for a second they did a weird dog-dance on the ice before they landed on the ground. They sat, looked at each other.

'Don't go back there,' Don urged. 'Not right now. Come to Abel, with me.'

Kennedy seemed to be thinking about it. At the same time, out the corner of his eye he was watching a figure who, out of the crowds around them, was headed directly at them. It was brown and orange and monkish, and waddled toward them unhurriedly, with patient determination. It stopped above them. A pair of eyes regarded them without animosity, an unsmiling mouth let out a long breath that made dragon steam over them. A gloved hand was outstretched to them. It smelt of coffee and the dirty deposits from market money.

'Okay,' Kennedy said, 'I will.'

Don turned his reach for the offered hand into a last-minute wave. The two men got to their feet without its aid and dusted each other off. Don made profuse apologies to the Turkish coffee lady. Even if the coffee was a work-in-progress, it still had to be paid for; he filled her hand with notes. Without a word, she took them and did a three-point turn and went back to her trade. Don and Kennedy resumed their walk to Gdynia station, and in a few minutes were on the train for Frozen Nutsville.

The slow train

'This is fun.' Don looked around, caught the attention of the woman sitting next to Kennedy. 'Isn't this a lot of fun?'

'Yes, much fun.' The woman really seemed to think so. In an elegant English not heard since movies in the fifties, she had already done the *what-brings-you-here-on-a-day-like-today-you-implausible-assholes* part, and had opined that they were ill-advised to be heading for Abel right then. 'It is a daytime place,' she had said firmly, and pointed to the blizzard out the window. 'You know, a summer place? It is not a place for the night, or for the winter. There is nothing to do there.'

'Oh yes there is,' Don declared, and at that Kennedy used his eyes to caution his friend. He did not want this to be like, *I'm a bigshot from Texas –* despite appearances – *coming to Abel to steal all your women away.* 'There's the sea, ma'am, the scrotumtigh – ' Kennedy cautioned Don with a kick this time. Don rallied quickly, 'My friend here, whose name is Kennedy, though he's not one of *the* Kennedys, not exactly, rather a, if you will…Ah, where was I?'

'Your friend here,' the woman prompted. She was around fifty, looked to Kennedy like the kind of woman back in Harrington, who, when she heard you were sick, called around bearing a pie she had made especially, using a recipe passed on from her grandmother, whose own grandmother had passed it on as she lay dying, an Apache's arrow through her neck. She had big hair, a bit Mary Tyler Moore, had big, even teeth, though what Kennedy kept noticing each time she spoke was the alarming half-inch-wide strip of her upper gum.

Kennedy put on a smile, saluted like a stage American uncle. He did not know why he was doing that, when what he really wanted to do was give Don another kick, a real good one this time.

'Lives in It's Damn Bull,' Don said. 'Right?'

'Yes,' she agreed doubtfully.

'In Turkey,' Kennedy made clear. She sniffed that she knew where it was, thanks.

'Lives right by the sea, like, the Black Sea?'

'The Sea of Marmara is more likely.' She raised an eyebrow at Kennedy, who nodded, and warned Don, 'I am a teacher of geography.'

'Oh, okay,' Don acknowledged. 'And it's his goal, his aim in life, if you'll have that, ma'am, to traverse this great continent of Europe coast-to-coast and sea-to-sea. That's this boy's ambition, to stand at the water's edge dreaming of the continent behind him and all its history and its…ah…doings, and I am, well, the humble pilot, with the privilege of steering him on this leg of his monumental trip.'

The woman scanned Don's face, and sent a glance at Kennedy as if to say, *What is he on? – I want some.* Kennedy relaxed when the woman burst into a loud, schoolgirl giggle. It cheered him to hear it, because he had just been thinking how, if he did not find this at all funny, then how was she supposed to?

Don bowed his head, went on, 'And after, he will head to France, and will go stand on Omaha Beach, will look at what the French call *Le Munch*, and then will continue down through France and then to Spain and, ah, thence to Portugal, to check out the windswept Atlantic in all its…ah…windswept glory, as it looks over to his homeland, the mighty old U S of A, God bless its fractured heart.'

Don's pause said *whaddaya thinka that, lady*? The woman kindly considered it a second. 'Bravo. It is called *La Manche*,' she corrected routinely. 'However, I still think your friend would have been better advised to make this journey in the summer months.'

'Well, he thought it *was* summer here at this time of year,' Don tutted.

'In January?' The geography teacher in her was poised sternly over that one, red pen in hand, awaiting Kennedy's answer.

'I was misinformed,' Kennedy borrowed from Humphrey Bogart's Rick in *Casablanca*, and that got another smile out of the woman as she gathered her stuff together. As the train halted, she wished them *bon voyage* then, and the best of fools' luck, and Kennedy thought what a gracious woman she was to put up with Don Darius, and not just sock him with her pocketbook. Funny, but nobody elected to rush into her vacated seat. A small kid was finally nominated; not yet having learned the true meaning of the word *idiot*, he sat there contentedly looking out the window as the snowed-under fields unravelled outside.

The train stopped at every break in the verge, every rabbit hole, every stack of rotting hay. People got off, wished one another good weekends, and smirked over at Kennedy and Don. Nobody got on, which did not surprise Kennedy any; not a sign of even the downest drunkest most beat old bum, and then Kennedy knew they were in trouble, or at least that they were nearly in Abel. He saw the station sign first through a gap in the snow, and then the train was sensing the end of the continent, and grinding gratefully to its rest, easing everybody toward the door and out of it.

Four

Abel

The first thing to do in Abel was to check out the tourist office, though Kennedy felt that it might have been better had they just ascertained where the hospital was. *This guy needs round-the-clock care*, he imagined telling the resident shrink. Not expecting even misinformed tourists, the office was shut. Off camera someplace, though, a soft but urgent call came out. Kennedy guessed it had something to do with the mere appearance of Don and himself, and was prepared to be weary all over again of people telling them they were in the wrong place at the wrong time. From a hole in the wall that stood in for the station café, a little guy was waving and wheezing at them. They walked over. He talked rapidly at Don, who blinked a few times before telling Kennedy that the tourist office was indeed shut.

'Oh, it is?' Kennedy swept a wide-eyed smile over both of them. 'Very helpful.'

'Now don't be that way, Kennedy.' Don's grin was pure Monterey Jack cheese. The guy behind the counter imitated it. He had no neck – no perceptible flesh at all between chin and torso. He had on a little green felt hat, a crushed feather like an egg-stain in its band. He had a day's snowy growth and clothes that looked like he had been shovelling coal in them. 'Says he can help us if we want,' Don translated. One of Santa's helpers in his off-season job, Kennedy guessed. 'Says we can ask him anything we need to know.'

'What is he?' Kennedy wondered. 'An oracle?' He had nothing to ask the man, except, *What happened to your neck?* 'No tourists,' he summarised instead. 'No information. That's the situation?'

'That's about the crux of it.' Don was not in a position to say much else. 'Hotel?' he ventured. Kennedy felt that he could have risen to that level of Polish himself.

The man was kindly writing something for them. Kennedy took a look around the station. People were making a way past them and out of there. There was nothing doing save the sounds and smells of the train that had dumped them there, diminishing as it settled into its rest.

They thanked their guide, and got out onto the street and back to their business. The snow had let up save for the occasional flake that acted as a calling card for more to come, but the wind blasted their eyes and cut their ears. 'We'll see her, man.' Kennedy thought it might be time to fix Don's dream date firmly in view. 'First person we meet it'll be her. She'll be carrying shopping,' he imagined.

'Oh, really?' Don's voice sounded like it was coming from a long way off, because he had turned his collar up over his mouth.

'Yeah.' *She'll be arm-in-arm with a gorilla of a guy who eats nails for breakfast and Americans for late lunch,* Kennedy wanted to say. 'She'll have a big coat on, big boots, a big hat…In fact,' it hit him, 'we'll never recognise her.'

'She's got any sense,' Don said, beating Kennedy to it, 'she won't put her nose outside the door till April.'

If she had any sense, Kennedy started to think, *she would never have gotten talking to Don Darius in the first place.* All he said was, 'Where are we headed, like…exactly?' He stood and watched as the people who had stepped down from the train disappeared into the lives they were about to carry on leading, getting smaller as they walked, vanishing into doorways and around corners. He envied them.

'Hotel,' Don hoped. He and Kennedy dragged down this street and that, and found the first place on the man's list after a few minutes. To Kennedy, it did not only look shut; it looked abandoned and ruined. Don pointed up at a sign just visible under the silt on the window.

'What's that say?' Kennedy guessed the sign had to mean, *shut, abandoned and ruined.*

'*Remont,*' Don read. 'Means it's being redecorated.'

It looked to Kennedy as if it had never been decorated in the first place. 'Think they'll have it finished by tonight?'

'Usually means the manager gave up and hanged himself.' Don sounded tired. 'Or ran off to Budapest with the takings and the receptionist. Well, let's head for the next place.'

'Might find a snowmen's hostel.'

A thing Kennedy was beginning to notice about Abel was the light. It came in off the open sky above the sea, and with the clouds, and the surface of the sea reflecting it back, it was an opaque silver. It reminded Kennedy of early mornings in old movies. He could see too that Abel was not a bad-looking little burg. Along the road that had to lead to that big cold sea, there were neat houses, and the welcoming light of a bar, unless it was a shoe store. Off the road stood the black tower of a church.

'Place we're looking for is right next to the change office.' Don squinted down at the paper in his hand. 'Right on this street here, I think. I really can't read this guy's writing too well. You see a change office?'

Kennedy did not. It was more likely people just exchanged rocks of amber for snowshoes. They crunched on. Kennedy would have suggested that Don ask somebody, but there was not a soul in the whole damn street, and the doors and windows that looked onto it gave off an air of impregnability, sealed against wandering fools, so they had nothing to do but keep walking.

They saw no change office, and therefore no place next to one, saw nothing at all that looked anything like a hotel. The town petered out and turned into layers of concrete, brick and stone, then just white and brown and grey, and the last layers were the sea and the sky, which loomed low and heavy. There was a scent of salt and fish and vegetation and ozone, a hint of rusting metal, a faint aroma of petrol, and a sense of nothing beyond but the elements. Don and Kennedy looked out, needles in their eyes drawn to north, said nothing, felt a wave of colder sea wind sweep over them.

Kennedy turned, looked at a squat apartment block, its windows making a chequerboard. The indistinct form of a man came out of a doorway, holding hard onto a bag. He slowed his steps and once-overed Kennedy and Don. He went on with his business when it looked as though Kennedy might raise a hand and say *hi*, and dumped the bag into a large trash can, the lid of which made a startling, violent clang. Kennedy watched him go back in, then was distracted by a figure that made its way down the glass-guarded stairway. It turned into a woman who looked like she was on the way to a wedding, in a pastel coat and a frothy hat, though on her feet were the obligatory moonboots that made her look, when she paused to button her mittens, as if she was standing in a plant pot.

'Where are we?' Kennedy knew the question was pointless, but he only meant it to prompt Don into turning back.

'The sea.' Don pointed uselessly, seemed helpless, in the face of it, to do anything other than obey Kennedy's silent bidding, and was already turning.

They trudged back toward the blocks, and became aware of a figure waiting under blinking yellow traffic lights at an intersection which, with its invisible sidewalks, looked vast, and almost monumental. It was a man, they saw, and, they knew, he was waiting for them. He had on a woolly hat, and a huge heavy black overcoat, a squeaky new pair of *Lives* with deep cuffs turned up, and snow-sneakers. His face, half-hidden by a scarf, was bony, his eyes contrasty and intense.

'You cannot go any further.' He said it in English. He pointed past them at the sea.

'No shit, Sherlock,' said Kennedy.

The guy said, 'Excuse me?' and made a doubtful smile. Then he stuck a hand out to Don, who was nearest, and said, 'This is Yatsek.'

Kennedy was going to be a smartass, and say, *No it isn't, it's Don Darius.* He got an inkling then that the man had painstakingly learned in his English classes not to say, when introducing himself on the phone, *I am Yatsek*, but had not yet mastered the art of face-to-face intros, when he was supposed to use, of course, *I am*. Kennedy made a token look around the guy, then caved in and said, 'Oh, uh, hi,' and followed Don in introducing himself, and shaking the offered hand.

'*Yatsek?*' he checked.

'You may call me Jack,' they were told. That suited Kennedy's sometime bad habit of calling everybody *Jack* whatever their goddam name was. As Jack fell into their walking rhythm, he told them that he had fixed on *Jack* because his name was actually spelled yot-ah-tseh-eh-kah, which meant nothing to Kennedy until he could see it written, later, as J-A-C-E-K.

'Snappy Jack – good call,' Kennedy agreed.

'I understand that you are lost here in Abel.'

These few words were as good a reading of their situation as any, Kennedy felt, but all the same, he said, 'How?'

Jack cleared his throat and said heartily, 'Because nobody comes here in the winter unless they're crazy or lost. I assume,' he laughed out, 'that you're not crazy.'

'Don't count on it.' Kennedy did the same silly laugh.

'Well, any suggestions?' Don asked, and Jack nodded vigorously and pointed back to town, and then they were all walking, with Jack talking away, to Don, mainly. Kennedy wanted to ask Jack what the hell *he* was doing wandering around out there, but was left to amuse himself by constructing the guy's biography out of the things he was saying. By picking out keywords and slotting them into utterances already half-formed in his head, he did it like the bad interpreter he sometimes got press-ganged into being in Istanbul. So, among other things, Jack was from Abel but was just there for a few days on a visit, actually lived in Krakow and taught English in a school there, was on a PhD program in linguistics at the university there, and for a time had lived in Britain in some town Kennedy had never heard of, and intended to live there again. Kennedy could see that the guy loved strutting his stuff in inhospitable English. It was as if they had inserted a hundred dollars into a learned but manic *I-speak-your-weight* machine. And were they aware that Abel was a place for the daytime, and for the summer?

'Jesus,' Kennedy managed to put in, 'listen –' but Jack monologued on, leading them into the maze of Abel's gloomy winter wonderland. They were off the main drag and onto a route that showed lights up side streets, a bright bar, a dark church, a dimly-lit store, a deserted kids' playground, a little white park, an empty but lit-up two-story office building with a neon anchor in its entrance hall.

A car whizzed past once in a while, but mostly the only sound in the streets came out of Jack. His voice was so loud that Kennedy half-expected to see people haul back layers of drapes and risk frostbite by putting their heads out to ask him to pipe down so they could listen to brass band music in peace. Finally, he stopped at an archwayed passage. At each side of the arch was a little stone gnome, face going, *Hah, Kennedy, you screwed up again, you moron.* Kennedy resisted the urge to give one a kick. He and Don followed Jack across a courtyard surrounded by yellow-lit windows, and went through another arch and up a staircase that smelled of cooking.

It struck Kennedy that if there had not been a Cold War, they would have had to start one, just to use the movie locations for it.

Jack's voice boomed around the echo-sounders of arches, stairways and lobbies. Kennedy was almost on the point of telling him gently that he was a real nice guy and all, and that he appreciated a lot what he was doing, whatever that was – he assumed there was some purpose to this meander – but could he please, just for a minute was all, hush the fuck up.

'This is a hotel?' he asked.

Jack turned and smiled. 'My home,' he said.

Chez Jack lay behind one of a lot of doors that faced onto a little lobby. Kennedy watched as Jack fumbled through a fistful of keys, Don trying hard to catch his eye as he made an experimental gesture of cheer.

Like the lobby outside, Jack's hallway was bewilderingly full of doors. On one was a curling poster repro of *Primo Bacio,* a painting by one of the Florentines, which showed two cute angels getting stuck into the eponymous first kiss. A seminal gay work, Kennedy thought it was smart to think, all angels traditionally being boys, until you notice that one of them, conveniently, is a girl. Jack followed Kennedy's gaze, and said, 'I bought this in Florenz, which is a fascinating city.'

'It sure is.' Kennedy too had a little piece of Florence, his Pinocchio keychain. It had been meant for his Istanbul neighbour's kid, except that the nose had suffered a break in Kennedy's luggage. He did not think Jack would want to know about that.

Anyhow, Jack was busy by then responding to a polite grunt by Don, and telling him all about his trip to Italy, about Florence, and Roma, and Verona, with Don going, 'Okay. Well, I know a lot of Italian girls too, Jack.'

Kennedy thought they might be stuck in that hallway for hours as Jack got out his vacation snaps, so he inquired, 'Uh, hey, Jack, buddy, what's happening?'

Jack had pulled off his outer clothes, and bared his head. They saw that he was maybe in his mid-thirties, his short, dark hair flecked with early grey. He looked disturbingly like one of Kennedy's uncles who robbed a small bank in…Newark New Jersey in…nineteen sixty seven, summer of love for some, first summer of a twelve-stretch in gaol for others. He stood expectantly. 'Your coats,' he said at last, slowly and pleasantly, as if talking to children. 'Your shoes, yes?'

'Indeed,' Don agreed.

'Certainly,' Kennedy pitched in.

They set to getting their boots off. Kennedy was happy to know that the Poles took shoes off before entering a place, just like in Turkey. To him, it was a mark of a civilised country when people had the respect not to bring in all the crud of the outdoors for their host to clean up. Don was relating a version of this to Jack, with the extra info that in Saudi Arabia one could get a sentence of thirty lashes for forgetting to remove shoes, plus a forfeit of three camels, female, in their prime, if it turned out the socks had not been changed recently. Jack thought about this a second, said, 'You are joking, of course,' and Don could not but concede happily that he was.

'Listen, Jack.' Don put a hand on Jack's shoulder, had on a solemn, confessional face. 'I'm the kind of guy you really don't want to believe a word of what he says, right?'

Kennedy watched Jack puzzle his way dutifully through the grammar to rest at the final clause. 'So.' He looked at Kennedy like, *Ha – caught ya.* 'You didn't go to Florenz, actually?'

'Got the Pinocchio to prove it.'

'Ah yes. Pinocchio.' Jack extended a finger for a wooden nose. 'You cannot believe anything he says also, isn't that true?'

Sick of it, Kennedy dropped his smile and asked Jack, 'Where's your bathroom?'

That seemed to throw the apartment open for business. Jack opened a door for Kennedy and showed him in. He heard Don's and Jack's voices receding as they entered another room. Washing was liberating. Kennedy forgot where he was and what he was doing there, and cared nothing about any of it for five minutes, as he pulled clothes off and washed.

He came out and crossed the hallway into a big living room with a high ceiling. It could have been a great room; it had a little apse at one end like a church, had big windows, Kennedy guessed, behind heavy drapes. One side of the room was taken up by two glass-fronted display cabinets that would not have looked out of place in a large store, cluttered with china and crystal, sets of cups and saucers, plus kitsch bone china chatchkas. Straight-backed chairs, tables high and low, magazine racks, bookcases or just piles of books, clogged up the rest of the space. Kennedy made his way in and out of them toward the end of the room. There, a couch and armchairs converged on a heavy-industrial TV set, hemmed in from the other side by a big brown stereo system and speakers that looked like they had come from the local stadium, plus a long row of record albums. *Where have I seen this before*, Kennedy wondered, then racked his brains to find Rogozhin's room in Dostoevsky's *The Idiot*, in the home of castrati and old believers: this was the place, exactly, albeit with updates.

'Neat apartment,' he said, mainly because he could not very well say, *What a dump.*

Jack broke off from whatever he was saying to Don, and turned. He smiled, and said, 'Unfortunately, it is not very neat at the moment. It must be tidied.' He sounded gloomy at the thought, which did not surprise Kennedy – it looked like a few weeks' work, after all – but became animated again when the idea occurred to him, 'You say *apartment*, but in British English they say *flat*.'

'What? Uh.' Kennedy tried to match Jack's wordsmith's enthusiasm. 'I guess they do, too.'

'They also say *arse-hewel*.' Don's declaration brought a look of anguished concentration to Jack's face. 'So I wouldn't worry my head about that.'

'I want to learn,' Jack said.

'Learn what?'

'English.' Jack laughed doubtfully. 'Of course.'

'Well, you can't.' Don was kidding, but his voice had a *my-decision-is-final tone* to it.

'But why not?' Jack's face was creased in its anxiety and concentration.

'Hey.' Don laughed. 'Listen, Jack. Sounds to me like you already have.'

'No, no.'

'Yes indeed.'

Kennedy dropped onto the couch, felt it give way and hug his ass contentedly. Jack ran stuff past Don and him; he wanted to learn English, all of it, properly, speak like an Englishman, or at least an American, a Canadian, an Australian. *Why*, Kennedy wanted to ask wearily, *what's the point? Jesus…Just…do like the rest of the world, all those Turks and Arabs and Eskimos and Chinese, Africans and Indians, and dwellers of the seas and steppes, and speak it any old way you can.*

He had to keep thinking, *Decent guy, just displaying a touch of…*aggressive *hospitality.* He sat there thinking how things had to shift; there had to be some change in relations between them, or they would just wind up remembering Jack as a dweeb who talked too much, and Jack in turn would remember them only as assholes who hogged his hospitality and gave back only smartass disdain. 'Hey,' he told Jack. 'Listen, man. Your English is way better than my Polish, just for a start.' Jack examined the compliment circumspectly, Kennedy saw, and added, 'In fact, it's excellent.' And it was, too, and he wondered what they were arguing about.

'It sure is,' Don agreed.

Jack shook his head sadly, but was appeased. He asked, 'Will you drink something?' Maybe he too had sensed the need for a change in mood and pace, as he cut to some kind of chase with this hackneyed remedy.

'I guess we will.' Kennedy entered into the spirit of it.

'Does the Pope eat pizza?' Don stopped Jack from considering the question seriously, went on quickly, 'Well, hey, now, but a shot of Jim Beam would sure make a golden trail all the way right down through me and hit some spot where it'd glow for an hour.'

'Excuse me?' Jack was confused, then anchored himself in the language at the mention of the Jim Beam, said, 'I'm sorry, but I have no whiskey.'

'Don't worry about that,' Kennedy joshed. 'We're not alcoholics.'

'*I* am.' Don's interjection made the hospitality leave Jack's face for a second. He stared at Don, uncomfortable with the phoney grin he was making. Kennedy made the same grin. He could not find it funny, and genuinely did not know what to make of it.

'How about some tea?' Kennedy knew he did not want any more booze. He also did not want Don to have any more – old killjoy Kennedy. 'You got tea?' Anyhow, he lived in Turkey, and he missed his regular glasses of tea all of a sudden. He saw Don's face cloud over, but Jack seemed to go in haste for the idea, and went off to busy himself in the kitchen. Staring at an unresponsive Kennedy for his trip through the room, and barking his shins at least once for his pains, Don exited to the bathroom.

Kennedy enjoyed the luxury of sitting alone and in silence for a few minutes. He did not know what to think, so he tried to have no thoughts at all. He did not want to feel hemmed-in by the room, and closed his eyes. He stretched his legs out. One of them hit something.

'I'm not crazy about tea.' Don came back in with a face on. Kennedy ignored him. 'Tea I can do without.' Kennedy ignored him still. 'If I wanted to drink tea,' Don risked, 'I'd go live in Turkey, right?'

'Whatever.' Kennedy kept his eyes shut. 'Why *don't* you?'

'Or China.'

'Wherever. Who's stopping you?' There was a lazy contentment evident in Kennedy's voice at the idea.

From behind a huge tray at the door, Jack made the superfluous announcement that tea was up. He brought it over to the little table in front of the couch. He poured. Kennedy sipped. Don sniffed.

'The hell.' Don did *shocked*. 'It's…*tea*.'

'But excuse me?' Their host looked flustered. 'You requested tea.'

'Take no notice of him,' Kennedy said. 'It's good tea.'

It was. It calmed Kennedy down in the way a decent brew ought to. It made him resolve again not to be an asshole to Jack. Not that he got the chance to open his mouth once Jack was back. Jack got stuck on some shit or other to do with things they could do in tourist Poland in the winter – instead of dragging around deep-freeze seaside towns – which seemed to involve going up a mountain, strapping on fibreglass planks, then coming right back down at speeds that could melt the fillings in a guy's teeth. Crazy. And then it segued into something interesting, as Jack told them that under communism a lot of people got into very dangerous stuff, such as skiing black runs, climbing the spikiest, iciest mountains, white-water rafting down the most swollen, roaring rivers, just to get the frustration out of their systems, and in places where fat-gutted pasty-faced commissars were too chickenshit to follow them. Kennedy was about to ask Jack more about that when he was off on some tangent or other, with Don in nodding overdrive, going, 'Yass, certainly, completely…totally.'

'Utterly,' Kennedy squeezed in. 'Say.' Cheap inspiration. 'Does your TV work?'

'Of course,' Jack said. 'But, you know, I have no satellite channels.'

'That's okay. How about checking out the news?'

The TV set looked like it ran on gas. A burglar with any decency in him, Kennedy thought, would have broken in and come back and brought a newer model. Jack coaxed the thing into life, and then – and Don saw Kennedy's logic here – almost shut up.

There was no news. When nothing major was happening in the world in general, TV news in other countries always seemed inconsequential, a satire of foreign TV news shows. It was a snooty, America-centric view, Kennedy admitted, though the local news back home had exactly the same desperation, news reporters and crews making it all up madly to keep their jobs. The three men closed in around the set for a second or two, then relaxed. Jack leaned over, flicked a channel, and was about to flick on when something on the screen prompted Kennedy to raise a hand and stop him. It was a black-and-white close-up of gaunt actor Elisha Cook Junior looking boyish and sore. The camera panned back from him, and

126

they saw that he was mad as hell at Humphrey Bogart, who was giving him the big sneer of the man who knew exactly where he was at.

'Hey,' Don said. 'I know what this is. What is it?'

Looking slightly bemused at the contradiction, Jack told him after a squint at a newspaper that it was *The Falcon of Malta*.

'That's the one.'

Kennedy knew the movie well. He had a memory of how he was at home in summer vacation and he was watching John Huston's movie of *The Maltese Falcon* on TV, fascinated at the story unfolding before him. What he did not know was that his dad had decided to drive him into town to see *The Jungle Book*. Kennedy did not want to go. He wanted to stay home and watch *The Maltese Falcon* and see what the black bird looked like. The unfortunate thing was that he had been bugging his dad the whole summer to take him to see *The Frigging Jungle Book*, and there he was being the kid from hell, and that made his dad even more determined to drag him there. He never got to see the falcon, nor what happened to the decadent and greed-haunted cabal in the movie, until a long time after.

Sydney Greenstreet's Casper Gutman was saying how Bogart's Sam Spade was a character, sir, a real character. What was weird about it, though, was that Kennedy could only hear that way down in the mix; what he was getting up front was some guy talking over it in Polish, and for a second he thought Sydney Greenstreet was being stalked and haunted on screen by the Polish Consul in Ostrava. 'What's going on?' he had to ask. Jack told him how that was what they did in Poland when they showed foreign movies on TV: they did not dub them, but had a guy intoning the lines over the soundtrack. 'Like subtitles for the blind,' Kennedy concluded. It was awesomely bad.

'A catastrophe.' Jack looked so embarrassed about it that Kennedy wanted to pat his back and say he knew it was not Jack's fault.

They sat and watched, lit up by blues and greys. Gutman was bringing to life the provenance of the falcon, and its origins with the Templar Knights of Malta; the guy speaking the soundtrack, however, sounded like he was going, *kilo of broad beans, can of tuna chunks in oil, box of cornflakes...and don't forget the crunchy health bars with the money-off-next-purchase ticket*. 'Catastrophe.' Kennedy repeated it Jack's way, with no *e* on the end – he liked that; they did that in Turkey, too – and Jack looked almost tearful.

Kennedy diverted Don and Jack by telling them about how there was a digression in Dashiell Hammett's book about the falcon-chasers. Sam

Spade and anti-heroine Brigid are waiting around in the gumshoe's apartment for creepy Joel Cairo, and Spade, killing time, it seems, tells Brigid a tale about a guy by the name of Flitcraft who leads a repeat life. 'No,' he had to put Jack and Don straight, 'not a double life. A repeat life. He has a wife, kids, job, a house, a car, a dog, then disappears without trace one day, but years later he's discovered in another town not that far away, with another dog, car, house, job, kids, wife, and all that, but, essentially, the same life.'

'So what happened?'

'Yes,' Jack said. 'Why?'

'Well, see, he's passing a construction site one day, and a beam falls down and hits the pavement near him, and that…makes him question how he moves in the world, and shows him how…stupidly *random* his death could have been.' Jack was gaping with concentration; Don's eyes were fixing to glaze. 'But that's not important right now. The thing is, it's got no bearing on the story of the falcon at all – it's got nothing to do with it. And yet Spade takes the time to tell it to Brigid.'

'And?'

'Well.' There were a lot of things Kennedy could have said. He had written a hundred-and-eighty-page thesis on Flitcraft's existential lives for his bachelor's degree. 'I don't think what this guy is saying over the soundtrack has any relation to the story, either.'

Don and Jack laughed doubtfully, and then they fell into a silence and watched the movie. Don's face fell a little as he saw the tale unfold, of incomplete people who chased a dream and were made to abandon it in disarray; the falcon-seekers were headed back to Istanbul, of course, and both Kennedy and Don were struck by the destination, and what it meant for each of them. 'Jesus.' The look on Don's face betrayed for the first time that, maybe, he regretted having come to Abel, that he had been reminded how seekers of dreams were cursed.

'Hey, Jack.' As the credits rolled, Don distracted himself with a new preoccupation. 'That little bastard called the munchies is beginning to gnaw away at my body and soul a little. You know what I mean?'

'Excuse me?' Jack sounded perplexed.

Kennedy recalled a time he was stuck on a Greyhound on the way to Boston with a bunch of French students who, after inviting him to speak French with them, yattered away rapidly in fast idiom and thought it a great joke at his expense. He wanted to remind Don that it was not a clever thing to do.

'That's okay,' Don said. 'I mean, you got any stores in the hold?'

'Excuse me?' Jack looked like he had just lost the gift of speaking the English he had amassed. A little worry worm worked its way between his eyes, though Kennedy thought he could see in the eyes the faint hope of the optimist-idiot that maybe Don was speaking Swahili just for the music of it.

'Got anything to eat, Jack?' Kennedy was not being entirely altruistic in coming to the rescue. Talk of food was reminding him that he had a cavern inside him as big as the Hollywood Bowl, with a little voice at its centre howling like a wolf.

'Of course.' Jack's face was illuminated with relief. 'What would you like?'

'I don't know.' Kennedy did not want to be presumptuous. A t-bone steak might have slipped down well, with potatoes duchesse and a side-order of creamed mushrooms, followed maybe by crepes Grand Marnier, all washed down with an unpretentious little carafe of Beaujolais. 'Food, mainly, I guess.'

'Excuse me?'

'Anything,' Kennedy said hastily. 'Whatever you got.'

'I will look.'

'Hey now, wait a second.' Don got up and blocked Jack. 'You've been kind enough to invite us here as your guests, Jack, and I recognise that certain, ah, host-guest stuff goes down here in this fine country of yours, stuff that shouldn't be messed-with at the risk of upsetting centuries of fine tradition, right, but –'

'What?'

Kennedy liked the little explosion Jack made with the word. He was glad not to be hearing that diffident *excuse me* one more time. Jack would either get used to Don, or would attack him soon with a sharp instrument.

That had penetrated maybe even Don's hide, because he went on, 'What I mean to say is, though, point us at the kitchen, lead us to the food and the open range, right, and we'll cook up some stuff for, like, all of us.'

'Hey, Jack.' Kennedy got up and joined them. 'What's the Polish for *long-winded asshole*? I sure would like to know.' This drew from Jack a formal little smile, and the building blocks of another disquisition, as they moved toward the kitchen.

The kitchen was small, dark and windowless, and had a neglected air. Jack confessed that he hardly used it, mostly grabbed food at a bar in town. They joined him in throwing cupboard doors open and finding….*stuff*, basically. 'What's this?' Kennedy showed Jack what looked like a display jar from a teaching hospital, indeterminate forms floating in it. Jack did not know. Mushrooms? They looked to Kennedy disturbingly like the intimate parts of women.

Jack diverted them by dropping a bag, and something went tinkle. 'Is that breakable?' Kennedy asked, and Jack took a peek in and, accurate to a fault, said, 'No, it is broken,' and started pouring the whole lot into the trash.

Soon on the counter lay a mess of non-specific meat, and potatoes, and carrots like the ones in Bugs Bunny, with long green flowers on the ends. There really was no room in there for three, and Jack and Don seemed to be having a lot of fun as they washed and scraped and chopped. In any case, they reminded Kennedy of those daytime TV chefs whose appeal was as much a mystery to him as who really killed JFK, so, unable to change channels, he backed out into the hallway for some respite.

He almost stepped into a woman. Her bright, fierce eyes were what he registered as he jumped out of his skin and had the momentary sensation of clinging to the ceiling like a fly. She was as tall as Kennedy, and was dressed in a throat-to-toe shimmery garment tied in the middle. She had long grey hair framing a face that startled him when he saw through the skin to her bone structure; it made her look like Death in the interminable Ingmar Bergman movie he sat through one time at college. He said, 'Uh, ma'am…' in a *sorry-for-being-alive* kind of voice.

She stared, did not need to say, *Who the frig are you and what the frig are you doing in my hallway?* Kennedy in turn did not need to say, *You're probably not Death in that crappy Bergman movie, so I guess you're Jack's mom.*

'Jack?' he called.

Jack and Don were sharing some no doubt hilarious master chef gag about what one could do with mushrooms that looked like vulvas.

'Hey, Jack!' Kennedy yelled.

The woman in the hallway pitched in and helped out.

'Who's dying?' Don appeared, big knife in hand making him look like the star of an old-dark-house slasher B-feature. 'Ah,' was all he had to say for himself as he got caught in the woman's stare.

'We are,' Kennedy said. Maybe it was to do with not really having had one of his own, much, but he had never been very good with mothers.

At that, the woman turned back to him, and broke out in a little smile. He did not know what it signified, but knew he ought to return it. He bowed his head, and nodded, and said, 'Hi, ma'am.'

Jack appeared, and took a stride over to his mom to give her a kiss on each cheek. Only after that did she ask him pointedly what was up, and a quick exchange buzzed out.

These are my friends, come to visit.

But look at them, for Chrissake. And don't they know Abel is a summer place, and a place for the daytime?

They were misinformed.

Out of here with them.

But mother —

I want them out of here before you can say 'Death' in the Bergman movie the fat one caught one time at college.

She sheeshed, and folded her arms. Kennedy thought for an idle moment that she might pull a shoe off and starting whacking Jack upside the head with it, and watched with interest. All she did was unfold her arms and raise them as if in surrender. Then she opened a door, backed into a room and shut the door behind her to make an exclamation mark. 'She is angry,' Jack did not need to explain.

'All I did was say hallo.' Kennedy said that only for the form of the thing; he had the memory of Jack's mom's smile.

'No.' Jack looked indulgent. 'She is angry because I didn't wake her up to tell her we had some guests.' Kennedy must have looked askance at that, because Jack swung a finger between the two men. 'You, of course. She is sick, so…in bed.'

Something came into Jack's face that was unseen by Don, when Don asked, 'What is it? Is it serious?'

'Rather possibly,' Jack decided to say.

Kennedy had seen it, though. He cut back to himself watching that Bergman yarn in the Syracuse Humanities campus movie theatre. He was there only because of the girl he was sitting next to in the dark, and he knew nothing about death, was ignorant of the strange pains his dad later made a foolish habit of dismissing, had not yet hooked up with his fellow fate-surfers who would kill themselves with heroin, would not in a million years have dreamed that he would one day see that power-driven shooting

131

on an Istanbul street. He saw Jack's mom's face again, saw how she had taken to her bed to lie there and watch her life go by in the silver light of her town, and how that was a dread and…*final* thing. He wanted out of there then, wanted to leave that place where Death had its boots off and sprawled in an easy chair, waiting.

'I'm surely sorry to hear that, Jack,' Don said.

Don had always displayed empathy with the bad fortune of others; there it was, underlining the blue in his eyes. Kennedy mumbled chorus.

'So we have an unexpected person for dinner, in which case.' Jack tried to look pleased about the idea. Kennedy squeezed back into the kitchen. He counted out knives and forks, got out glasses and wiped the fog off them. He was ready by then for a drink of some kind. He spotted no beers in the icebox, no vino. Don knew better where to look, though, and out of the freezer compartment Kennedy saw him make a face of triumph as he pulled out a pale bottle of what had to be vodka, and weighed it appreciatively in his hand.

When Kennedy went in to set the table, Jack's mom was standing by the living room window. She had pulled the drapes back. A streetlight, that had to be right next to the window, made the snow into a yellow blizzard. She turned and gave Kennedy a long look. 'So, Jacek's friend,' she said in cool English, 'what did your mother call you?'

The verbatim *You little schmuck* would not have been a very appropriate thing to relate, so Kennedy kept it straight and said, 'My name is Kennedy, ma'am.'

'Just Kennedy?' She laughed huskily, but refrained, Kennedy was pleased to see, from making any vacuous comments about presidents. 'Okay.'

'Just Kennedy.' He was sometimes caught off guard when people wanted to know his first name, sometimes looked so hesitant about it that it was like he had forgotten it. From the age of sounds perceived and words spoken he had been Kennedy, even to his dad, except when the old man was mad at him, of course, when he became *Nolan*; this pattern had recurred in his various relationships with women, oddly enough.

'You're American,' she knew. 'From where?'

'Vermont,' Kennedy confessed. 'A town called Harrington.'

'I didn't ever go to Vermont.' She made it plain that Vermont was a no-account kind of place in her book. 'I lived in Detroit.' She shut her eyes for a second. 'Five years – rather, five and a half.'

'You did?' Kennedy would not have wished five years in Detroit on anybody. 'What took you there?'

'I was in the motor industry.' She laughed gently. 'Of course.'

'Right.' Kennedy saw the Motor City blues in her face, though in the sweater-and-skirt combo she had put on, plus neat little buck slippers in black, and with her hair tied into a girlish ponytail, she no longer resembled the haggard Lily Munster he had seen in the hallway.

He thought, *Shame on you for thinking that, ya big...*nincompoop.

As if having exposed herself to a surge of sci-fi energy, Jack's mom had taken twenty years off. Kennedy still saw her skull through her face, though he saw too that one thing she had done was go put some teeth in. She set fire to a cigarette, and the car exhaust impression she did led Kennedy to ask her, 'What did you do there, like, in the motor industry?'

'Science and technology...um, research and development.' She addressed Kennedy's dumb look with, 'Gases, emissions from exhausts,' and launched into what sounded like a wearily-repeated summary; it had been to do with deposits in the works of engines, and finding a lube that would evaporate more cleanly, and stuff like that. She stopped, and said, a little acidly, 'But, you know, that was another life.' The words made Kennedy feel sad. He felt even worse when she let out almost casually, 'I left it all behind, to come back to the new Poland.'

'Hmm.' Kennedy let out a breath. 'Right.'

Jack's mom looked closely at him, and laughed, at his discomfort, he guessed.

'The new Poland will...take time.' Kennedy almost heard himself swallow. 'I guess.'

Maybe he had a gift, he reflected gloomily, of hitting the exact spot when the time came to say the wrong thing. The face Jack's mom reverted to for a second let slip that the one thing she did not have was time. The clothes and the ponytail and all did not hide that.

'Well,' they both started to say.

Jack's mom asked, almost at once, 'So, what are you doing here in this new Poland we have? Are you living here?'

For maybe ten minutes, Kennedy made her a child's collage of Istanbul. She told him that she went there once in the sixties, lifted up a corner of the Iron Curtain and crawled under it and escaped, told about her eyes wide to see all the stuff they had in Istanbul, the food and the drink and the mosques and the markets and the clothes and the people – millions of people; she shook her head, shook those images into the room. Kennedy was looking then at her own collage. '*So I have sailed the seas and come*,' she quoted from W B Yeats, '*to the holy city of Byzantium*,' and Kennedy thought that was neat. 'What a place.' She left the poem hanging. 'You can't explain it.' Kennedy took that to mean that they were through talking about it. 'But maybe you can,' it struck her, 'because you live there.'

'Not me. It's the kind of place nobody can explain.' Kennedy had the relief of his own laugh, at the very idea. 'And I live in modern Turkey, ma'am,' he had to admit, 'as dreamed up by Kemal Atatürk.'

'Of course. Do you think he would be pleased with the place today?'

'I guess not.' Kennedy thought it was kind of cool that she had even heard of Atatürk; he was the dictator the world always forgot. He thought about the question, and went on, 'Too much religion, and not enough…marching.' Mustafa Kemal Atatürk had embodied the nineteenth-century soldier in his bones and brows; that was the paradox of Atatürk, though: nineteenth-century man forcing his country into the twentieth century at the point of a gun. 'But then, you know…I think he was a very…*exacting* guy, and I don't think he was ever pleased with anything much.' Kennedy thought of the dour old despot pacing the halls of the Dolmabahçe palace, muttering to himself, *You bust a gut for people, and they what? Just let you down…*

Kennedy's reverie and conversation were interrupted by the arrival of Jack and Don bearing platters that steamed, Jack saying, *Please*, and Don trying to say, *Voilà*.

'Smells good,' Kennedy called. It was true. Kennedy was not exactly amazed, just…surprised.

Jack placed his dishes on the table, and approached, said to Kennedy, 'This is my mother.'

'We have already met, Jacek.' Jack's mom said it much more imperiously but still somehow more kindly than Kennedy might have, and dismissed the occasion with a wave. 'Of course.' The look she sent Kennedy was shorthand for a whole series of utterances culminating in something like, *Okay, he's gauche compared to you sophisticated western types, but he is just saying things that reveal the process of which we are all a part, and what is more he is doing it in a foreign language, so it's okay for him to say dumb things, and what's more he is my kid, and don't you dare diss him.* 'And now please introduce me to your other friend.'

Don hustled himself over to be announced, and he and Jack's mom segued easily back into the Motor City conversation, which accompanied them over to the table.

Once everybody was seated, Jack's mom was demanding to be told about Don's name. He went into his raconteur part and told the story of how his grandpa on his dad's side made the damp crossing of the pond from Gdynia to New York way back in ragtime. He had the Christian name of Dariusz, pronounced *dar-ee-oosh*, and the family name of Pszczynski, which went *pish-chins-kee*, both of which just looked fearsome and barbaric written down. The Ellis Island officials had as little success as Kennedy in getting their tongues around the names, and wanted to knock off for the day and go home, so they just put his first name down on his papers, and, unhappy too with the s and z combination, chopped off the z. It was a familiar tale to them all, but they found themselves caught up in it all the same. Jack reminded them that their hot stuff would become cold cuts if they did not start in on it. 'Here,' Jack's mom laid down the law to Don, 'you will be Dariusz again.' Don said he would be more than happy to take on one little z.

It was more than Don's name she wanted to know about, it was clear to Kennedy; she wanted to examine Don's status as a Pole. Back in Istanbul, especially after Don had announced his intentions to go live in Poland, Don would tell anybody who asked that he was a Pole, as well as a Texan. 'I mean from my family,' he would elucidate. 'Grandparents and all. And my mom, too,' he would add, almost as an afterthought.

Kennedy was just looking politely in Jack's mom's direction when he had a vision of Don's mom gazing out the doorway of that hut in Auschwitz, rake-thin and frowning, her eyes large and yellow, as a Chinaman invited her out for porridge. Don did not mention his mom to Jack's mom. He seemed content to let her assign his Polishness back to a ship that left Gdynia in nineteen ten, full of people with names that sounded like tongue-twisters sent to try bureaucrats.

'You will call me Krystyna,' Jack's mom commanded. It was a good trade; Kennedy was glad she was not going to be Mrs Mouthful-of-Consonants.

'With a c, mother?' Jack and his mom fielded grins, some private gag going down to do, Kennedy worked out later, with her anglicising her name in Detroit from the Polish spelling to accommodate people who got easily confused.

'With whatever you like.' She waved it past her.

Jack had both quieted down and lightened up in the presence of his mom. Kennedy thought their rapport was cool, Jack only putting in his two cents' worth when he thought it might help. At the table, Krystyna castigated Don for not having liked Istanbul, and even his usual bravado provided no refuge; Kennedy enjoyed the way he flubbed and flustered his answers. They talked about her own travels, and saw where Jack had got his wanderlust from. Krystyna told them different things about Warsaw and Krakow, and of the luck and determination that had preserved them. There was nothing earth-shaking, just the usual dinner-party thing, really; Krystyna mentioned a pal who did this or that or went there or here, a cousin who said this when she wrote her…She talked about a wedding in Connecticut she went to, and a christening in Philadelphia she missed, a suit she bought near New York's Delancey Street, a wild night out with some Chicago Poles, an ice cream sundae she ate in Lindy's at Times Square, a show she saw off Broadway…Jack's dad was not mentioned, so Kennedy and Don guessed that he had been rubbed out of the scene entirely.

Another thing they did not talk about was whatever was wrong with Krystyna that had laid her in her bed. Some kind of cancer, both men guessed. Whatever it was, they did not pick up any hint of bitterness from her. She hardly glanced at her food, though, and Kennedy saw that Jack had been ready for that in giving her only the tiniest of portions, and not making with any *you-eat-that-up-now* variety of table talk.

All in the descent of a second, Krystyna looked chalky-white and red-eyed. When Jack went out to dump dishes, she said she would hit the hay. When Don got up and stuck an arm out for her to lean on she made no protest, stood holding onto it, and then nodded to show him that he could leave her to it.

'I'm glad we met you, ma'am.' It sounded very final to Kennedy as he said it – there he was again, out with exactly the wrong thing – but there seemed no other way to put it.

'A privilege, ma'am.' That was the southern gentleman in Don.

'Thank you, guys,' Krystyna called back through the doorway. 'Me too.'

She was gone. They stood and listened to nothing. They did not catch each other's eyes. They sat down carefully.

'Well,' Kennedy said.

'Yes,' Don agreed.

Jack stayed in with his mom awhile. Don sortied to the kitchen to brew coffee. Kennedy squeezed in and did the washing up. They tried so hard not to listen to the low hum of voices coming through the hallway that, for a time, it was all they could hear. Don found a radio with nothing to be wrung out of it but morose tunes which only made them ponder Krystyna all the more.

Jack came back in clutching three shot glasses and a bottle, and Kennedy knew that they were to give some of the night, and their brains, over to the hard stuff.

'What else can you do?' Don had always been fond of saying that.

There were a few things they could have done, but it seemed plain to Kennedy that they were not going to do them. He forgot them. Jack poured, carefully.

'To Krystyna.' Don raised his glass solemnly, and Kennedy and Jack joined him in the toast.

Kennedy looked at the vodka: beautiful. So far. Don and Jack knocked their shots down. Don eyeballed Kennedy's, its one sip gone. 'For Krystyna,' Don entreated him, and then down went Kennedy's, pausing at the back of his throat to trip the switch for his central heating system.

'Krystyna,' he said.

'Fine lady,' said Don.

'Very fine.' Jack took a look over to where his mom had sat down. 'And now...'

Kennedy and Don looked at him.

'Now...what?' Don asked.

Kennedy looked away.

'Now is the time for me to appreciate her...finally. You know?'

'Yes,' Don claimed.

'You understand?'

'Yass. Totally. Hey, Kennedy? You understand?'

'You know it.' Kennedy watched as Don poured them all another shot. 'Hey, Jackski.' He pulled out the stash of dope Don had provided. 'You cool with this?'

Jack sent Kennedy a bright-eyed look that said he was more than cool, so Kennedy reached for one of Krystyna's smokes and, mixed thus with tobacco in the English manner, fixed them a j. He lit up. It tasted faintly of petroleum, but it was extremely okay, he decided. He passed it on, and set about building another.

Anxious maybe to get it done before he got too slaughtered to splice together words, Jack started telling Kennedy and Don about his mom's finest hours. Because she had been born in Poland at the wrong time, the Second World War had to be faced, and there was no going around it; there she was, orphan girl in forced labour in a factory outside Lodz. Then she was marched east to serve the Third Reich in Ukraine till the Nazis started getting their butts kicked by the Red Army. On their way back to Germany, those petulant Nazis burned every last blade of grass and ear of corn they saw, razed every building, shot every last man, woman and child. Grey in her hair already, Krystyna found a strange moment in a field full of fire and smoke and parts of bodies, during which nobody in the world was looking at her, and just walked away and parted company with the master race. She headed for the forests west of Ukraine, east of Poland, and lived in them, joined a band of fighters, carried a gun, lived through times nobody could begin to imagine, nor bear to remember.

One good thing could be said for the Second World War, Jack broke off to say. He was convoluted, but his main point was that people caught up in it had seen a world other than their own.

'They sure did,' Don agreed quietly.

'Wait a second,' Kennedy had to interrupt. 'Let me get this straight. You're telling me that the war was a…*character*-building exercise?'

That was it: it was partisan Krystyna's line exactly, Jack confided, and proudly.

Don seemed to Kennedy as if he was about to talk Jack's statement back at him and tell him about his own mother, cowed by history-in-the-making, and the guy who never survived to be his uncle, and her friend who got shot even though she was in love. Kennedy saw him let it go. Don just shook his head, took a drink, bade Jack, 'Go on, Jack. More.'

With the first of her interesting times done-with, Krystyna's character was steely enough to let her see through the bullshit of Uncle Joe Stalin-style communism. That did not make her popular in the Poland being rebuilt by Soviet brown-noses, and they threw the little red book at her whenever they could. She had invoked the help of Saint Sebastian in daring them, *So shoot me*, and, Jack had the idea, they came close. But she did good stuff in her studies and research, made contacts in business who despised the system as much as she did, and who placed and kept her in jobs. When the Italians sold the Poles the blueprints for the pygmy Fiat one-two-five-p, it was a team fronted by Krystyna that they called in each time they wanted them modified; that was her baby for a long time, along with baby Jack. Krystyna put in the year upon year at Polski Fiat until she outgrew it and went to Detroit.

Jack waved a hand as if to say, *Enough of this nostalgia*, but Kennedy found himself wanting to think all over again about what Jack had told them of his heroic mom, wanting to make memories from the story's images.

Jack and Don cut themselves off from Kennedy, and any more logical discussion, by drinking at what Jack dubbed *Polski tempo*. It was a challenge Don was only too ready to take up. Kennedy declined by making only token efforts, puffed all the while on his magic dragon. He did not want to risk the *tedious ridicule* stage into which heavy drinkers nearly always stumbled; the pleas to get it down you like a man – *what*, he would always think, *the kind of man who wants to actually run out of his liver and senses?* Kennedy wasn't exactly proud of it, but he only ever got drunk by accident, taken by the moment and the atmosphere, and never by determination. His strategy paid dividends, and after a little while he was able to refrain from the vodka without Don and Jack noticing, they were getting so smashed. Meantime, Kennedy withdrew into a little world of his own in which he watched a flickering movie of partisan Krystyna in the forests, spotting her creep around trees, a Saturday night special in her hand. Wild.

'Here's the thing, here's the thing,' Kennedy heard Don say at different points in the proceedings. 'There's, like, a…*philosophy* to drinking.' He felt pretty glad to be missing out on that wisdom. 'And, ah, to the, ah, things that become…clear to you when you are…ah…what was I saying?'

'Where is the thing?' Jack managed once, but mostly he was helping, going, 'Yes – rather yes, it is so – ah-hanh,' a lot of the time during Don's spiels, so Kennedy knew it was giving Jack the bypass, but that neither Jack nor Don cared.

Kennedy listened without hearing. He saw the table all scattered with debris, the light showing up every shadow like in a black-and-white movie, and in the middle of it he thought he saw Dashiell Hammett's enamelled Maltese falcon unwrapped, pieces of its skin scraped off to reveal it as a sham. 'The stuff that dreams are made of.' He recalled Sam Spade's judgement of the bird. But it was only Don Darius talking, eyes blazing one second, squeezed up in helpless laughter the next.

The stuff that dreams are made of. Like Ola. Kennedy projected the name of Don's flyaway woman at the window, and followed it. He really hoped she was out there someplace. Then he knew at once that, if she was, she was hidden: she would stay an enigma. He found himself at the window, looking out on the snow, his nose against the cool glass, and then his cheek, then his forehead. 'So cool,' he called back. He got a Texan whoop, and then a very Polish *rather yes*.

Kennedy's memory of the evening went a little fuzzy after that. He was in an extended phase of *zonked*, and was reasonably content. He spent what seemed like a very long time in the bathroom trying to get his contact lenses out, till he remembered that he had not in fact put them in that day. He knew then that it was time for him to pass out as gracefully as possible.

Kennedy's last coherent memory of the night was of hearing Don cough out to Jack, 'Hey, my dear Jack, tell me now, is that *Polski tempo* too?' as Jack threw his guts up someplace. In the bathroom, Kennedy was hoping, as he hazed off to sleep.

The clatter of crockery forced a gentle way into Kennedy's consciousness, melded with the smell of coffee and Don's voice near his ear. He also heard Jack nearby, yattering happily away. Exuberant bastards.

Kennedy sat up, said something like, 'Fuh.'

'Couldn't've articulated it better myself, good buddy.'

For a few seconds, the face above Kennedy looked blurred. Then it morphed into full-on morning-person Don Darius. How the hell did he maintain that?

'Coffee,' Don announced, then made a pause. 'Ah-ah.' He wagged a finger. 'Breakfast in bed is cancelled on the Lord's day. Coffee awaits out in the kitchen, as does bread which can reasonably quickly be transformed into toast. And listen.'

Kennedy did.

'In the bathroom there is water in which you can sloosh the stuff out of your pores and creases and wrinkles, if you have any, and what-all. It's good,' he tried to persuade his friend.

Kennedy thought for a moment; no, he had not forgotten what water was.

'Shit.' Kennedy was only saying the word because it was something you said in transit from a late night to an early morning. He had a bit of sloeberry dryness in his mouth, but did not feel too bad, truth be told.

'No.' Don was already out of the room. Kennedy thought he could hear his voice echoing in the passageway, saying, 'Shit will happen, I am almost convinced, later.'

Through a fault-line in the drapes, the light outside was bright with the snow. Kennedy knew what to expect, but all the same took a step to the window, pausing only to snag his foot on some low piece of furniture. He pulled the drapes back. The snow was glorious, looked at from the warmth of an apartment. There was snow back in Istanbul, but it did not look like that. And they had it in abundance in Vermont, too, but…well, that was just no-account kind of snow.

Even though she had never been there, the thought of Vermont brought to Kennedy a picture of Krystyna that took the light out of the day for seconds. Maybe she would make it out to breakfast? But he did not want to look Death in the face anymore; Death was for the night-time, and Kennedy wanted to troop on into the day without it.

He had a whirl at making himself look presentable. Then he figured that it did not matter one bit, seeing as out in the snow he would look like an Arctic explorer. You did not go to a town like Abel, anyhow, and try to outsmart its natives in their winter Sunday best. Even supposing they gave half a damn.

In the kitchen, Jack looked slit-eyed and slept-in, but was heroically ignoring the pulses that had to be beating out a *Polski tempo* behind his forehead. He was enthusing away to Don about something or other to do with his PhD, or the school he worked at, or both; Kennedy was not interested enough to mind getting thoroughly confused. The radio was on low. After a lot of tinny chat, so much that Kennedy assumed it had to be talk radio, a piece of classical music began. It set his teeth on edge, and hurried him back to the living room.

He had caught the look on Don's face as he nodded along to Jack's spiel. He knew what Don was preoccupied with, of course: there he was, poised on the starting blocks for this wild skirt chase.

Not for a moment, Kennedy knew, was there any hope of it; not in ten thousand snowbound winters was Don Darius going to run into the girl of his dreams in a nowhere town like Abel. Did Don really not have any sense of that? Kennedy listened for signs of it in the things Don was managing to shove into Jack's pauses, but could not detect anything that spoke of his hopes at all.

What did he know, though? Don was deep; really, Kennedy would not have been surprised at anything Don said or did, or achieved. He had come to realise how all the time he had known Don in Istanbul, and thought he had him read like a book, albeit one he had tossed aside quickly, he had been wrong. It had taken Don's own book to show him that.

Soon it became apparent from the scraps Kennedy could hear that Don had sketched out part of his plan to Jack, who had abandoned his monologue to do *incredulous,* at first in the unusual silence from his part of the kitchen. 'I'm serious,' Don kept saying. Jack began to sound like a stubborn motor launch engine, *but but but.* 'Really,' Don insisted.

'Crazy man.' Jack let the two words rest. Kennedy did not hear Don trying to argue the toss on that one. He went out to the kitchen in an effort, maybe not to rescue the situation, exactly, but simply to give Don a little support.

'Just tell us where the churches are at,' Don was almost pleading. 'You don't have to tag along.'

'We're in Poland.' Kennedy was seeing one more time the sky over Silesia, full of crosses. 'You can't move for churches.'

'Very true.' Jack seemed to like that. 'Don, I can understand you wanting to go to church.' He spread his hands. 'That's okay. But, you know…to both of them in Abel?'

'What did you say?' Kennedy asked Jack.

Don had not been paying attention. 'I've been to all the churches in Warsaw,' he made the outrageous claim. 'And listen. Here in Abel, I…ah…want to go to all of them too.' Kennedy and Jack looked at Don almost in pity as he went on, 'Not a lot to ask, it being Sunday and all.'

'*Both* of them, he said.' Kennedy caught Don's attention at last. 'Do the math. That means, like, two.' He emphasised the number with a finger and thumb. 'You know, not three. Or four. Or the square root of three hundred and nineteen thousand.'

'What?'

'Two churches.'

'Why?' Jack's persistence seemed reasonable enough.

'Two.' Don let out a little cowboy growl.

'But why?'

'Ah, well now, Jack, that's because…' Don improvised his way back to the matter in hand. 'That's the way I make my, ah, particular path to the Lord.'

Jack took a long look at Don, who crumpled under it almost at once. With as little joy as a Chinese midwife, Don said, 'It's a girl.'

'He's looking for a girl,' Kennedy spelt out cheerfully for Jack.

'A girl?' Jack said.

Don said, 'Well, in fact, a woman.'

'Excuse me?'

'A woman who lives in this town and…ah…goes to church in this town.'

'I don't believe you.' Jack did his incredulity great justice.

'You're a character, sir.' Kennedy conjured up Sydney Greenstreet, mainly doing Caspar Gutman in *The Maltese Falcon*, but the one in the Polish consulate in Ostrava too. He thought how even then, in a room with two ringers for guys who had never existed, the day ahead of him had seemed more comprehensible. 'A real character. One never knows what you'll be up to next, 'pon my word.' Don turned a suffering glance toward Kennedy, but Jack grinned like a chimp that had just seen another chimp's ass.

'What is her name?' Jack asked.

'Ola,' Don told him. 'That is, Aleksandra.'

'Yes.' Jack sounded patient. 'But you know, probably three hundred women in any district in Poland have this name. I mean, what is her family name?'

'Well, see, Jack, now, that's the problem.'

The three men shared a look, and a second of silence.

Jack said, 'You don't know?'

'Not…as such.'

'What?'

'No.'

'I don't believe you.' Jack showed tonsils as he laughed. Don showed the top of his head as he bent it in a kind of submission.

Kennedy left them to it, and got the rest of his church-going clothes on. Out the window and down the street a way he spotted the dark bulk of a church. That would be the place to start, he guessed. He heard Jack saying, 'And so, are we going to go to every mass today? And are we going to stand next to the priest, so that we can see everybody? Will we ask his permission for this, or shall we hope that he doesn't notice us? What is your idea, please, Don?'

Harassed, Don came out of the kitchen looking nearly as stupid as he probably felt. Kennedy joined him in putting coat, hat, scarf and boots on in the hallway. Jack seemed to be doing the same. Don took a look at Kennedy, who declared, 'I'm not saying a thing, man,' and then the three of them were out the door and on the cold stairs and on their cold way.

It was going through Kennedy's mind that they ought to have said goodbye to Krystyna. They had said it the night before, it was true, but it had felt unfinished. Kennedy had the urge to go back, write her a note.

With the snow falling, it was not as cold out as Kennedy had expected. At least, not until they turned a corner into a white-flecked headwind coming in from the sea. The streets were calm and quiet. Cars grunted along timidly as if hungover, and people walked with their heads bowed to the elements, toward that church that lay before them and maybe drove them from inside, but, in any case, not expecting a guy with as frivolous a mission as Don Darius's.

Don was trying to describe Ola to Jack as best he could. Jack offered statistics: did Don know there were three thousand people living in and around Abel? 'What are their names and addresses?' Kennedy cracked. Jack paused long enough to look bewildered at the question, then gave Kennedy an *oh-shucks-you-old-joker-you* look. Not all of those people went to church, Jack rattled on bravely, but say two thirds of that number did, and so on and…did Don see what he was getting at?

'Describe her again,' Jack asked. But when it came down to it, Ola's was a routinely universal form. 'It is a pity she has no…distinguishing mark of some type,' he thought out.

'Yeah,' Kennedy said. 'Like a hump. At least we'd know to look in the bell tower.'

Don threw that the kind of gaze it deserved.

'Damn.' That was all Don seemed able to say in the face of the stats. Then he exited a silence, murmured, 'You're right. I mean, what can I say?'

'Nothing.' Jack's suggestion was sincere. Unable to help himself, Kennedy stuffed his scarf into his face to quell a laugh.

They stopped and stood, getting speckled with fine snow.

Kennedy had to remind himself that he had at some point decided that he really did not care where Don dragged him in Poland; so he had spent another day on trains, had woken up with a stiff neck on a stranger's couch – it was not the last time in his life that it was going to happen, he had to assume. He felt sorry that he could not help Don, and thought he should at least make an effort.

'Listen. We're here.' He adopted a rallying tone, and at the same time prodded Don into walking again. 'You dragged me up here to this summer place – that's what you told us, right, Jack, and a daytime kind of place? So, well, we got the daytime. Half's not bad. Where was I? And here we are on the way to the Arctic Circle on the trail of the woman of your dreams, and you what? You're too pussy to go seek her out? That isn't the Don Darius I know.' Kennedy paused to reflect on that; it was kind of true. 'We've travelled hopefully, man, *and* have arrived. So let's go do it, huh?'

'Are you sure?' Don peered through the snowflakes into Kennedy's face.

'Sure I'm sure. And if I am, you can be, too.' Kennedy nearly added a playful *dumbass*, but knew it was a time to be solemn, or something like it. 'Come on.'

Echoing Kennedy, Jack pointed toward the church, which had thrown them into shadow with their last few paces, and he ushered them up the few steps, through the door, and into the crowd inside.

They stood surrounded by brick and stone, statues in niches, offerings of medals, rings, watches, pipes, keychains, penny whistles, enamelled badges and brooches, and bullets and buttons and ships' brasses, all fixed to boards on the walls; there were wooden pews, tatty books of hymns to sing; there were the people of Abel, cheeks pink as babies' butts with the cold, eyes squeezed tight in headaches and prayer and song the way only those of churchgoers can be, going through all that stuff that Kennedy, as an Irish American, would never quite escape.

He stopped in front of a large tapestry of the Pope, whose eyes seemed to follow him. He moved away from it quickly.

It was in Kennedy's bones, and his bones responded by letting him in on what had drawn those good people out of their beds to go greet Jack Frost in their nicest winter garb with their hungover hangdog faces. He was at ease in the church, and decided he might as well try to enjoy the experience.

Kennedy soon lost sight of Don. He wandered and walked, then would remember where he was, and stand for a minute and listen to the call and response, familiar even when disguised in a language foreign to him, all the time watching people. He gradually became aware that there was a lot of in-and-out movement; people dropped in for ten minutes or so, did little more than greet others with a wave or a whisper, bend heads to say a prayer or make a response. Then they left. Maybe they were all looking for people they had met on trains one time – maybe Abel was the place a Polish girl said she lived in if she wanted to show guys the door.

Jack occasionally made his own greetings and, Kennedy saw from his respondents' faces, was trying to cram in everything that had happened to him since, like, fourteen eighty five.

'What do you think?' Kennedy asked Jack, once the kerfuffle that signalled the ceremony of communion was under way. 'Think there's a chance?'

'You can never know.' Jack was trying not to sound too pessimistic. 'A crazy idea, but…You know, it can take only one second of good luck. And then Romeo can meet his Juliet.'

'You never know, right enough.' Kennedy tried to match Jack's attack of feelgood. 'But, see, I'm an optimist.'

'And that is what has allowed you to have been brought here?'

'No.' Kennedy was too impressed with Jack's convoluted use of the passive mood to reply right away. 'See, the other side of being an optimist is being an idiot. I guess it was the idiot in me that allowed Don to drag me here.' And he again remembered Dostoevsky's idiot, and Jack's living room influenced by Rogozhin, saw Krystyna standing there amid the jumble, and again felt glad that he was in Abel, and felt too that he no longer had anything to beef about. Accordingly, he turned his complaint into a gesture of cheery dismissal.

'Well.' Jack put a hand on Kennedy's shoulder. 'An idiot, perhaps.'

'Yeah. Thanks.'

'But a friend, too.'

'I guess.' People overseas didn't have friends, though, did they? Kennedy tried to think of people in Istanbul he would rather have been with right then, and, except for Ling, there was nobody. He got a memory then of the two of them having nixed a walk one Sunday, then going back to his place and spending the day in bed. He was startled by the pain it brought. He really hoped Don would find his woman, and that he would have the same kinds of times. 'I mean, like, what are friends for?'

'You are a good man.'

'Yeah yeah.' Kennedy's double-positive negative was lost on Jack. He felt a hurry to change the subject, and said, 'Hey, listen,' and he had been going to remind Jack that he too was a friend indeed-and-a-half, and ask him what he had in fact been doing wandering around near the sea the previous evening when they had all met. Instead, he made the declaration, 'Don's going to be famous one day.' Jack moved his features, meaning to be polite; Kennedy thought Jack already had Don and him down as prime candidates for the ding house. 'No, listen. He wrote a book. He's written several, and – well, I don't know about the others yet, but, well…the one I read, it's…' Kennedy closed his eyes. He could see Don's Saudi book in print already, and that made him feel weird, and only slightly jealous, and got Jack's interest. 'It's going to come out, and it's going to make people talk and think and argue with one another.'

'Which people?'

'Huh?' Kennedy sent Jack a sharp look. Americans, maybe, for a start, he thought, and people overseas in general, and anybody who was in a place where they just should not be. 'Well, I don't know their names, yet.'

'Excuse me?'

'Just…people who read *books*, Jack.'

'Is this true?' Jack sounded like a schoolmaster right then, which made Kennedy recall that he was one.

'I know it. I don't know how. And all I'm telling you this for is…' Kennedy was not actually sure, but he went ahead and said, 'But listen. Tell your mom that, will you?'

'My mother?'

'Tell her he wrote a book that will pull him together a little and make music come out of his ears and the sun shine out of his ass.'

'What?'

'Just tell her about Don's book, for Chrissake.' Kennedy looked around him. 'Uh…sorry.'

'Okay.' Jack laughed cautiously. 'I will. But why?'

'Why what?'

'Why must I tell her this?'

'Just so she knows.'

'So she knows…what?'

'Just so she knows he isn't just some…aimless *bum*.'

'But why?'

'I don't know.' Because they had been there, Kennedy thought, and had met Krystyna and sat at her table and ate with her and talked with her and later heard about all she did, and drank to her, and…all. 'Just…*because*, man.'

Because it was a way of…explaining Don Darius: it was a key. Why Kennedy felt the need to offer it, though, he really did not know. Not right then. All this went through his mind, and he tried to form the words in there to relate them to Jack.

'Okay. I will tell her,' Jack decided. 'I don't know why, but you are probably right,' it dawned on him, 'and it will make her happy in some small way, perhaps.'

'*Perhaps* is all an optimist needs, Jacko.' They had worked their way outside by then, and were in the porch among smokers and chatterers and stampers of feet.

'Hey, listen. Are you, uh, religious?' it occurred to Kennedy to ask. *Here we are*, he was thinking, *me and Don Darius, self-absorbed and flippant, dragging Jack round churches in search of a woman, and not for a second did we stop to think if that might be offensive to him; what a pair of jerks.*

'Sometimes,' Jack said. 'For many years, not at all. When I was climbing,' he remembered, 'and perhaps, it seemed, in some danger, of slipping, perhaps, of falling, even then God was far from my thoughts, although I had colleagues who thought of God at such moments as these. But then, on a mountain, what could the church do to help me? It couldn't stop my life being so…unhappy and unfulfilled that I wanted to go up the most difficult mountains. But now?' He turned, reminded himself maybe that the church was right behind him. 'Now, I go to church, and, yes, I think about God, and how he can help me, and if he might help me, and I think sometimes that he does.'

'Well.' Kennedy threw hands up as he took all this in. 'I mean…we're getting you to schlep round the churches today, and…You know…Sorry.'

'Why?'

'Uh, well, see, I guess it's kind of…profane.'

'Profane?' Jack puzzled over the word.

'Disrespectful,' Kennedy tried.

'Oh. But why? I think God has no problem with this. Did you not see people who spent less time in the church even than you and Don?'

There, Kennedy's and Jack's thoughts were crossing, and, as always, Kennedy felt a shiver go through him at the thought, and a spark of kinship light up.

'These people will go away for a week,' Jack continued, 'and feel like good Catholics because they put their faces in the door and came from the cold and made the circulation of their blood…circulate again. And if that is enough for them, and if they act well during the week, and do some good things for some people, well, then, who can say that God has a problem with this? The church is not only a place for bishops to preach at us. Really.'

'Right,' Kennedy agreed, then remembered the enquiring eyes of the Pope. 'Not even, like, the bishop of Rome?'

When Kennedy was little, his mom had told him that, if the Pope died, a world war would happen. He had accepted this absolutely, and with the required dread, and had prayed hard every night for the Pope. When he talked to his dad about it, years later, his dad had laughed, and had sketched out a Catholic mothers' plot to get kids to pray for the Pope.

'Our saint?' Jack seemed to ponder the idea for a moment. 'Well, he is a man, at the end of it all.' It was said like a challenge.

'Yeah, a regular guy, I guess.'

'Probably.'

'Albeit in a dress.'

'Hmm. Yes.' Jack processed the image and the words, thought about them, and squeezed out a laugh, and then they were silent.

They began to freeze in the porch, but agreed tacitly not to go back in. They watched the faces of women as they snuck in and out; there went Ola, Kennedy guessed, hiding in plain sight.

When Don appeared, he looked a little sour as he bellowed, 'Not there, guys.'

'She isn't?' Kennedy took a look around Don to make sure.

'Ah, very funny.'

'Well, there's always the other church.' Kennedy mentioned it gently, but stared the task into Don's eyes.

Don hid his face in his collar, pulled his hat down with some emphasis.

'Where is it?' he asked Jack, whose body-language told them that he was not about to let them wander round Abel like even bigger schmucks than they were; he was going to lead them to the other church like the Samaritan he was.

'Hey, listen, though, Don.' Kennedy put an arm around each of them, and they huddled. 'She might be a ten-minute girl.' Kennedy told Don then, with Jack nodding along, tales out of school about the people who did not stay for the whole shebang; Don would have to stand at the back and be there for the whole thing to really be sure if his Ola looked in or not. 'And that's, like, how many services, Jack?' One per hour, Jack told them, in each church, till twelve, and then time out for the afternoon, and then a few evening services – he was not sure about the times. 'You see what I'm getting at?'

'I think I'm getting the message.' Don's expression did not say anything like *romantic, impulsive genius at work*; he looked more like a kid trying to puzzle his way through making a model airplane having sniffed all the glue. 'It's impossible,' he said at last. Kennedy really did want to help, so he resisted doing a slow handclap. Don looked at him as if he had done so just the same. 'Who was it told me it was a crazy idea?' It sounded like an accusation. 'Was that you, Kennedy? I believe it was. Someplace in the haze of the past couple of days I think I recall you telling me that in terms that would leave me in no lack of certainty. Well, thank you, anyhow.'

'Sorry, man.' This time there was no spiel from Kennedy about time and distance and trains. 'I really am.'

'I know.'

'Well, you tried, right?' *Not so very hard*, Kennedy thought, but refused to let it show.

'I tried.'

'You got to try.' They impressed Jack, Kennedy thought, with their unison, but it was only that shared breath of words from the end of a Lyle Lovett song. Jack looked from one to the other.

'We used to be in a barbershop quartet, this man Kennedy and I.' Don stood tall next to Kennedy. 'And from that venture we gained our Siamese twin-like presence of mind and harmonious purpose of movement and gesture.'

'Excuse me?'

'You're excused,' Kennedy told Jack, and shook his head and dismissed Don with a wave. 'You really are.'

Nudged out of the church doorway by a flood of homegoers, the three men slushed through town. They got engulfed for moments by incoming churchgoers, got splashed by their cars. Abel looked crowded all of a sudden, full of matchstick people on dirty snow.

Kennedy said to Don not to quit right then, to keep the little winking light on in his brain to kid housebreakers that somebody was home. Don risked nasal frostbite to search the passing faces, but they were not going to return the compliment, and it was as Kennedy had suggested the evening before: every passer-by was so well wrapped up you could not tell if they were men or women or bears or buffalo.

They shoved into a little bar around a corner, which by then was as packed as the church had been. It was way too early for anything other than coffee, but most guys in there were hitting the beer, and several were on the local moonshine. By their addled looks and slo-mo voices and movements, it was plain that they had been freshening their glasses assiduously. One group kept going *ah-hargh* like stage Long John Silvers. Kennedy could not help but admire their fortitude; how did guys who had no livers left keep up with the day-to-day traumas that had driven them to drink in the first place?

It was a long, dark place under a low ceiling. There was a smell in there redolent to Kennedy of Turkish tripe soup, and it turned out to be the Polish version. Kennedy was careful to remind Jack that he would eat anything but tripe soup, as Jack ordered coffee and chow for him and Don. Both had the simultaneous idea of treating Jack to a meal and a drink in some attempt at recompense for his hospitality, but he did not sit down. He told them he would have to go check on his mom. 'I am not sure how long I will take,' he said. 'So – you know – don't wait for me. Carry on and…do the things you have come here to do.' Kennedy thought he made them sound like the hit men in Hemingway's story about killers.

Jack was saying goodbye in his own way. Kennedy was glad about that, and not glad too. Part of him thought that a goodbye ought to be effected the way Jack had just done it, all terse and manly and northern European; another part of him, though, wanted Mantovani and bear hugs, tear-choked promises never to forget the things they did, and to remain in touch daily, and be godfather to first-born children, and all that. In truth he was happy either way, but the first was a lot less trouble.

'Hey, Jack.' Kennedy held a hand out, and they shook, and Don shook Jack's hand too.

'We'll be here,' Kennedy told him. 'But if not, though – you know.'

Jack nodded, but looked puzzled, and said, 'No. What?'

'Thank you, man,' Kennedy spelled out. 'For the bed and vittles.'

'And the booze,' Don added.

'And – you know – for us getting to meet with your mom.'

'Well.' Jack looked embarrassed, but he knew what they meant, and he almost bowed as he backed his way through the town's diehards and out of there.

Don quieted Kennedy with a hand up, then went and added a couple of vodkas to their order to warm them up. Kennedy was about to point out the early hour, then realised he craved the instant fix of the spirit's warmth.

'To Krystyna.'

'Fucking A.' They drank. Kennedy raised his glass again, and toasted, 'To the churches of Abel.'

'Yes.' Don looked bleak for a second, then said graciously, 'And to all who pray in them.'

'Even if it's only for ten minutes.'

'Hey, Kennedy, listen.' Don leaned over, his face threatening confidences. 'You came here with me.'

'Yep.'

'You helped me.'

'Hey.'

'Thank you.'

'That's okay.'

'Thanks.'

'It's cool, really.'

'Thank you. I mean every word.'

'Sure.' Kennedy couldn't resist pointing out, 'Uh, it's only two words.'

'All the same, anyhow. I mean both of them.'

'Right.'

'But hey, you know what it's like, though.'

'What?'

'You got a girl.'

'Old Flat Face,' Kennedy quoted.

'Now don't call her that.' Don raised a finger. 'You love her? Really?'

'Sure I do.' That was the one of the few things Kennedy was sure of. And there he was, a whole continent away from Ling, and time running away. What a klutz. 'Why?'

'You're lucky.'

'I know it.' Kennedy was not lucky, though. He would never find Ling among the Chinese billions. He would be stuck in a scenario horribly similar to the one Don was in at that moment, would just follow Chinese girls through the streets his whole life and always be a sad tomato who loved one time but lost the plot of his romance because of geography. Okay, and economics, maybe.

'Real lucky.'

'Yeah.' A guy who was never going to make it to China, not in ten thousand years. 'Right.'

'Listen,' Don said brightly. 'Tell me about China.'

'What about it?' Not in ten million years was Kennedy going to get to China. Who was he trying to kid?

'*All* about it.'

'*All* about it?' Kennedy sent Don a *get-outa-here* look. 'I can't do that. Even Chinese people can't do that.'

'Okay, then. Some. Tell me *some* things about China.'

'They have good classical music,' Kennedy thought up.

'They do?' Don guffawed. 'Like the names of all those Chinese composers spring immediately to mind.'

There was no answer to that. 'Their tea's good,' Kennedy said.

'It always tastes fire-damaged to me.'

'Eh?' Kennedy was slow, but guessed that Don had in mind the smoked leaves of Lapsang. 'Uh, okay. Fun-*ny*. It's green, though, mostly.'

'Oh. Green. Okay.'

'They learn English, and speak it to one another.' Outrageously wacky, Kennedy had always thought, but true, and a great testament to their determination to get out there in the world, somehow.

'What, all thousand billion of them? All babbling away in English the whole time?'

'I didn't say that. But, see, there's nobody else to speak it to, only one another. There's a park in Beijing, right, and when they want to practise their English they go to this park, and they're not allowed to speak Chinese, only English.'

'Freaky. What's the drill?'

'You go there.' Kennedy saw Ling telling him about it, her posture, the olive green crewneck sweater she was wearing, and the light shining pinkly through one of her delicate white ears. She had been seeking his approval, willing him to say what a great thing it was, the English park in Beijing, even though she had allowed herself to file it under *absurd*. 'You stand around. You speak English. That's about it.'

'Weird.' Don was impressed. 'What else?'

'I'm going there, man.'

But all Kennedy saw was himself in that Beijing park, searching for Ling among the flat faces in the crowds.

'You're what?' Don said. 'No. Really?'

'Oh yeah.'

'But they cook dogs there.'

'They do *not*. And even if they do…No, listen. I'm going there. Do me a favour, and drink to that.'

Don would do that for anybody, so they drank. Their stew, when it came, could have done with a little meat to balance out the fat and gristle, but it was hot, at least. People made their Sunday noises around Kennedy's and Don's heads, and once they had eaten they were dragged into the proceedings by a group of hairy guys who looked like the results of a union between Roseanne Barr and a roadie with Metallica. They wanted to know in the first instance what the hell Kennedy and Don were doing in Abel at such a time of year and day, etcetera, which broke the ice, despite them being surrounded by the stuff. Don and Kennedy claimed to have come there to visit their old pal Jack, a guy who lived over there and up that way a little, round that corner and up on Wherever Street.

'I know him,' one of the men said. 'He is a professor in Krakow.' The group's noises could have been taken any way; they were scathing, envious, admiring.

That was the fellow, Kennedy and Don told the men. 'And a fine professor he is, too,' they had no compunction in saying. *We teachers stick together, see,* Kennedy was fond of declaiming in Istanbul, *as you'll find out if one ever terrorises one of your horrible kids,* but he decided it would be wise not to impart it to the hairies of Abel.

The men asked and talked about Kennedy's and Don's trekking around their country. It seemed an awful lot to Kennedy, though in truth he had seen little of it but trains and bars and the occasional shoe store. The men listed places for them to go, probably all the places Don's student Peter had told them about way back in Warsaw, when the idea of them being anyplace near Abel was something Kennedy, for one, had settled on not even considering.

Outside, the to-ing and fro-ing of mass-goers was chimed and timed by the church bells. Kennedy sent Don a look each time this happened, but hell, Don could tell the time. Or most of it. Don returned a look that told of time not meaning a thing when you were with good guys and having a drink. Those guys were by then spouting stuff that sounded like sharp bursts of poetry, then busting their considerable guts laughing. Don said they were telling jokes so old he was considering getting a historian in to laugh at them.

Watching them all getting into this with the enthusiasm of first-grade kids, Kennedy rustled up a round of whatever it was they were on. He was only half-listening to the grizzled little man inside his head with Buster Keaton's face, who said he did not give a damn how luckless his charge was in love; if Kennedy got shitfaced again he would be there with all his levers to pull: dry heave, full upchuck, right up to full Jimi Hendrix and goodnight – he had them all oiled and primed and ready. He told Kennedy to flag any use of the words *Polski tempo*, and be very wary of them. Luckily, most of the guys had homes to get to for Sunday brunches, had mothers and wives and sweethearts, who waited behind doors with either kisses or rolling pins poised. Not even Don's laughter could hold them there, so they drifted off the back of the field, leaving Kennedy and Don at a corner table on which empty glasses seemed to fill every space.

When Jack walked back in, to that thinned-out straggle of drinkers and drawlers, he was indeed Professor Snappy Jack. He signalled to Kennedy and Don, but stopped at the bar to get the bartender over with a bottle of firewater and three shot glasses. He surveyed the rows of glassware on their table, shook his head and laughed, and peered closely at the two men.

'You are here,' he observed as he sat down.

'Sober, though,' Kennedy declared. 'I think.'

The bartender did his stuff.

'To sobriety, then,' Kennedy toasted, and Don followed suit, and they downed their drinks in one, just like heroic Russians in movies.

The bartender liked that so much he went to pour them all another. When Kennedy put his hand over his glass, the bartender glared at him like an Irish uncle. '*Polski tempo*?' Kennedy thought it might be a good idea to ascertain. Jack looked like he was remembering the obvious point that when it went in at *Polski tempo* it came out that way, too.

'Way too early for that,' Don, of all people, warned. 'No, just this one for the road, to keep that frost out before we shove off out of here…Ah.' He got it down him. 'Now, well. Yes – this sure is good.'

'Very good.' As he said it, though, Jack poured his second vodka into Don's glass.

'And very good,' Don echoed, 'to see you again, Jack.'

'Thank you.'

'Certainly,' said Kennedy, but he could not hide the question in his voice.

The bartender went back to his pirate pals at the bar, and Kennedy was glad. He really had had his fill of consuming stuff. He felt his body twitching in protest, saying for the love of Christ to give it a rest.

'You are here, still.' Jack had a big bunch of keys in his hand. He isolated one, and tapped it on the tabletop. 'You missed some masses, I think.'

'You do, hah?' Don looked at him in frank resignation. 'Well, Jack, we have a saying in English, goes, *if at first you don't succeed –* '

'Yes, I know this,' Jack said.

'*Then fuck it, do something easier,*' Don finished.

'Hmm.' Jack radiated approval of Don's having reached a succinct turn of phrase at last. He smiled, then let out a laugh, shut his eyes as he committed the phrase to memory, Kennedy thought, for use later on. 'Well, you know, I went to see my mother.'

'Yeah,' Kennedy said. 'How is she?'

'I don't know.' He apologised for that with a movement of his shoulders. 'I never know. She never complains, not to me, anyway. She speaks to the doctors, I suppose, the nurses, about how she is. But never to me. I look at her, and she seems as she was always. And then perhaps I see that she has eaten nothing of the food she has asked for, or that she has fallen asleep while listening to the opera on the radio she has waited all day to hear. Today, however, she was awake.' Jack hesitated a second, watched their faces, then took a plunge. 'I told her about your book, Don, and, like Kennedy said, my mother was pleased for you.'

In response to this, Don whizzed a pissed look at Kennedy, then put on a neutral one for Jack, who went on, 'She asked me if that was what you were doing here in Abel at this crazy time. Were you writing another book? I said no. So I told her of your real reason to be here.' He fended off a grand inquisition from Don by pushing on to say, 'She laughed.'

'I bet she did,' Kennedy said. He was in truth a little pissed at Jack, too; he had only meant for Jack to tell his mom about Don's book, and certainly not about his lovelorn headless-chicken-in-Abel business.

'This was very good, Don,' said Jack. 'It was good to see her laughing.'

'Well, good.' What else could Don say? 'Great.'

'She said you were going about your search in the wrong way.' Jack seemed confident that he would elicit no protests. 'And my mother and I discussed it, and decided that it was one of the bases of comedy, people doing stupid things to reach their goals.'

Kennedy and Don sent Jack a look that said, *uh hal-lo*? They waited for him to cut to the chase, and he did, almost at once.

'We agreed, however, that in comedy people must finally reach their goals, or it is no longer comedy, but tragedy. Do you agree? Whether in Shakespeare, or in Charlie Chaplin, always the same.'

'Oh, okay.' Don sent Kennedy a look that let on that all he knew about Shakespeare was that he had kept a bookstore in Paris one time. He raised a hand, helplessly. 'If you say so, Jack.'

'My mother is a scientist, you remember, and so she suggested a more logical way of finding the lady for you, Don.'

'She did?'

'What?' Kennedy felt the hair stand up on the back of his neck.

The two men drew closer to Jack.

'A foolproof way,' Jack claimed.

Kennedy recalled the wisdom that every time something foolproof was invented the world just produced an even bigger idiot to fuck it up.

'Foolproof?' Don seemed to be up for the challenge.

'Yes. But I must ask you something, Don. Are you sure that the lady comes from Abel, that she was born here?'

'Said she was.'

'And she lives here?'

'Well certainly, Jack – well, of course, or I wouldn't be here now.'

'Nor would I,' Kennedy reminded them, but they were not listening.

'She went to school here?' Snappy Jack was back on track.

'Well, I guess so.'

'And how old is she?'

'She's anything between twenty five and thirty two, thirty three.'

'What's the deal, Jack?' Kennedy demanded.

'My mother is a scientist,' Jack said. 'But we're in Abel and, as you know, it is a holiday place. There are no scientifical institutes such as you can find in any big town in Poland. So she didn't work as a scientist here when she came back from America. She is…not well at the moment, as you know, and she is not at work, but in fact she is still employed in the public records department at the town hall.'

'Oh.' Don looked a little impatient at this digression. 'Okay.'

'Hey – neat.' Kennedy performed a high-school *doh* at Don, who made a gape into a smile that did not quite trust itself, and looked from Jack to Kennedy to see what the joke was. 'Public records. *School* records,' he spelled out for Don, and the two words were repeated between the three men for a time.

'Correct.' As if he had been waiting all his life for the moment, Jack held his bunch of keys up. Kennedy thought maybe he ought to grab a chair and stick it into Jack's grin, in case it swallowed up the whole bar. They were on their feet then, though, and, pausing only to pay their check, were out of there, resuming Don's business.

With everybody at church or at lunch, the roads were wide and welcoming, the streets sparklingly empty of all but footprints. It was like the day had thrown itself into helping Don with his search, because it was beyond doubt that to sneak into the town hall and root around in its records was not a very kosher thing to be perpetrating in any place that took a pride in its bureaucracy. 'Oh boy,' Don kept on loudly into the crisp air that, in the silent town, made his voice carry. 'School records – *yeah*!' He made Texan rodeo whoops. Jack had the bright idea of telling him to shut up, please, proving that he could offer a little role reversal when it suited him.

Abel's focus being the strand and the sand that fringed the Baltic, the town hall was not in the town centre. Jack led Don and Kennedy through backstreets to a tidy triangle of space hemmed in by squat red-brick offices, a snow-laden tree at its heart, presiding over stone benches and chess tables that could have been ice sculptures.

Jack stopped opposite a building with a mock-gothic façade and swore. Kennedy stopped too, and at once saw a figure in the building's doorway. Jack walked on slowly, making it up as he went along, Kennedy guessed, and wondered how he thought he was going to bluff his way in. Kennedy and Don followed. They saw that it was a woman, her eyes the only feature visible in her wrapped-up face. Jack spoke to her, rapidly and angrily, and she spoke back in the same tone and spirit.

'Quickly, quickly,' Krystyna threw out at them. 'I am frozen waiting here for you. I am asking Jack what kept you so long.'

'Jesus,' Don said, which had to be better than *vodka*.

'Are you okay, ma'am?' Kennedy asked her.

'Yes. Okay.' Kennedy had already gathered from what Jack had said that Krystyna did not like to talk about her illness. He learned only later that Poles generally did not do the *how-are-you* smalltalk; unless people were truly feeling on top of the world and looking down on creation, the questioner risked eliciting their entire medical history. Even though Krystyna had done her time in America, she was not going to flout the conventions just for Americans. 'Give me the keys.' She held a gloved hand out to Jack. Kennedy and Don caught each other's eyes for a second, mirrored each other's droop-lipped shrug, then watched Krystyna's back as she bent and scraped metal, then pushed buttons to disarm the alarm, and then they were following her in.

Once through the hallway and its monumental marble, the building gave up on *grandeur*. Gloomy down-at-heel corridors ran the length of offices glassed-in down to shoulder height, led to a central hall full of desks piled with the shabby accoutrements of office life.

Krystyna talked without hushing her voice. She said it had been obvious to her that, unless they knew where to look, they would be still there sifting merrily through papers when everybody creaked in to work the next morning, so she had called a cab and hauled herself out to meet them. She knew Jack would have nixed the suggestion and, while she made it plain that she could hold her own in a dispute, she had not wanted to be bothered with one. She brought them through the central hall and out back to another corridor, then ushered them into a room full of shelves burdened with thousands of files.

She asked Kennedy, 'Did you see this woman?'

'No, ma'am.' In the church, Kennedy had started off scoping all the tall, dark-haired women, but he knew the description had been way too vague. He would have felt distinctly foolish repeating it. 'Only Romeo here knows what she looks like.'

'Well, take a seat,' was her advice. 'I think we will be here for some time.'

There was no sense in not getting comfortable, so Kennedy and Jack chose desks, scraped chairs out and planted themselves. They could hear Krystyna guiding Don to the section he needed, hear him going *oh wow* and *Christ*; they could hear Krystyna's dark, mannish laughter leaking out.

Jack continued his earlier theme: it was good to hear his mother laughing. Kennedy nodded, then asked Jack what was wrong with

159

Krystyna, and of course it was the crab. 'Eating her alive,' Jack quoted her. She suffered courses of chemo at the oncology hospital in Gdynia which made her feel like she had been on a five-day booze binge. What she felt about her treatment most days, Jack sensed, was that it was just putting off the inevitable. 'She told me once that if it became too much for her, and for everybody else, she would walk into the sea,' Jack whispered. The whisper was scary, and the image scared Kennedy too, because from the little he knew of Krystyna it seemed to him that she was serious. Jack had taken leave from his job when his mom's cancer had first been diagnosed; he had stayed with her a month until she kicked him out and told him to get back to Krakow and on with his life. A cathartic row got him onto the train, and yet when he called her the same evening she was back to her regular self. *It's for the best*, she had told him and, as usual, the cliché rammed home the sense of a terrible truth.

Jack went into a gloom, and Kennedy left him to it. He picked up a pen and doodled on a blotter, then practised his Chinese characters, wrote Ling's name, and what he could remember of a simple poem from his study book, about a crane, or a stork, maybe, that delivered hope on a thirty-day free trial, and took it back from the undeserving.

He got up to stretch his legs, and to gauge some idea of Don's progress. Guided by Krystyna, who sat on a low file cabinet, Don was pulling out gigantic envelopes and opening them to look at student files, or more specifically, their photos, which were situated somewhat inconveniently a few pages into each file. They were not split by gender, it became apparent to Kennedy, but into class groups, and in an alphabetical order of surnames that was no help to Don. Kennedy checked the time, was surprised to see that they had been there over an hour.

Don groaned. He took five, and explained that some of the files had no photos in them, and at that Kennedy imagined some school administrator someplace in Abel with his bedroom wall plastered with hundreds of passport-size photos of the faces that had appealed to him. Don had just come across the first *Aleksandra* file with no photo in it.

'Can I do anything?' Kennedy didn't know what. Could he pass Don stuff, put it back, crack witty gags to make the time pass more quickly, something, whatever? Don was not in need of any help that Kennedy could give, though, especially with the gags, he made it plain. Don had a lot of classes to get through, so Kennedy went back to the office. Jack had uncovered the makings of tea, was engulfed in steam.

Kennedy brought cups of the murky brown stuff for Krystyna, and for Don, who forgot his disdain for the drink and took time out to gulp it down. 'We're Goldilocks,' it occurred to Don. 'The bears'll be in tomorrow, going, *Who's been drinking our tea, who's been creeping through our files?*

And who the fuck has been writing goddam Chinese poems on our blotters, Kennedy thought to add, *badly,* but refrained.

'Hey, listen, now.' Don seemed excited. 'Imagine doing this not even – what? Three years ago?'

'Of course.' Krystyna loved the idea too. Three years before, she explained, the files in the town hall would have contained a lot of other info, useless crap gathered by obsessive communist officials from beleagured informers, festering away just on the offchance it could be used against people. 'That was madness, right? Crazy madness, and now, when people from that time are asked to explain themselves, they can often say nothing, and, you know, I think now that I believe them when they say that there is no explanation. They really don't know why they did such stupid things so zealously.'

'That's the story of bad ideologies,' Don observed. 'People doing dumb and pointless things with a lot of energy, and not questioning why.'

'Of course,' Krystyna noted, 'but the communists, the individual communists – I'm not talking about the ideology, you understand, nor the people at the top of it – they were always rather stupid people, and they really were too dumb to see what they were doing, and the consequences of it, just hoped that out of it some kind of gain would be given to them somewhere in the scheme of the system. They are still here.' She dismissed them with a movement of her shoulders. 'Still here in the town hall, working, still all over Poland in offices, factories, institutes. There is no other place for them to go. However, gentlemen, it isn't only here that stupid people put a lot of energy into doing nothing that benefits anybody. I know from my time in America that within its systems there is plenty of scope for stupid people to make their mark.' She changed tack. 'I like you, gentlemen.'

Jack looked up and smiled at Kennedy, sent a look to his mother, looked at his watch, looked up at the clock and synchronised them. Then he sank back onto his elbows.

'I like you, too,' Kennedy told her, and Don parroted him over his shoulder.

'But listen,' she said. 'I like you because you're not stupid in that way. It's very crazy, this thing you are doing here in Abel, but it's not stupid. That's why I like you. Let me tell you something about me. Can I do that?'

'Sure.'

'I am a scientist. That is a good thing in itself – do you agree? The communists thought so, anyhow, and educated me for these special talents, you see, so that I could use these talents to serve them. Our world was to be run on science. Culture was all very well.' She dismissed it apologetically. 'But science was the real thing. When I was young I was full of the arrogance of this idea, which is permissible when you are young, I believe. Do you know, I went to Moscow on a visit, and I was presented to Comrade Brezhnev, and this man who would one day be king of the dumb people, this hulking, murdering *petit-bourgeois*, he shook my hand – I was one of his pet Poles, one of his loyal and foolish subjects – and he told me that the world he was directing could not exist without me. For a minute, I believed it, and for that minute all was good with that stupid world. What else did I need – what else could anybody ever need when they are young, except to know that the world is good, and that they are helping to make it that way? In America it was the same thing, though, and other people, as dumb as the First Secretary, shook my hand too, and told me the same thing, even as I helped them with their car exhausts, polluting the air with a more benign pollution, helping them use up the world's gas. I hardly met anybody who thought of anything but how important we all were, all we scientists.' She laughed lightly, went on, 'Listen. A fuel specialist I worked with got so carried away by his enthusiasm that he blew himself up thoroughly enough to disappear without trace. He was working on a propulsion system that would improve the zero-to-sixty performance of a car by a mere fraction. But, anyhow, I think you see what I mean.'

'Jesus,' they heard Don say, and they broke off even from breathing to make a pregnant silence.

'Found her?' Kennedy asked.

'No, I – you trying to be funny, Kennedy?' Don thought he ought to check. 'No. I was just admiring your…story, ma'am. Made me wish the Los Alamos crowd had done the same thing.'

'But then,' Krystyna said with a laugh, 'we may never have had so much fun with the Cold War.' As if the effort of laughing, or just talking, had tired her, Krystyna suppressed a yawn with a hand. She was resting her head against the wall. 'Well.' The yawn got her anyhow, and she said through it, 'I admire your story, too, even now, as it is happening.'

'Mother.' Jack still had an eye on the clock, and Krystyna's bag in his hand. 'The cyclo.'

Krystyna took the bag and looked into it unhurriedly, brought out a bottle and shook out a pink tablet, held it on her palm before getting it down her with a mouthful of tea. 'Cyclosphosphamide.' She did a *silly-me* wave. 'I learn all their names.' She seemed wide awake again then, saying, 'It's a good story. Next week at the hospital, when I am lying there with them doing whatever they do, I will tell them, perhaps.' Her eyes fell shut abruptly. 'We always…struggle to find things to talk about.'

She was rapidly in a deep sleep. Kennedy and Jack went back to the office and talked on. What was Don going to do once he had found the woman of his dreams, they wondered. 'Hearts and flowers time,' Kennedy speculated.

'Hearts and flowers.' Jack seemed to like the words together.

That made Kennedy ask, 'How about you, Jack?'

'What?'

'Well, no Polski maiden you got your sights on?'

'Excuse me?'

'No woman in your life someplace?'

'There is a woman.' Jack seemed to be thinking hard about it.

'Oh? Where? Here?'

'No.' Jack looked a little scornful – *the very idea of it*, he seemed to be saying, *some local hick of a girl*, then maybe remembered Don's search, and the scorn vanished. 'In Krakow.' He looked beleaguered and sad for a second, then made a smile of sorts.

'What does she do?'

'She is a nurse, for children.'

'What does she look like?'

'She is very beautiful.' Jack grinned. 'Of course. What do you expect?'

He started to tell Kennedy a little about her, then quit describing her to whip out a wallet sweetheart pic, and Kennedy saw a shy-looking woman in her twenties, dark blond hair, with high cheekbones, kind eyes, a very natural, vivacious smile. Jack resumed his description, cramming in as much as he could, much as he had done when he had first run into Kennedy and Don in the street the previous evening. It was mainly to shut him up that Kennedy pulled out his photo of Ling, but he was struck dumb when he realised that the most significant thing he could say about her was that she would soon be gone from his life. He was left with the usual relationship universals, then, and he went though them dutifully.

That filled in the time till Don appeared in the office. Kennedy could see from Don's face that Jack's woman was no longer on their agenda, nor Ling; Don was bringing his own wish-fulfilling woman to the fore.

'Got her,' Don said quietly. Kennedy and Jack yahooed, got up and crowded Don in their efforts to see the little photo in his hand. Solemn, somewhat determined-looking girl of sixteen or so, they saw, dark hair, eyes a little squinty, kind of…powerful-looking nose, and real nice lips, with a big bow to them; she had all the keenness of high school there, and there was something about that which touched Kennedy, somehow. 'That's Ola,' Don hardly needed to tell them.

'Wow,' Kennedy offered.

'Where does she live?' Jack asked.

Don rattled off an address, and Jack grabbed some paper and wrote it down. He thought he knew it, a place close by the sea, and held his hand out for the file. He studied it.

'Do you know her?' Kennedy thought to ask Jack, and he said her face said nothing to him. Her surname was Bruzhevska, and he thought he knew some of them someplace, but shrugged out that it was a common enough name. She was going on thirty, he worked out, which made Don six years older.

'But why are we delaying?' Jack handed the file back, and stretched. He was master of the hunt. 'Shall we go and call on the lady?'

They did not wake Krystyna. Jack took the keys and left, saying he would be right back. Kennedy discovered that the filing racks looked as if Hurricane Don had just swept through, so he gave a hand in putting the files back so that they at least looked neat. He doubted if anybody ever looked at them anyhow, had the feeling that he and Don had been the first and last people to scrabble among all those yellowed, autumnal papers.

Jack was back in a half-hour. He had borrowed a car from some acquaintance too passed out under a table by then to even remember they invented the internal combustion engine. Gently, he woke Krystyna and got her to go first down the corridor. She did not know any Bruzhevskis or Bruzhevskas either, but reminded everybody that her exile had made her almost a stranger in town. She primed the alarm and shooed them all out onto the porch, and surveyed the street, just like in TV crime dramas. Getting the men to put all their weight on the doors – a thing they were glad to do, loving the chance to revert to being mere boys – just to check,

Krystyna left the place secure. Then they stepped over to the only car in the square, waiting for them in six inches of snow next to where the sidewalk might have been.

The family connection notwithstanding, Kennedy was hoping that Jack had not gone and brought one of those baby Fiats, and he had not. Their ride was a Volvo, a fine achievement of a car, he had always thought. This one was a big square gas-guzzling jalopy maybe thirty years old. Once they were settled into its seats Jack cranked the key, and it let out a modest *ahem* and purred away, ready for its any-weather business.

Jack and Krystyna started almost at once on an argument, and Kennedy guessed what it was about, knew that Jack would lose it. Krystyna was along for the ride, her curiosity getting the blood circulating around her.

'Are you just going to walk up to the entryphone and tell this lady who you are?' Krystyna asked Don. It was a good question; entryphones were probably invented exactly for occasions like Don Darius scudding his way into your life out of a snowstorm.

Don seemed to think about it. 'Well, ah…I thought so,' was all he could come up with.

'It will be a surprise,' Krystyna said. 'A nice surprise? Or not?'

'Not,' Kennedy suggested, which earned him a whack on the top of the head from Don.

'What else can I do?' It was not just something to wonder; Don was really asking.

Nobody knew; even Jack held back from filling the space with an answer.

As Jack inched them through Abel they all thought about it, but it was only ten or so minutes and they were there. Jack was pointing across a road to apartment buildings right out of Kafka, saying a superfluous, 'There.'

He killed the engine. It ticked merrily, the loudest thing in the street.

'So,' Kennedy put to Don, 'what's happening?'

'I don't know,' he replied.

'Uh, right.'

Krystyna suggested Jack go announce Don, and reassured her son, 'They don't kill the messenger anymore, I believe.' Kennedy began thinking that this could easily revive the practice.

Then Krystyna put herself forward as the pigeon.

'I could tell her,' Kennedy pitched in, 'come to that. Or you could,' he brought it back to Don. 'They seem to be the four alternatives.'

'Rather not,' Jack said. 'You have her family name, and her address. It will be easy to find her telephone number from this. Yes? Then you can phone her, just as in your original agreement.'

'That wasn't the agreement.' Kennedy thought Don was stalling in stating this. 'She was supposed to call me.' But there was a world of difference between a guy calling a girl and a girl calling a guy.

'You're a writer.' Everybody let Kennedy's comment hang a second. 'You could write her a letter,' he illuminated. 'But hey, aren't you forgetting something?'

'What?' they all asked.

All Kennedy was thinking was how Don had dragged him all that way through the snow on the train to be right there and right then in that deep-frozen Ben-and-Jerry town, sat in that car, just so that Don could do the very thing he was now procrastinating about. He tried to shine all that out of his face. The three of them looked at him.

'Well, Einstein,' Jack was challenging Kennedy. 'What?'

Kennedy said, 'You're here, man. Face-to-face, one-to-one. No operator, no mailman, no tricks, no smoke, no mirrors. What are you,' he half-joked, 'a man, or a big scaredy-cat?'

'A big scaredy-cat?' Don ventured.

'Hey, come on.'

'*What* kind of cat?'

It was too complicated to explain to Jack at that moment.

'Mister Dariusz.' Krystyna spoke calmly. 'May I make a suggestion?'

'Suggest away, ma'am,' Don said.

Krystyna said nothing to Don, nor to Kennedy. She just spoke softly to Jack, which got him to fire up the engine and roll them down toward the sea.

'You see, Jacek?' When Jack made no answer, Krystyna touched her son on the shoulder. 'You see this, what is going on?'

'Yes, mother.' The look on Jack's face said that what was going on was just him driving a bunch of crazy people around a grim town he had all but washed his hands of. It said he would much rather have been in a dive in Krakow with his girlfriend and his pals, sipping coffee and tapping his foot to jazz. 'In fact, rather, no, mother. Please tell me.'

'These romantics.' The look on Krystyna's face betrayed her enjoyment of sharing in people's foolishness. 'We have here a modern Keats and Shelley. And here we are,' she went on into Jack's silence, 'driving them to destiny.'

Kennedy thought how Keats had been immortal for four years by the time he got to Kennedy's age, and Shelley, a guy who loved the sea but who, fatally, never bothered learning how to swim – well, that kind of said it all about him. They were Laurel and Hardy, more like, he thought, just two dumb hicks who should have stayed back on the farm.

'Yes, mother,' was Jack's only comment.

'You have a sweet way of putting things, ma'am.' Don seemed to go for the analogy. 'Keats and Shelley on the road, huh?'

'They wrote stuff, too,' Kennedy aimed at Don. They did not spend their time gadding around nowhere towns through blizzards under clouds of acid rain in Volvos, he meant, got down to it and put into words that whole Romantic vision of Nature as the driving force, pure and unsullied; couldn't conceive of Henry Frigging Ford or giant chimneys stoked by five-year plans.

They were all out of road. The dull silver late sunlight revealed a ruined building on their left, fishermen's huts and closed-down kiosks on their right, and the expanse of the sea ahead. Jack stopped the car, and it seemed plain that they would have to get out. Kennedy gave Krystyna a hand; she held it, then let it go. She grabbed the car roof for a second, then was walking.

There was nothing on the water apart from a guy in a rowboat some way out, fishing, they guessed, crazy, certainly; maybe he had been there since New Year's, frozen to his boat, with nobody screwy or sober enough to go reel him in.

Kennedy recalled the Baltic beach scene from Gunter Grass's *Tin Drum*, shit-stirrer Oskar and his mom watching a longshoreman fish off a shore a lot like the one he looked on now. The guy had a rope tied to a horse's head and had let the sea carry it out; he reeled it in and it was full of black eels, trapped by their greed in gristle and bone. The sight of it made Oskar's mom barf, turned her brain on the spot and drew her into suicide. Kennedy thought the scene was meant to have convinced her that the world was a corrupt and evil place; never mind the fact that the entire continent was in the grip of Nazis at the time.

'Sand.' Jack drew their eyes with a finger, right to left. 'For twenty kilometres, maybe.'

Kennedy cracked, 'Looks more like snow to me.'

'It is under the snow.' Jack took a long look at Kennedy, and almost smiled. 'Of course.'

'Uh, right.'

'Mountains of sand.' It was generous of Don to enthuse about sand, Kennedy felt, seeing as how he had lived in Saudi, a place the size of Europe full of the stuff. 'Or so I heard.'

'Hills, actually,' Jack corrected.

Kennedy joined in the fun with, 'You don't mean dunes?'

'Dunes?' Jack clicked fingers, and smiled. 'Oh yes. *Dunes.*'

Sick of sand, maybe, Krystyna pointed at the ruin, said, 'That was the church of Saint Barbara. I went there every week, when I was young.'

Don and Kennedy drew their attention to the building, a skeleton of fused, blackened bricks and stone, and burned wood that resembled leather. It was held up by rusted scaffolding. It looked forlorn and dangerous.

'It could sure use a lick of paint,' Don said, and Krystyna turned to him and let out a bark of a laugh.

'In the summer after mass we bought candy from stalls along there on the front, and the adults bought beer, and we played on the beach and paddled in the water, and the day seemed to go on for so long. It was like a…festival, and we looked forward to it very much.'

'Well, that was one way to get you all to church,' Kennedy said.

'Oh yes.' Krystyna nodded. 'They were not foolish, those priests and parents of ours.'

'What happened to it?' Kennedy asked.

'A German ship,' Krystyna told him. 'It shot at the pleasure boats in the yacht marina first. That was the day the war started. I think when we saw that, we knew that we were not fighting against…gentlemen. Then it turned the guns on to the church. It was just for fun, or maybe target practice. The ship passed up the coast, toward Gdynia, and then people came running to put out the fire, but they were too late. They were aching to get on with it, those Germans, we could tell, when they shelled Abel. And then we were very afraid, and we knew that it was the end of our lives as we had known them.'

Poland was full of churches, though, Kennedy was about to observe, but prudently muttered only, 'That's too bad.' He tried to imagine what it had been like, stood on the edge of the land, gazing out at the start of the Second World War, heard Don say a soft *Jesus* next to him.

'Why do you write?' Krystyna, tired of the war and the idea of it, or just used to it, maybe, aimed the question at Don.

'Why?' Don deflected it at Kennedy.

Kennedy did not know why Don wrote, just knew that he should. The movement of his shoulders probably failed to put that over.

'You,' Krystyna said. 'Keats, Shelley – why?'

Dumb question? Probably. Kennedy did not know. He saw himself up nights, lit by a square of screen that displayed what at the bottom line was just the end of a series of mechanics: brain, fingers, binary numbers, stuff that looked like words. And why? He saw Don in that kitchen in Bakirköy, tapping out a version of his life that had been altered by the fears in his imagination…but why? Just so it could be the start of a process that had led him to that shore, a continent away from anyplace he could call home, trying to think of an answer?

And why were they stood on the edge of that frozen land talking, when they had come all that way in the name of action? Kennedy would rather have known that. Who cared what anybody wrote, when others were fishing and freezing, dying indeed or just luckless in love and dying inside?

'I don't know.' Don realised how underwhelming that had to have sounded, and hurried out, 'Just get the urge one day, write down the thoughts going through my head, change them around a little…Not a natural urge, I guess. I mean…Well, take a look at Barnacle Bill out there.' He pointed to the fisherman. 'Sits and reels in his fish. He has thoughts going through his head, right? But he doesn't feel the need to come and spill them out so other people can know them.'

'Maybe he does.' Kennedy thought Don was being unfair to all the little people who got exactly that same urge one day, just like Don himself, and wound up writing books.

'No. Sure, he's got thoughts, like anybody else, but he isn't going to spot us here on shore and row like a fool to come share them with us. Not going to write them down, either.'

Krystyna nodded, waiting for more, though Jack was not bothering to pretend that he was anything other than cold and agitated, and worried about his mom.

And Kennedy was thinking, *Out on the water in the sub-zero, unless you're truly certifiable, all you think about is keeping warm enough to reel in those frozen fish fingers. Hey, but then you'd need to be certifiable in the first place, even to be out there…*

He sent a look to Jack that said, *See the kind of thing I have to put up with, huh?* He was not surprised to see the same look returned.

'The urge finds you,' Don said. 'If that's what it wants to do. And if you're willing. He knows.' He tossed his head at Kennedy. 'He writes, too.'

'A little kid's urge.' Kennedy was glad to junk lofty old Keats and Shelley. 'To tell what he sees.'

'To show the world how smart he is.' Krystyna had a leather-clad finger aloft to say *ah-hah.* 'For scientists, the same thing. There is no point in doing it, we used to think, unless everybody knows you have done it. My point, Mister Dariusz, is prompted by another question.'

'What question would that be, ma'am?'

Krystyna said, 'Do you want to find this woman just to show her that you are a clever man, and can find her if you want to? If that is the case, then I think you should go there now, and she can answer her door and you can examine her face to see if it is delighted or not.' She laughed. 'Or her husband's face, to see if he too will be as pleased.'

Kennedy almost applauded the trap Krystyna had opened in the middle of what he had been dismissing as highbrow small-talk. There they were, then, back on-topic at last, without even realising. He and Jack perked up and closed in on Don just a little.

'It's not like that at all.' Don's face looked a few clicks short of delighted. 'Listen. I'll tell you straight. I liked her. That's all.'

'Rather a lot,' Jack put in, 'it seems.'

'Rather a lot.' Don laughed, looking surprised at himself for doing so. 'But, you know, now really, my intentions,' he summoned up that corny old southern gentleman to help him announce, 'are totally honourable. Hey, I just want to do what most people on the planet want to do. Go out on a date, talk a little, see what transpires. Now, somebody tell me if that's too much to ask, hah?'

'Well, do it, then.'

For a second, Kennedy thought he himself had said it, but he had only thought it, and it had come from Jack. 'Do it.' Jack put a hand on Don's shoulder. All of them made a circle around him. 'You are here. So do it.' Jack did not add, *And let's all stop freezing our fricken asses off here, huh?*

Kennedy felt, though, that Jack was by then getting genuinely worried about whether Krystyna could handle the elements around them.

Don looked like he was thinking. It did not last for long. Out came that *man's-gotta-do-what-a-man's-gotta-do* cowboy stuff, when Don said, 'Point me there.'

'You will go there now?' Jack checked.

'*Oh* yes.'

They traipsed back toward the car. Kennedy wanted to run, get some spikes of warmth back into his limbs. Krystyna was suddenly the tourist who climbed up a hill but could not get down a mountain. Jack was helping her along, refraining, Kennedy could guess, from reminding her that she should not have been there in the first place.

When they were settled back in the car, Jack turned to Don and asked, 'What is your idea?'

'I have no ideas.' Don said it like a boast. 'Ruled by the heart, that's me. We go there forthwith, I get out of the car, I press on her entryphone, and I say her name loud, but not brash, and announce my own.'

'Well, okay.' Jack's sense of logic had been challenged. 'But that sounds to me like an idea.' Before anybody could change their minds, he had fired up the car and was bringing it into a careful turn, and then they were cruising back along the road. It was only a minute or two before Jack eased them to a halt, saying, 'We are here. Well, Don, so – '

But Don was out there already. He cut a momentary man-with-plan shape in the swirl of the snow, and then it closed over.

Krystyna gave off the silence of sleep, so Kennedy and Jack talked in low voices about nothing much. What did Kennedy think of Poland, etcetera? Kennedy thought they had covered all that the night before, but was glad enough to take refuge in it. He told Jack a little about Istanbul, and what a place it was, and how Jack had to get there sometime, and when he did, Kennedy would borrow a car too and drive him all over the city, show him every last little nook and cranny in it. *Oh, is that so,* a little voice intruded, *but you're leaving Istanbul, ain't you, Marco Polo, off to wander the world like a forsaken fool, I thought?*

'We were near here,' it occurred to Kennedy, 'last night, when you saw us,' though he wanted to laugh with the thought that, just like in his home town of Harrington, anywhere in this town was near anywhere else.

'Yes.' Jack moved his head to indicate the direction.

171

'What were you doing?'

'Last night?'

'Yeah.'

'Only…walking.'

Jack gave Kennedy a nod and his sad smile, in which Kennedy at once saw a whole melancholy world of sickbeds and silence and dark furniture, the yellow light from the street, a longing for the chimneys and churches that marked the way to Jack's real life, the one in Krakow. And so indeed then why not go out and just walk?

'Well…it was good news for me and Don.'

'Well, good.'

'Yeah.' Kennedy pitched into silence, and tried to ignore the trouble in his thoughts; he was trying to picture his own life, his life with Ling, but only saw himself walking around Istanbul, just walking. He became aware of Jack talking softly.

'What do you think will happen?' Jack was asking.

She'll leave, was Kennedy's answer, *and my heart will cave in and break and not be fit for anything again except beating its way through endless, miserable nights.*

His answer to Jack was, 'Chase a wild goose, and a wild goose is what you'll get.'

Jack seemed to dig that, but said, logically enough, 'Nobody can catch a wild goose without a gun.'

'Well, Don's from Texas.'

'What?'

'I went to Texas,' Krystyna said. Kennedy and Jack took a look around at her. Maybe Jack remembered getting her dumb Texas postcards: the rodeo cowboy riding a giant jalapeno pepper, a recipe for baked armadillo – yee-frigging-ha.

Kennedy said, 'I never went there.'

'I didn't mention it to Mister Dariusz.' That begged a *why-not* from Kennedy. 'I had a bad experience there,' she said, and Kennedy was impressed, he realised later, that she didn't laugh it off with bad-girl bravado; it was the strain that showed on her face as she told her tale that made it ring so true.

Krystyna had stayed in a motel near Houston with a girlfriend, another scientist. They had been meant to hook up with some other people someplace in Houston itself, but they had not shown. A confusion of highways and turnings had led them to the motel, and they had called for a takeaway and turned in early. What they did not know was that they were on the notorious Telephone Road, which was a twenty-mile strip of bars, poker dens, strip-joints and cat-houses that grew up to cater, initially, for the body-and-soul demands of itinerant oil-workers. Rip-off artists, grifters, panhandlers, psychos, pimps, muggers and murderers were the strip's natural by-products: Krystyna and friend had wandered into the whole Tom Waits songbook. They were woken in the night by the sounds of a vehicle getting trashed. They got out of bed and looked out the window, and their nervous giggles stopped when they saw that it was their hire car suffering the damage. Three hombres, all muscles and tattoos and leather vests, were banging the car with iron bars. Krystyna – who at age fifteen was scaring the living shit out of Nazis with a home-made rifle – put a bathrobe on and leaned out the window and asked these guys what the hell they thought they were doing. The meatheads were too off their faces to recognise and deal with a rhetorical question; they began banging at the door to the room, and it looked like things were about to get very ugly. Krystyna's companion was meantime on the phone to the motel night clerk. Luckily, he was as big as a cigar store Indian, and strolled out carrying a baseball bat, persuaded the guys to get out of there. He told Krystyna and her friend they ought to get gone too; the assholes would almost certainly be back, and he for one was not going to stay up all night waving baseball bats…The travelling ladies took that advice, threw their stuff together and drove the wreck of their car toward Austin, along the full neon glory of the rest of the Telephone Road, only then, at four in the morning, revealing its full Dantesque circus.

'It was senseless,' Krystyna said. 'But, you know, that was my first bad time in America. When I had finished feeling very shocked and scared, I began to wonder what kind of society could produce such people. I thought then of all the men here in Poland who are like that in their hearts – violent, senseless, and with no positive thoughts in their heads – and that maybe the society we had here, which repressed them, maybe that was the right kind of society after all. What do you feel, Mister Kennedy? Do you think that our society here will ever become like that in America?'

'It *is* becoming like that,' Jack said. 'Mother, that kind of society is already here.'

'Jacek, no,' she scolded. 'Surely you are being…theatrical?' She dismissed whatever her son was about to say, and turned again to Kennedy.

'I don't know enough about your society to say so, ma'am,' Kennedy said. 'Hey, though, I know a guy who thinks he *does* know. And unless I'm mistaken, here he comes now.'

Don did his looming snowman part and banged on the car roof, pulled the door open and slipped into the back. Jack, fearful surely not of the Volvo's motor freezing and stalling, but maybe of his own, set it humming.

Kennedy and Krystyna turned to Don and said a simultaneous '*Well?*'

'It was the place.' Don twitched a thumb.

'You have seen her?' Jack asked.

'Not...exactly,' Don admitted.

Kennedy asked, 'What *exactly* does *that* mean?'

'I saw her in her mom's face.' Don shut his eyes, watched Ola in his head for a second, Kennedy guessed, in youth and age. 'I saw her face there, maybe thirty years from now.'

'Not a pretty sight?' Kennedy ventured, which got a laugh out of Krystyna.

'On the contrary.' Don sounded offended. 'A pretty sight for certain. I look in the mirror sometimes, see my face thirty years from now, and that's no picture.'

'It's no oil painting right now.'

'She has gone out?' Jack got them back to the pertinent.

'You could say that.' Don anticipated the trio's laughter. 'She's in Warsaw.'

'Oh.' Kennedy tried not to laugh, then just had to. 'Wow.'

'Just for the weekend.' Don's audience thought through the few words. He answered the silence with, 'She'll be back tonight.'

'Well, you are here.' Good old snappy Jack, straight to the point.

Kennedy thought, *And so am I.* 'So what now?'

It seemed for a time that all of Don's adrenaline had gone into marching up to the entryphone to do his cap-in-hand lover thing. After a pause for a study of the backs of his hands, he recounted the bare bones of it: the sad-faced woman who invited him in and listened politely to his inquiry, got intrigued, then got smiling, which set her up for what must have seemed like a weird clutch of questions. First up, was Ola, ah, free, no...special gentleman in her life? As far as her mom knew, she was. Had she mentioned him at all, the klutz she met one time on the Laikonik express? Ola's mom spun Don the kind yarn, *Yes, now I think I recall that she did, maybe quite possibly certainly.* She had coffee cooked already, poured him some, got out poppy seed slab cake, had him stuff some down. She had looked at his red eyes and asked had he been drinking at all. He said it was the cold made his eyes that way, mostly, but that he had indeed taken a tipple just to be polite with these friends of his…He had jumped up back into the real world as he remembered those friends out in the car. He got the phone number he needed, and left.

'Bravo,' Krystyna offered.

'Yeah,' Kennedy sort of agreed. 'Good. But, uh, what now?'

Don looked at him blankly, said, 'Now?'

'Yeah.'

'I got her number.' Don suddenly did not sound too enthusiastic about the idea; he sounded beat. 'I can write a letter.'

'But you are here,' Jack pointed out again.

'And she will be here,' said Krystyna.

'I'm here.' Don looked up at the roof of the car, looked out at the snow, checked the backs of his hands again, agitated. 'But I got to be in Warsaw at eight thirty tomorrow morning.'

'Oh – *no*, Mister Dariusz, surely not.'

'But you're kidding. *Why* the hell?'

'I got a class to teach.'

'But hey.' Kennedy could not see that bothering Don in the least; he would just give somebody a call, wouldn't he, rearrange the class, meet up with them in some bar?

That was not the deal, as Don explained, with his three-days-a-week gig at the Warsaw Polytechnic. It was his only job that paid well, and was the one he enjoyed the most. It also featured beetle-browed director-types who eyeballed the clock when he rolled in, tapped fingers on desks and looked at him as suspiciously as they would a nine-year-old boy. It sounded to Kennedy like they had him figured out all right.

'It's a…' Don raised hands.

'Fuck-up,' Krystyna suggested.

'Yes ma'am, couldn't've put it better myself.'

'I'm sure you could.' Krystyna laughed.

Jack was looking up at the block, and Kennedy just stared at the dash. Krystyna put a hand on Don's shoulder. The silence went on longer this time, broken again by Don, saying, 'Hell, there's always next weekend. What do you think, Kennedy, old man?'

'Yeah, you do that.' But Kennedy was at a distance from the idea already; he was Bogart's Sam Spade in *The Maltese Falcon*, watching Caspar Gutman and his cronies start all over again for Constantinople in search of the stuff dreams were made of, declining the venture with a shake of the head. Except that it was Kennedy who would be in Constantine's city by the next weekend. The idea brought it back to him that he had a pulse. He laughed out, 'But phone ahead, maybe.'

'But what now?' Jack repeated for them all.

'Now?' Don smiled, and said softly. 'Why, to your perfect little railroad station, Jack, my man.'

Jack raised a hold-on finger, and rummaged in a pocket.

'You are a character,' Krystyna said, just like Caspar Gutman. 'You really are.'

'Thank you, ma'am. I guess I am.' Don sounded amazed at the idea. 'But, ah, listen, now. You're not exactly lacking in the attributes of character yourself.'

'It must be the company I keep.' She let out a laugh, stopped it becoming a cough.

Kennedy assured her, 'We could never've done it without you and Jack, ma'am. Uh, whatever it is we've done here. Might've been at that church till Easter.'

'Not a nice thought.' She was serious for a second. 'I don't trust the company of priests. Not even if they become Popes – in fact, especially if they become Popes. Listen. Will you come to the apartment before you leave? Do you want to eat or drink something?'

Kennedy was relieved to hear Don decline. He really needed to make tracks away from that big cold sea full of eels, and from that town that truly should not have been seen on a winter evening. He also did not feel like eating or drinking a single thing ever again.

Jack turned, a little book in his hand.

'No, but listen, ma'am,' Don was improvising bravely. 'I'll be back – I got a really strong feeling about that. I really do get the distinct impression that I'll see your town in all its summer…glory, right, and that…and that…'

Kennedy looked down as Don got caught up in his words. That was what went down sometimes when you were spontaneous, he guessed. He had wanted to turn around and put a face on to stop Don going there, or let out a line of *harrumphs*. He gave in and turned anyhow, and saw Krystyna make a smile that kindly hid the words on her lips to tell them that she would not see another summer in Abel, or anyplace else.

'I'm certain of it, Mister Dariusz,' was what she did say. 'And when you make your trip, I'll be here.'

'That's a date, ma'am. But listen. We got us a trip right now, on that old Laikonik express.'

'Perhaps not.' Jack waved the rail timetable at him. 'I may have bad news.'

'What?'

'*May* have?'

'Hmm. I think you will not catch the Laikonik tonight. It will be necessary for you to arrive in Gdynia in...' He took a quick look at his timetable. 'One hour and twenty three minutes. You have just missed the train from Abel. And the local trains are very slow in any case, and they depart only once every two hours on Sundays.'

'Ah.' Don set up a show of thinking, but just hummed and hawed and faffed. Kennedy wanted to say something like *Jesus, and while the train was leaving we've been sitting here in this cold old jalopy listening to you babbling on like a fishwife, you dope.* As he did not have to say it, he refrained.

None of it mattered, though, because Jack and Krystyna were having another of their quickfire exchanges. Hip to the rhythm of it, Kennedy guessed what would happen next.

The road

Jack filled up with gas at a station on the edge of Abel, and then they were motoring along the crepuscular road to Gdynia. Krystyna went through bursts of animation as she told them a little about their vanishing surroundings, how over there was this place, up ahead that one – and did Jack remember something that happened way over there, to some family, and did he recall which horrible party official once lived in this place here? Jack did and didn't, he grunted and hah-hmmed. They were nowhere places with nothing to offer but stories that ran out of steam halfway, his sighs seemed to say. After a time, they all eased into a roadtrip torpor that comes over anybody in a car when there's zilch to look at out the window except the dusk alleviated by yellow lights. Kennedy half-dozed, and Don too, by the sound of his delayed, disembodied replies to conversations that had passed a minute before. Krystyna fell in and out of sleep.

177

Kennedy woke, asked Jack if they were going to make it, and Jack looked at his watch, said there would be no problem...probably.

Don was awake too. 'I don't like to leave things unfinished,' he said between Kennedy's and Jack's heads.

'Yes.' Jack did not take his eyes off the road.

'You know what I'm saying here?'

'You like to finish things,' Jack translated absently. 'Okay. I understand that. It is good. I too like to finish things.'

'You do?'

'Yes.'

'She'll be on the Laikonik express,' Kennedy spelled out for Jack.

'Oh yes.' Jack flashed out *eureka*. 'Of course.'

'Book a table at the station diner,' Kennedy suggested. 'Dress up in black tie, get a waiter, candles, caviar, champagne, get a band playing the music from *Doctor Zhivago*. Man, it'll be the date of her life.'

'Huh,' Don found for that.

They drifted on, fell once more into torpor, for ten, fifteen minutes, or time that would go on until a word or a jolt on a pothole broke it, a railroad crossing, a headlight coming at them from another vehicle. Sounding almost alarmed sometimes at the silence, Jack broke it, talked almost to himself about how Krakow was a town in which everything was in walking distance, and how he hated driving, and had lost both the urge and the expertise. That got Don offering to take the wheel. 'Listen,' Kennedy snapped to full attention and warned Jack. 'Don't go there, man – do not for a second let him drive.' Jack murmured assurance that he had no intentions of doing so.

The thought of a boozed-up Don Darius at the wheel must have put Kennedy in mind of road accidents. For a long five minutes he looked out anxiously to try to make out the extent of ice under the wheels, and whether or not friction would be maintained.

One winter night at Syracuse in freshman year, Kennedy was going to an off-campus party, and a whole bunch of people were headed there in a whole bunch of cars. There was no room for Kennedy in the car he had originally been going to ride in, as some horny-looking babe had wiggled her butt into his place. He had sulked along in a following car. His original ride went too fast over a patch of black ice, turned over and over and wound up on its side down an embankment. The girl who had stolen Kennedy's place had broken her spine; from then on, nobody would see her butt, hidden as it would always be in a wheelchair. Kennedy was about to tell this story, then stopped himself; he was ashamed of the ending, which was that he, along with everybody else, had still gone ahead and partied.

They were alone on the road most of the time. Approaching lights from either direction usually meant trucks, empty, they could tell by the way they skimmed and rattled along like pebbles on cobblestones. The moon was coming up, the fields were white; the grey light changed to yellows and oranges as they passed through little settlements, and they all joined together as they got into the suburbs of Gdynia, which took but the wink of a drunkard's eye to become the city itself.

Gdynia

Jack weaved his charges carefully in and out of Gdynia's little streets and across its wide avenues, and then even Kennedy could recognise where they were. He spotted the market, dimly-lit and deserted, and caught sight of the shoe store still twinkling redly like a bar, and then of the bar with the sardonic bartender and his talk of summer and the daytime. Jack rumbled them to a halt at the entrance to the station.

Almost at once, he stated flatly, 'I think I had better not come with you.' He took a look back at the reclining Krystyna and added, 'My mother, you understand. I don't want to leave her to wait here.'

'You will do no such thing,' Krystyna sang out. 'I have had a fine sleep, and I am ready for another walk. And besides, if we are to meet the train, and this wonderful princess is to be on it, I want to see her, and I want to find out what the fuss is all about.' She sounded to Kennedy like the narrator in a play, full of the *know*. 'You see?'

They guessed they did, and showed it in various ways; only Jack's face was agitated.

'Now let's get out,' Krystyna continued, making movements in the back. 'Let's get ourselves a coffee, or even...You know, I think I would really like to drink beer.'

'Mother,' Jack began.

'It is so long since I drank beer.' Krystyna did a great job of ignoring Jack. She reached out for Don's arm.

'I know that feeling.' Don sounded sincere. Kennedy turned and looked at him in admiration at the claim. 'And, ma'am, it sure would be a privilege to sink a beer with you.'

'Mother,' Jack said, although the emphasis he gave the word had no substance. He had given in, and was round by the car door, ready to take her other arm and help her into the air.

'So Romeo,' Kennedy scolded Don, 'you're going to breathe beer fumes all over Juliet, huh?'

'Never.' Don reached into a pocket, pulled out a frizzy-haired rock-and-roll toothbrush.

'You are like a scout,' Jack observed. 'Always prepared.'

'Never know when you might get the chance to kiss somebody.' All three of them looked at Don, trying to work out the depth of his levity, but his face was unreadable as he went on, 'Hey, folks, come on, then, and let me go cheerfully to my humiliation and doom.'

Don and Jack went to scope the ETA of the Laikonik, and to get reservations for Warsaw while they were at it. In the meantime, Krystyna had a hold of Kennedy's arm as she led him toward the station café. On a quick look around, Kennedy discerned that it was like any station café anywhere – they always had the same vibe – but that it had curtains, and a stove going, had tablecloths, and in short was welcoming, and the vanguard of this was in the smile of the babooshka who stepped forward and had to have been asking not what in the name of Christ they were doing there but what she could get them. Encouraged, Kennedy did the hospitality part, mainly with his fingers, and ordered four beers. Krystyna took banknotes out of his hand and told him their values in the holy dollar, and he had a bash at repeating them; they were in the thousands with a lot of scratchy, shchushy words which sounded good to Kennedy, maybe because it was money she was talking about, and any American would do absolutely anything in service of the stuff, specially when counted in the thousands.

Krystyna also talked about who was on the mugshots on the money – Chopin was there, and Marie Curie too, but it was mostly a lot of people Kennedy had never heard of.

'Is there one with that general guy on it?' he wondered. 'The guy who wore shades the whole time?' At one time, Kennedy had privately felt that the Polish dictator with the shades had looked relatively cool – superficial or what, he was prepared to admit. But shades were shades.

'General Jaruzelski?' Krystyna looked real happy to be able to say, 'No. And now there never will be.'

'How about…uh, the shipyard guy, with the…'

'Lech Walensa? No. But I am sure he will be there. Maybe in time for our next big inflation,' Krystyna joked.

'And how about the Pope?'

'Our own latter-day saint?' Krystyna shook her head, leaned over to Kennedy and whispered, 'A family man, you know.'

Kennedy said she had to be kidding.

'Not at all.' She had practised that conspirator's face; it was a good one, Kennedy thought.

'No way.' Kennedy did not believe it for a second. It was just the kind of build-em-up-to-knock-em-down thing that circulated in any society that worshipped, and at the same time hated, celebrity.

'Well.' Krystyna moved shoulders. 'I have known people who have known people who have known people…But listen. It's the kind of subject people *must* talk about when they drink beer.' And she laughed long and loud, and she asked, as their beers were placed on the counter, 'Would you agree, Mister Kennedy, that the drinking of beer is a serious business?'

'No doubt.' As Krystyna was posing as a serious drinker, Kennedy thought he might, too. He lifted his glass, and Krystyna slammed hers against his.

'To the little John-Pauls,' she concluded the toast.

'Here's to them,' Kennedy concurred, 'running around the garden, playing at mass.'

'A wonderful thought, Mister Kennedy.' Krystyna really did look pleased. 'I shall think of it when I am unhappy.'

'You do that, ma'am.'

Krystyna was more than welcome to the thought; it was an absurdist home movie. Kennedy guessed that she had a few unhappy times scheduled. It was only with some difficulty that he stopped the swelling of a lump in his throat; he was thinking of his dad, and the way he died, out of his head on diamorphine, or heroin, and poised as ever on the verge of some high that would be lost on everybody else. Meanwhile, Krystyna was laughing those times away, and Kennedy thought how that was a thing nobody could put a price on.

'You've got to think happy,' he advised, lamely. 'To, uh…be happy.'

'I will,' Krystyna promised.

Don and Jack came in and broke the mood. Krystyna made them toast the proactive Papa. That got Don, an instant believer, sparkly-eyed and laughing, but got Jack rolling his eyes to the ceiling with his *oh mother* like a hook from a fifties sitcom. 'Don't listen to her,' Jack entreated, and that got Krystyna pleased all over again.

'Every word is true,' she asserted, 'and every word is a lie. That is how the world *was* here, and that is how it will be from now on, too. The new world will be the same as the old. You don't believe me?'

'No,' Don protested. 'It'll have more money.'

'It'll be dressed better,' Kennedy decided.

But they were happy to believe her, even as she abandoned her teasing and forgot it with the wave of a hand, and the pointing of a finger that revealed the three men as having been caught out.

'How's your beer?' Don asked Krystyna, and then they all noticed that she was just holding it there.

'It is perfect,' she declared. 'You know, it is a symbol of the new Poland. Bright and golden, and...desirable. What do you say to that, Jacek?'

Jack's face said not a whole lot, but he drew his glass up gamely, and said, 'Cheers, mother. *Na strovyeh*,' which means, literally, *to your health*. Krystyna said at once that she had better drink to that, too, closely followed by Don. Kennedy too caught on, and raised his glass. They seemed to be stuck into that Polish thing, and that Irish thing, with drinking being both focus and conduit of their hopes and dreams.

'Ten minutes before the train gets in.' Don looked big-eyed through his glass. 'Time for another brewski, or what?'

'For me, no.' Jack was not going for the drinking prize. He had the drive back, with the fragile load of his mother to think about.

'Me either. Hey, come on,' Kennedy admonished Don. 'Keep a clear head, man. You don't want to come on like some drunk...*asshole*, do you?'

'Well, no,' Don sniffed. 'In fact, I'd kind of prefer not to come on like *any* kind of asshole, if that's all the same to you. But okay. I can't argue with your logic there. Logic is rare coming from this guy,' he confided with a wink. 'Really. Hey, but, listen. How do I look?'

'You look fine,' Krystyna said. 'You look...*natural*, Mister Dariusz. You look like the man of the world that you are.'

'I do?'

'*Yes*. Dashing and daring and out here in the world, where you belong.'

'Ah. Okay. That sounds kind of...*good*. *Thank* you.'

Natural was not the word Kennedy would have hit on, exactly. *Dashing* and *daring* also would have been low on his list. He scrutinised Don in the same way maybe as how Don's mom would have: his pal was in need of two nights' sleep and three days' rest – like shit, in short – but, what the hell, there was not much anybody could do about that.

'You will charm her,' Krystyna said, 'with your words.'

'Yeah,' Kennedy joined in. 'Heart of gold. Tongue of silver.'

'Head of Texas beech.' Don tapped his temple. 'I know.'

'Hey, have you got a good feel about it?' Kennedy asked Don.

'Well.' Don pondered that one a little. 'No good going into it with a bad feel.'

'Go ahead,' Krystyna urged Don. 'Get away from us and our opinions, and from Mister Kennedy and his fraternal jokes. Think about what you will say to this wonderful woman.'

'Goddam it,' Don ventured. 'Yass.' He downed the remnants of his beer. He got his toothbrush out and, holding it in his hand like a lance, got up and galloped over to the john, leaving his friends with a wave, leaving them spectators.

'You wait.' Kennedy did not actually believe what he was saying, but he wanted to. 'He's going to come out of there, see, and he's going to look like a movie star.'

'Gregory Peck,' Krystyna favoured.

'John Travolta,' was Jack's offer, 'in...*Saturday Night*.'

'Humphrey Bogart in *The*...uh...*Falcon of Malta*,' Kennedy said. 'Hey, though, but listen, and I'll tell you something weird. Don was born the day Humphrey Bogart died.' He waited for it to sink in. 'January fourteenth nineteen fifty seven, and the exact same minute, though I forget the time. How about that?'

'So, do you believe in reincarnation?' Krystyna laughed.

Kennedy had to admit that Don's and Humphrey Bogart's cosmic confluence did not provide much evidence for it. 'Hey, though,' Kennedy asserted. 'I believe in carnations.'

Kennedy did not know it, but that was a good thing to say, as the Poles were a people that appreciated flowers. They were all laughing about it still as Don emerged from his ablutions and went to make a step over toward them. They fell silent. 'No.' Krystyna put up a hand. Kennedy could see the bones in it as it was caught for a second in the light. 'Go,

Mister Dariusz, away from our influence, and the terrible things we will say about you.'

'But wish me luck,' Don called.

'Luck, man.' Kennedy, Krystyna and Jack elevated those glasses one more time. Krystyna and Jack pitched in with something in their own language, but Don was not looking anymore, was walking over toward the trains, hands clasped with the appearance of wisdom, behind his back.

Wordlessly, and with only a flurry of fuss, Kennedy, Jack and Krystyna moved to the window, where they could face the track and spectate and speculate. It felt kind of weird to Kennedy, but then he knew that Don, for any number of reasons Kennedy could only guess at, wanted to be witnessed.

'I can still not believe it.' Krystyna said in a pinch-me voice. 'In my time in America, I never met anybody like this – true, Mister Kennedy. I liked the Americans, okay, of course. I liked their good nature and informality, but a spontaneous people? Never. I liked their logic, and their straightforward approach to problems, but never did I meet one who made things up as he went along in such a way.'

Kennedy knew plenty of people who had done just that – his dad had been the original one in his life – but they were mostly grade-A screw-ups. He did not feel that America gave much space to people who made up their own way. Brits claimed that their country did, but Kennedy did not believe a word of it. He made this into a concise version for Krystyna, who did not look too convinced.

'Do you know how I feel at this moment, Mister Kennedy?' Krystyna was not asking him. 'I feel as if I am acting in a movie – as if I am a character in a story. Yes.' She let out a giggle that startled Kennedy and Jack, it was so loud. 'And it's a good story.' She leaned back in her seat, looked, for those few seconds of utterance, radiant, and not sick at all with anything at all. 'And – do you know what you must do?'

'Yeah.' He thought about it. 'I mean, no. What?' Kennedy asked for the…*form* of it, but he thought he knew what was coming, and was wrong.

'You must write it.'

'Eh?' Kennedy had had some idea that Krystyna, practical, scientific, logical, was about to tell him to get Don to snap out of his dreams and get on with his life. He had forgotten their conversation by the sea about writing.

'Yes.' She put a hand out, pressed Kennedy's arm. 'You, not him. He is too close to it to see it, to see how it is...telling itself.'

'I agree,' Jack piped up. 'He can not see how it looks. And, in any case, it would not look well in the...first person.'

'Uh, right.' Kennedy, about to get lost in a vague daguerreotype of himself in a room, late at night, stuck for ideas, was glad to be able to latch onto this question of technique. 'But he could do it in third.'

'No.' Krystyna was adamant. 'It must be you.' She squeezed Kennedy's arm. 'You are the observer. You can see the parts of it that are hidden from your friend. And you know the parts that are hidden from us – from Jacek and myself. Promise me that you will write it.'

'I'll try,' Kennedy began.

'No, not good enough.' She squeezed again, but already Kennedy could feel her strength ebbing. 'You must promise.'

'Uh.' *This is dumb*, Kennedy was thinking, *way out there dumb*, but even so the word *okay* was escaping from him. And then he felt it might be something to think about after all; his man-writing-alone-in-a-late-night-room picture flashed into his head again, in any case, much clearer. 'I promise.'

'Good.' Krystyna let go of him, and relaxed. 'I always wanted to be in a story.' She got lost then in a coughing fit, but managed to say, 'I think I would look very good in a story.'

'Uh, well, me too.' That was, of course, just a thing to say. Nobody, he thought as he looked frankly at her, bent, wheezing, grey and red and purple and white in the face as she was, looked good, exactly, when they looked like that. She was near the end of her own story. But then, it hit him, she could live on in another yarn, and that might not be a bad thing. But anyhow, she was already there in the history of her own country, a little of her in every partisan legend, and in every tale of people pissed off with the stupid systems they had to weave their way through all those years. 'Way to go.' The words were out before Kennedy recognised one of their possible meanings, but neither Jack not Krystyna seemed to notice. 'Right, Jack?'

'Whatever that means,' Jack kind of agreed.

'You can be in it too,' Kennedy told him. 'In fact, you'd have to be.'

'It's decided, then?' Krystyna sounded anxious.

'Signed and sealed, ma'am.' Kennedy took her hand. He was going to give it a big shake, mock the idea with it. Then he felt the bones in it, and had an inkling of how fragile they had to be, how painful. He held it a second, long enough for her to look expectantly at him, and then pleased, and then he carefully let it go.

'Look,' Jack said.

They had heard the rumble of the train, Kennedy realised, but they had been taken with their plotting. By the time Jack spoke, the Laikonik express was pulling into the station in all its screeching glory, filling the place with its presence. There stood Don by the track, a figure spotted easily among the little crowd waiting for the train. Krystyna went into excited schoolgirl mode as she said something that sounded like *oh boy*.

'Viva Shelley!' Jack seemed to have adopted the same tone.

'Go get her, Perce.' Kennedy gave in to the Shelley schtick.

Saint Ola of Abel had to have been in the front car of the train, because she was in view before the watchers could get many more words out. She was tall; that was the first impression of her. When Don hailed her, she pulled off a woollen hat to reveal short dark hair. 'She's stopped.' Kennedy stated the obvious out of relief. He did not think he would have been able to handle the sight of her showing Don her back right from the off and just walking right on out of there without a word.

'They are talking.' Jack was compelled into the commentary. 'Do you see this, mother?'

Of course she did. Krystyna put up a hand to silence them, as if she might be able to hear what was being said, satisfied herself that all seemed to be well and truly as good as it could be, then turned back to Kennedy and Jack. She picked up her beer, toasted, 'To Mister Don Dariusz, lover, and writer of books,' and Jack and Kennedy put their empty glasses into a trio. They watched, and again excitedly did the commentary, saw Don and Ola obscured for seconds by other people, then visible again, facing each other, and talking.

'What now for you, Mister Kennedy?' Krystyna did not take her eyes from Don and Ola.

Nor did Kennedy as he tried to think through the question, which branched off at once to make a hundred questions. What indeed? There was work to do on Don's books. That was easy. There was also stuff to work through in his head; there was the leaving of Istanbul to consider, the changing of his life, there was the void he would have to enter in a life without Ling; there were high places to contemplate, purely because you could not throw yourself from low places: all kinds of things. 'See more of Warsaw,' was all he thought of, all those little plaques to mark the places of murder, to read and respect and remember. Not taking her eyes from whatever was going on over at the track, Krystyna asked him if he had seen this place in Warsaw, visited that one, passed by another, marvelled at yet another. Kennedy was mostly not sure. 'We just walked around a lot,' he confessed.

'It's a good place to walk,' Jack said.

Over on the track, not much seemed to be happening. Don was still talking, Ola was listening, then she talked and he listened, and all the time people hid them and revealed them, made them move this way and that, made them move back, got them facing the watchers, or backs turned.

'See, we both do stuff like that,' Kennedy reflected, then explained. 'Go to a place and have it all in the background, see it out the corner of an eye, then open a guidebook later and go see it again, look at it properly. I was in Istanbul a year, maybe, before I went in the Blue Mosque, but I had, like, a...*feel* for it already. I'd passed it a thousand times and just liked it being there, you know?'

'I understand that.' Krystyna nodded.

'Right. I can't make out people who go on a tour of Europe, right, with, like, eight cities in five days – it's insane. It's mostly Americans,' it occurred to him. 'I mean, why?'

'Yes, but, Kennedy.' Jack sounded tetchy, and Kennedy had a quick vision of him on one of those very tours, bounding out of the bus, his eyes sparkling to see Florence and Rome in a day. 'You must realise that most people don't have the opportunity to live in another country and take the...landscapes for granted in such a way.'

That was true enough, Kennedy was about to turn tack and agree. Krystyna put in, though, 'Yes, but maybe more people should have the courage to do what Mister Kennedy and Mister Dariusz do, and go to live somewhere new, the way I did, and the way you yourself have done, Jacek.'

'Hey.' Kennedy felt ashamed of what he had said. 'But, you know, Jack's right. People do what they can, right?' He also remembered that, back home in the land of the free, people generally got two weeks' vacation a year. 'Maybe it's better to spin crazily around Europe in a week than to never see it at all...But hey.' He had a sudden stab of anxiety at the wandering of his eye from the events on the track, had momentarily lost sight of Don and Ola. 'What's happening over there?'

The crowd on the track had cleared, and the couple they watched were now clearly to be seen, still talking up a storm, pacing, pausing, turning. The gestures were telling tales, though, a dialogue made of arms, hands, shoulders, shakes of the head, out of which the observers made their own script. Ola made a brief turn away as if in disbelief, and it was starting to look not so good from the stalls. 'Show of thumbs?' Kennedy suggested, and Krystyna and Jack narrowed eyes at him. 'Like the Roman emperors at the games?' he prompted. Jack's thumb was turned down without hesitation and, with a deep, sad breath out, Krystyna too downturned a thumb. Kennedy was not about to make an eejit of himself by going against the whole of the imperial box, thus risking his own neck in the arena. 'Oh well, poor old Don,' he said, as he too showed the thumbs-down.

'Well, we don't know, yet.'

Both Kennedy and Krystyna turned to Jack and stared.

'Hey, Jack.' Kennedy laughed. 'I didn't have you down as an optimist.'

'I'm not one.' Jack did not quite make it into a boast. 'In general. Remember, Kennedy, this isn't your story. You're not writing it yet.' To both Kennedy's and Krystyna's nonplussed looks, Jack spelled out, 'I mean that nobody knows the end of this story.'

'Hmm, right. Well, whatever happens, I think we're going to see it in the next few minutes.' Kennedy looked around for a clock. 'Hey, how long have we got before the train goes back?'

'Perhaps fifteen minutes.' Jack sounded moody.

Railroad workers were going up and down the train already, banging this and checking that, drawing jets of water and spills of oil, and cleaners were emerging from the cars with full garbage sacks. Train arrivers and greeters had been replaced by city leavers and wavers. The track was filling up again, and once again they could barely see Don and Ola.

'Come on, then, baby.' Kennedy focused on Don. He and Ola were still talking away, and making their hand-movements. Ola laughed; it did not look to Kennedy like a dismissive kind of laugh. Those hands kept going up, though, and Ola's were defensive, blocking her body, and maybe her mind, from Don and whatever talk he was conjuring up to hold her there. She seemed to Kennedy like a fine-looking woman, and maybe this went some way toward telling him that, despite what Ola's mother had said to Don, she was not just hanging fire with nothing and nobody in her life, waiting for Don Darius to dare his way into it.

With no warning, Don pointed over to his audience and, like a bunch of kids playing at spying, Kennedy, Krystyna and Jack ducked their heads down and giggled – they could not help it – then raised them slowly. Ola was still looking toward them, distracted momentarily by the audience they had formed in her honour, and they saw her bark out an oval-mouthed expression of what had to be disbelief, hands thrown up toward her face.

Then she waggled a finger at Don, spoke angrily now, it seemed to Kennedy, and then very suddenly she was swinging her ass out of Don Darius's sight, and his life. Don had a try at bewitching her back to him with a word or two, but it left him as a stark, solo figure on the track, in sharp relief against the backdrop behind him of metal and stone and people, his hands slightly raised. Kennedy had to go join him because of that alone. Also, Don had the tickets. Kennedy rose.

'Yes,' Krystyna said. 'You were nearly forgetting that.'

'What?' Kennedy and Jack spoke together.

'No matter how things have worked out, it's back to Warsaw for Mister Dariusz to get some more inspiration for his romances.' She sounded wistful. 'And back across the continent for you, Mister Kennedy.'

'Yeah. Well, eventually.' Kennedy had a sharp and savage vision of himself on trains, his eyes shaded and steely, and of getting off at Sirkeci, head poisoned with his thoughts. 'Listen. Thanks. It was…great.' He reached down to Krystyna, gave her a kiss on the cheek. She made a noise and held on, made him kiss the other one. 'In fact it was awesome. Thanks,' Kennedy told Jack too, and shook him by the hand. So much to say, as ever, but time was all up and his mind was full of clocks and clouds.

He turned and walked and pulled at the door to the little café; it would not budge, there being a Texan the other side of it, also pulling for all he was worth.

Don did not have it in him to treat Jack to any more of his mystifying English, which had to be good. He shook his head to answer the unspoken question, and said a quick thanks, and they shook hands and clapped shoulders. He bade Kennedy wait, then bent down to Krystyna for his turn at that double kiss. Then he and Kennedy were together again, and legging it to arrive breathless at the track.

Kennedy looked down the sleek length of the Laikonik express. He would soon know what was on Don's mind, and the thought both wearied and intrigued him. Right then though he was getting alarmed at signs showing how that iron monster was snorting away and just raring to get the hell back down the line and home for the night. Kennedy thought they had better make sure they got this part right, and took Don's arm to lead him up steps to the nearest car.

Both were looking back, all the same, into the station, at the two figures framed in the doorway of the café, smiling, arms raised in farewell. And they too waved, and wavered, distracted despite their wishes.

By the time they found their seats they were way up the middle of the train. Kennedy leaned over a guy ensconced comfortably in a corner, and looked out the window. He could not see the café, nor any sight of Krystyna or Jack. He hoped they were still smiling.

Five

The Laikonik

Their companions were the usual muddle of people with nothing to do on a Sunday evening but traverse the wastes of their big country on trains. A little old fellow took his eyes from his paperback to blow his nose volubly into what was surely a foot-cloth souvenir from the *Gulag*; a cardboard-faced wire-haired woman in a leather jacket, marbled jeans and shiny white boots sent them a look almost hidden by pouches under eyes roomy enough to house a baby kangaroo; they got a glance too from a whey-faced little man in a dark suit that did not go with the tan shoes he wore. They all exchanged a round of *good evenings* in the grave style to which Kennedy had by then accustomed himself.

'So good to be on one of these lousy trains with you again,' Kennedy commented to Don as they settled. He did not honestly know what to say. If some little part of him had at one time looked forward to the letting-out of a triumphant *I-told-ya-so-ya-big-loon*, it had been subsumed into a feeling of sympathy. 'Huh?' He gave Don an experimental jab in the ribs.

'Travelling fools,' Don breathed out.

'So.' Sympathetic or not, Kennedy thought he might as well open up the inquest.

Don said, 'Yes. I asked if I could kiss her.' And there he was, Kennedy thought, beginning in the middle, the way he wrote his postcards. And his books, come to think of it.

There was no more for a half-minute, so Kennedy said, 'Well, look at you. I wouldn't let you kiss me, either. So what else happened?'

'She said it'd be better if we didn't.'

'Uh, right. But…I meant, what happened from the whole…*thing*?'

'Could have been good to have just one little kiss.'

'True,' Kennedy humoured him. 'But what else?'

'Sang me that song,' Don mused, and Kennedy, and everybody else there, had to look at Don as he rumbled out, '*Na na na-na, na na na-na, hey hey-ey, goo-oodbye.*'

'Enough of that.' Kennedy felt kind of disturbed.

'Nutshell version, right?' Don grinned, seemed to be gathering his thoughts. 'She said the time wasn't right for her. Nor the place.'

'Well, that's…well…That's kind of cool, I guess.'

Though time and place were, when it came down to it, all that people had, when they were face-to-face. 'I mean, it wasn't *you*, in that case.'

'Nor the person, she said. Said she wasn't about to go walking out with some hick like me. If she wanted a hick, she could find her own hick back in her own hick town. Well, not in so few words – it was in her eyes. Said I wasn't going to stick around Poland just for her. Said I was just people overseas, stay in her country a couple years, laugh at its customs and trash its traditions and insult its religion, then get out of here.'

'Okay.' Kennedy smiled, shook his head. 'And *is* that the plan?'

'Said I seemed like a nice guy.' Don brightened up a little at the memory. 'But that I should head back home, find me a nice cowgirl to settle down with.'

'Uh-huh.' Ola actually sounded to Kennedy like a bit of a ball-buster. 'Well, listen, man.'

'I only wanted to, ah, remind her of our, ah…sweet meeting, and ask her out on a date next time she was in Warsaw. Or Krakow. I'm a guy who's prepared to get on trains. Did you notice that, Kennedy?'

'Listen, man.'

'I really didn't necessarily want to drag her down the aisle of a church in sight of God and relatives and spend the next fifty years with her. I mean, not right now, anyhow. Go out, was my idea, have a drink, something to eat, shoot the breeze and see what might be what and might be not. That was all.'

'Listen, man.' Kennedy did not know why what he was about to say had occurred to him. 'When she sees your name in lights, she'll remember you all right, huh?'

'I guess she would.' Don's little-boy face started to say, *Is that really going to happen to me? Are you sure about that?*

'You'll be the one that got away, then.'

'Sure, but, you know…'

'What?'

'That wouldn't bother her none. She's a person of…*integrity*. I can tell.'

Kennedy was really not sure if Don had met one of those before. But Don was right, if he thought he was. And Ola was, too. They were both right, and Kennedy saw then, saw it all real sharply, what he had to do about Ling.

'And I'll tell you something,' Don said. 'I wouldn't want that to bother her. She wouldn't be the person I think she is, if that kind of thing bothered her any.'

'Uh-huh.' *The fuck I would care by now*, Kennedy was thinking. Whatever bothered Ola or didn't, she was right, and they were all just people overseas; they had no right to impose themselves on other people's cultures the way they did. What would Ling do in the US – what was Kennedy going to do in China, for Chrissake? No. Ling was Istanbul, where she was people overseas, too, and that was that and that was fine. *I'll love you, Ling, I'll leave you, Ling, and you'll love and leave me too*, Kennedy thought. Too many ls, but it would have to be said. It would hurt, and go on hurting. Then one night the hurt would stop, and that was their path, Kennedy's and Ling's, through pain to a scented Chinese garden that would exist only in some place in Kennedy's mind and, probably, in Ling's too, in a land shorn of all its vegetation. 'Well, uh, right.'

'She said I was crazy, certainly.' As Don Darius often did, he answered a question Kennedy had not yet asked. 'Said you were crazy, too, whoever you were. I told her Jack and Krystyna would probably give her a ride back to Abel, and she said no way, she wasn't going to get into a car with crazy people.'

'Right.' Kennedy thought dully how that imagined car ride could have been a chance for his friend: the real Don Darius relayed to Ola via the good opinions of a war-heroine and her decent, level-headed son. But there it went, up some other road. 'Listen, though. Are you…uh…happy with the way things panned out?' It seemed entirely like a dumb question, and Don looked it right back at Kennedy. 'What I mean is, like, happy that you did all you could?'

'Well, hell, no.' Don studied the backs of his hands. 'Time,' he stated. 'I had enough time to be witty, right? But then any clown can be witty. I didn't have enough time to be...*eloquent*. Women like witty,' he confided. 'But they like eloquent too, and...Oh hell.' A new thought came to life. 'I forgot to tell her I went around to see her mom.' He bit on his lip. 'Hoo, well, now, hey. That might easily make her mad at me.'

'Well, madder, anyhow,' Kennedy agreed. 'It might. But listen to me. You got her address, man. You can write her, tell her anything you forgot. You can be eloquent then, man. Hey, listen, but I know you can be eloquent, given a page to write on.'

'I can?' Don murmured. 'I *can*. I *will*. Oh, yes. I'll tell her. I'll let her know, all right. So listen.'

'What?'

'Let's talk about something else.'

'Okay. Like what?'

It was an idea that appealed to Kennedy, but in fact it took a while. The train guard came, marked everybody's tickets with the crocodile jaws on his little dingus. The old fellow went back to his book and his hellish snotrag. The woman took her boots off and put her feet up and slept and dreamed maybe of bouncing boxing baby marsupials. The guy in the suit got out a Walkman that leaked what sounded like a public meeting.

'Hey.' Kennedy marked a memory. 'No way is J D Salinger Thomas Pynchon.'

'He sure is.' Don looked sadly knowing. 'For certain. Ever read *Gravity's Rainbow*?'

'I tried.' Usually, Kennedy did not like dissing books that a lot of people felt strongly about enough to love, but he made an exception for TP's revered tomes, partly because the man's disciples tended to be so righter-than-thou. He honestly could not think of a better description than, 'It was a crock of shit.'

'No way.'

'A crock-and-a-half of shit.'

'No.' There was a whole new Don Darius there: a fan, up in his seat, eyes blazing. 'It's a book that, ah, sets out the whole schemata of...human existence. War, history, geography, the fluidity of continents and nationality and...layers of the stuff that makes us what we are and shows us that to be human you got to be...*inhuman*, sometimes, and...Kennedy, you got to read between the lines a little, but it's worth it.'

'Huh. Listen. I'll take your word for it, man.' Whatever *GR* was, it was also a book that was nothing like anything J D Salinger had ever written. 'I shit you not, but reading just the lines themselves gave me a headache. And you could be right,' Kennedy seemed to allow, 'about it setting out the whole human whatever. But it's still a crock of shit. What makes you think Pynchon is Salinger, though?'

'You don't know about that?'

'No.' But of course Kennedy knew: the tired rumour about the most private public figures in American literature had had currency for years. Kennedy was simply interested to hear whether there had been an update on it or not. The full story, as far as he could recall, was that it had originated from some essay by the novelist John Batchelor back in the seventies, an exercise in scholarly mischief; Salinger closeted away from the world, Pynchon never photographed: must be the same guys...Yeah, right. Don rattled this nonsense off for Kennedy without referring at all to the Batchelor article.

'Ever go on the pilgrimage?' Don broke off to ask.

'Go stare at Salinger's wall?' Kennedy snorted. He did not care what the venerable author got up to in his fortress. The published Salinger, in his view, was fine stuff, all right, but it did not make Kennedy want to help in turning the old grouch into a religion.

'You don't have to settle for that.' Don was by then in the role of disciple. Kennedy was glad. And not glad. 'What you got to do is bring along an ailing child, and then Salinger'll invite you in and entertain you the whole day.'

'The hell he will.' In fact, Kennedy had heard that wish-fulfilling yarn: a guy drove miles to Cornish New Hampshire and knocked on Salinger's door, and when the feisty hermit started to shut it in his face the guy said to give him a break, huh; he had a sick eleven year-old with him. So Salinger asked them in to watch TV and eat cookies. Personally, Kennedy would have told a guy dumb enough to bring a sick kid on such a frivolous mission that he would give the kid an aspirin and then kick his dad's ass for him. 'Well,' Kennedy laughed out, 'I haven't got an ailing child, as you might've noticed. So, what, tell me. You abducted a child and went there?'

'Not exactly. No. We were all set to go there from college one weekend, but the car broke down just three miles out of Austin.'

'Uh, right.'

'And so we, ah, we went drinking instead with the money for gas.' Don laughed, almost embarrassed.

'Well, there's dedication for you.'

'Okay. Good point. We couldn't even *read* by the time we were through, let alone remember who Salinger was. But, you know, Kennedy, it's still a good *idea*. You know, it's an expression of our...wish to ratify, to praise. You know? What's the difference between doing that and going to see, say, Victor Hugo's house in Paris, France?'

'Well, Victor Hugo's not going to come out and tell you to fuck off, for a start. Hmm, but listen, pal.'

'What?'

'Forget all those venerable deadheads. Back to the future, man. That is, to now. Forget Abel. It's over. I mean, the chasing of wild geese, or at least...' Kennedy ruminated a little, serious now. 'It's gone through this phase, right?' He reached over, gave Don's shoulder a pat. 'What now? What happens now?'

'Easy,' Don said. 'Head home. Make plans.'

'About what?' Kennedy saw Don in a writer's pose, in shirtsleeves, in front of an old typewriter rather than a PC: nerd on a dust jacket stopping people buying the book.

'Amsterdam.'

'What?'

It fell to Kennedy to remind Don that it was honestly not the best time for him to be heading for Amsterdam. Kennedy knew it was Don's kind of town, knew that Don got there at least one time a year. His first visit, Kennedy remembered, was in the summer of eighty eight, and Don saw *über*-beat Chet Baker's last ever gig. The next day, the craggy junky trumpeter had fallen out of a window and leaked his last notes away on the cobbles. Don had even seen the last crowd Chet ever pulled, up a side street, people gathered around the dying jazzer. Since then, Don had fixed on the city as a place where he could go and get truly wrecked without having either to try too hard or to answer to anybody. 'But not as wrecked as Chet,' he was fond of adding.

'Need a vacation,' Don asserted.

'Like hell you do. No.' Kennedy tapped on Don's arm, got his face out of dreams and giving him its whole attention. 'Now is not the time for you to be heading for Fuckupsville. What you need is a publisher. What

I'm going to do is help find you one. You can go on vacation later.' The promise seemed to calm Don down. 'For now, you got rewrites to do and hard copy to print, you got letters to sign and some people to talk to on the phone.'

'I do?'

'You *do*.'

'Ah...right.'

'Right. Let's jump to it, Donski, the rest of your life. I mean, it's out there, man. We just got to find it.'

'That's all?'

'That's all. If you don't blow it.' *If you don't head for Amsterdam and blow what's left of your mind*, Kennedy thought, *you big fool*.

The guy with the pinched face had stowed his Walkman, and was by then reading a magazine covered in exclamation marks. It had a picture on the cover of the Brit fiddle player whose name Kennedy could never remember, the one with the Vivaldi and the stupid punk teenager hairdo. The man glared at Kennedy and Don once or twice when they got loud, and could hardly have been pleased either, Kennedy guessed, at their somewhat unprepossessing appearance. The other guy sniffled on, oblivious in his book. The woman slept. Kennedy looked at her, and envied her concentration on whatever was inside her head.

Their business done, in a way, it seemed a simple thing for Kennedy and Don to lie back in their seats and shut their eyes. 'No.' Don sat upright. 'Don't sleep on this train, Kennedy,' he warned. 'We miss Warsaw, next stop is Krakow. And that sure is a nice town, but I don't need to tell you it'd be a little, ah, inconvenient to wind up there tonight.'

Kennedy was not so sure about that; it might have been cool to check out venerable Krakow and its towers...but no, maybe not right then. He too straightened his back.

He thought they might be able to keep awake with a little conversation, though he was keen to keep Don off the subject of Ola. He did not need to worry: it was Krystyna who gradually filled up their thoughts and manifested herself in the things they said. They lauded Jack's mom for a little while. Then they lapsed; they capped each other's puns featuring the names of fish, finished off lines of lyrics from obscure songs, but nearly always heard their words trail back to the time they had had in Abel in the kind care of Krystyna and Jack. In this way they barely noticed the train around them, forcing its way through the darkened land to the truly eternal city that defied tyrants and lay at its centre.

The magazine reader creased his mag shut and stashed it away carefully. As he got up to disappear into his overcoat, he said to Kennedy and Don, 'Gentlemen, do you know what it was that I did today?'

'Would I, sir?' Don asked, reasonably enough.

'I learned English.' The man's glare was somehow familiar, and they realised that he had been eyeballing them in the same way throughout most of the trip.

Kennedy said up to him, 'What, so you mean you're, like, *fluent* now?'

'I learned English,' the man repeated. 'However, I have listened to you gentlemen throughout this journey.' He made a pause straight out of Stanislavski. 'And I must say that I can not understand a *word* you have uttered. Thank you, gentlemen.'

'Our pleasure,' Don said.

'Thank you. Very much.' The man exited. Kennedy pictured him going home and burning his English textbooks.

'Must try harder,' Don recommended to his retreating form.

'Down a snake, no mistake,' Kennedy decided; the man would be up a ladder the next day – language learning was like that, he knew from his Turkish.

The train winding down into Warsaw East gave Kennedy and Don pause in their journey, and guided their other two companions out of their lives with civil *goodnights* that were almost cheerful. Kennedy got a sudden sense of them with their own preoccupations to go on to, of people weaving their thoughts into tapestries, which would become templates for the actions they would take. He saw the fisherman out on the freezing sea off Abel for a second, wondered if he was still there. And none of these people figured on being right there in Kennedy's mind right then, nor on being preserved in grotesque miniature on a page he might write, trapped like flies in amber.

'Tired.' Kennedy did not think he had ever heard Don Darius admit to that before, not in all the nights they had run into the ground in Istanbul. 'I could sleep.' Don's face lit up as if he had just had a startlingly original idea. 'In fact, I believe I will.'

'Sure you will,' Kennedy ordered him. 'And me too,' he volunteered.

They got their stuff together, got up and joined people in the line forced on them by the layout of the train. They waited for Warsaw centre to appear out the windows to welcome them to something that, for people overseas, had the alien feel of home.

Six

Warsaw

'Great little place right by the station.' Don was thinking once more of Chet Baker, Kennedy thought, when he added, 'Plays great jazz. Does great food.'

'Right.'

'Has great beer.'

'Not for me. And hey, not for you, either. No, man.' In the mirror window of one of the little stores in the guts of the station, Kennedy saw himself in bonnet and crinolines, wagging the finger of the old Vermont schoolmam who took up residence in his brain from time-to-time. 'Home.' He repeated the word as he led Don up into the main hall of Warsaw Central station, through its sparse travellers and loungers and out to the road. He stopped at the edge of the sidewalk. 'We go back to your place, that's what we do, heat some water, take a shower, get some coffee on.'

'That was exactly what I was about to suggest,' Don protested. '*But instead*, I was about to say, *what say we eschew jazz and fried chicken and beer and head homeward.* Hey, Kennedy.'

'What?'

'What are we doing, standing here?'

'*Duh.*' Kennedy dropped his jaw. 'Like, waiting for a cab, maybe?'

'*Duh* yourself. Cabs are to be found around the corner, at the cab rank.'

'So why didn't you tell me, you *eejit*?'

'Eejit, your*self*. Mor*o*n.'

'Moron your*self*, *ass*hole.'

Bickering happily, they walked around to the rank and made their own line, stood under the station's concrete awning. They were soon joined by a wrapped-up Gypsy kid in a plaid shirt and bluejeans, doing his best to look like the all-American boy-next-door, albeit an Eskimo one. He asked Kennedy for a dollar. He had a pleasant face and demeanour, and looked like he really could use a dollar. Kennedy tried to oblige, fished in a pocket and remembered that all his dollars were back at Don's. He gave the kid instead a few faded little hundred zloty bills, that looked like they had been through the mill with Poland itself. 'Have you got another one?' the kid seemed to be asking. Kennedy and Don stared at him, but the question was reasonable enough, and so Don found a few more for him.

As they settled into their cab, Don told Kennedy how a Brit guy who worked with him at Warsaw Polytechnic had been in the habit of chucking any fifty or hundred zloty bills he wound up with into the trash. Don brought to life a picture of some long, cool slacker dude. Anyhow, seeing money in the trash pissed off the school cleaners when they emptied the garbage, and they had complained. Kennedy could see why. 'So he quit that,' Don continued, 'and then what he started doing with all those no-account bills was throw them in a box and, when it came time for him to leave for the Christmas vacation, he got the box out, counted the bills up, right, and found he had enough for one bottle of beer. So he took this box full of bills to the twenty-four-seven and asked for a beer and handed the box over, thinking how he was glad to have gotten rid of it all. Seemed to me that was a real important part of it for him, a little bit of…closure, right? Okay, and, by the time he was through drinking, the people in the store were through counting, and they said the money was right, so he put the bottle down and went to walk out of the store, okay? And they called him right back, gave him three hundred zloty. It was the deposit on the bottle. That freaked him out, a little.' Don shook his head. 'But never mind him. What's certain is that it's got to do something to a nation, right, when its money seems so goddam worthless.'

'Certainly.' Kennedy had been thinking the same. He was busy by then checking in pockets for more of those little bills, see if he had any left. He nodded toward the cab driver. 'I guess this guy won't refuse them, though.

They still drive the economy forward, right, only, real slow. A bit like this driver, in fact.'

But Kennedy was only griping for the sake of the analogy. The driver tippytoed them over shiny dark ice through town and down the hill to Don's soon enough. Back at the apartment they showered and drank the coffees they had promised themselves, which attacked their nerves and kidded them into the notion that they were wide awake still. They talked quietly about Don's books, which inspired Kennedy into getting carried away and deeming the Saudi book to be perfect, and ready to go. He started on the mammoth task of printing it out. He woke in the middle of the night surrounded by sheets of paper, the printer firing out blanks where the cartridge had run out, and Don snorting out snores where he had run out of the talk that wired and drove him.

Kennedy did not want to disturb Don. He also fancied a sleep in something that resembled a bed. He went and lay in Don's bed and slept again.

A guy stood over Kennedy later that morning, saying, 'You got the bed.' He was wearing a graduation gown and mortar board hat, held a stick under one arm and in chalk-dusted fingers clutched a Latin primer. 'Means you get the breakfast, too. And listen, I'll be back from the old *polytechnika* around one thirty, and will be expecting a spread fit for a king.'

'Hey…what,' Kennedy drowsed out, and the teacher figment faded, revealed only plain old Don Darius, coated, hatted, gloved.

'Not a very bigshot king,' Don allowed. 'Bakery store downstairs. Up the street a way is a minimart where you can get eggs, ham, mushrooms, kind of stuff. Beer.' A golden light winked on behind his eyes. Kennedy raised a hand, did not want to see a beer light so early in the day. '*Voodka.*' The Polish way of saying the word recalled *Polski tempo* for Kennedy.

What was more, *Polski tempo* showed a little in Don's face, like an old car running on fumes, but Kennedy was no longer afraid of the spectre. Whatever Don had found in Abel, Kennedy had the notion that he had shaken himself into some kind of focus somehow, and that he was not going to let anything fog that up. Not that day, anyhow.

He went back to sleep and got up around noon, felt his way into its moody light. He gulped down some juice, then some deadly coffee, took a shower and felt ready for the rest of the day. As he dressed, he looked over at the sleeping screen of Don's computer, but resisted the urge to wake it up. He went out and skated up and down the street, his bag getting heavier and heavier, and by the time he creaked back up in Don's elevator he found his pal waiting, a cheery, patient look on his face as they made greetings.

They worked their way through their food, made it into breakfast all day. Don surveyed the neat piles made by the stuff he had scribed, saw it all getting beyond him, not out of control exactly, but assuming a control of its own.

'Am I really going to be a writer?' It was as if the idea had never occurred to Don. 'Is that really what's going to happen?' Kennedy said he guessed so. 'Well then,' Don decided. 'I guess I am, then. Listen, though, Kennedy.'

'What?'

'I trust you.'

'Yeah?' Kennedy said. 'Good.'

'I…respect your judgment.'

'Yeah? Good.'

'Do you hear what I'm saying to you?'

'You think I'm deaf?'

'Ah, no. But…as long as you know. You say I'm going to be a writer, then, well, okay, hell, that's what I'll be.' He looked out the window at nothing for what seemed like a long time. 'Kennedy?'

'Yeah? What?'

'Don't get me all wrong here.' Don worked his thumbs, had nothing else to twiddle. Kennedy looked pointedly at them, made him stop. 'But listen. There may be one little flaw in your, ah, very good and…very kindly and considered advice.'

'There is?' Kennedy thought he knew what was coming.

'Maybe. You're giving me all this…hope. You're telling me this thing, and I'm believing you. Right? Okay. But what about you?'

'What about me?' A good question was being implied, though: if Kennedy was so hotshot knowledgeable about writing, about what was good or bad or great or plain crud, why was he still just an English-teaching bum, and not a great book-writing bum? He had stories out, didn't he, with some warm reviews, and there was the novella, bought by people in double-figures, almost, and he had placed articles here, essays there. But so what? When was he going to set about the big one? He did not know, and was not at all sure that he had one in him, but he said, 'Listen, pal. You don't need to worry about that. I got a story in mind.'

'Oh? You do?'

'Yeah.'

'What is it?'

'Hah.' Kennedy snorted. 'Think I'd tell you? So you can just write it down in one evening and sell it for money? No way. But hey.' His tone softened. 'Maybe I'll tell you one day, when you got less on your mind.'

'You will?'

'Well, maybe.' Kennedy followed that with silence.

'Right.' Don grinned, looked like a man who had things all figured, and it was cool for Kennedy to see him safe, at least in that moment, from the corrosive effects of doubt. 'Well, good. So, then, we're both going to be writers.'

'You, mostly.' Kennedy had to be honest. He reminded Don that first he would have to attend to the little detail of selling the books. At that, Don looked dismayed, as if watching himself going around bookstores hawking boxes of the things. 'I guess we'll just stick to the conventional way and sell them first off to a publisher.' Kennedy made it sound like a stunningly novel notion. 'And they'll do the hawking for you.'

'Ah, well, I guess anybody can sell some old book,' Don said bravely. 'Just depends on the spin they put on it, right?' Kennedy thought Don would be hurt without his agreement, so he gave it. He imagined agents he knew, all the same, sitting genially behind desks, looking at Don, their faces saying, *Who is this clown?* It was clear that Don might need a little coaching before he exposed his pale body to the shark-infested waters of publishing.

'Anybody,' Kennedy assured him. 'You don't need to worry your head about that.' And that was true, in a way. But Don was no longer listening, was on his way to the icebox, glasses in his hand.

'I want to write the kind of book,' Don said later, 'you're reading it, right, and you're feeling all the time that life is getting in the way.' Kennedy liked that, and immediately set about putting it into the covering letter he was trying to finish.

'You will.' Kennedy caught sight of the printouts. 'In fact, listen, and I'll tell you. You have, already.'

'Eh?' Don was genuinely startled, and then puzzled. 'You're sure about that?'

'I'm sure as milk.'

'Oh. Right. And, ah, what the hell does *that* mean?'

'It means, like, very sure.' It was a thing Kennedy's old man had liked to say. 'Like, extremely sure indeed-oh.' And Kennedy *was* sure, too, knew he wouldn't have been there unless that were the case, knew he would never, if that were not the case, have seen Poland at all.

Seven

Warsaw

It ended at that point in Warsaw, that phase of Don Darius's first book. Once Kennedy had spent hours on the phone to various people in New York, and had typescripts and disks bagged up, and had placed them into the careful mitts of functionaries in the Polish mail system, things changed in Don's life. Not overnight, of course, because things no longer happened that way in publishing. It was a couple of months before Don got the call to get his ass across the pond to gripe at agents, contend with publishers and bicker with editors, and another while before he was able to nitpick through galley proofs of the Saudi book, but that was it from then on: as people overseas, Don was on borrowed time.

He went back to the land of his ancestors only one time. He flew to Warsaw, got to Warsaw Central station, hauled himself up the steps of that laconic, iconic express to take the trail through Warsaw East, Mlava where his mom hailed from, Dzialdowo where Kurt Vogel chirped the first bars of his sad song, Gdansk, Gdynia, got on the hedge-hopper to Abel and paid his last respects to Krystyna. Don had no thoughts of the ever-mysterious Ola, whose face, he told Kennedy in a rare letter, he had forgotten, but he would remember the other woman in Abel, he said, all his days. Don and Snappy Jack hit the hooch and celebrated not Krystyna's passing, of course, but her having been there. They sat by the window she had liked to look out of, and watched the crowds of party-coloured trippers having a time in a place come into its own the way it did every year, in the daytime, in the summer.

For some reason, Kennedy remembered every detail of that breakfast he had made himself and Don that day in Warsaw. Every man he knew gave good breakfast, and held religiously to it in a way that women seemed unable to – he could never make out why that should be. Don agreed. 'I meet me a woman who knows what breakfast is about,' he had once told Kennedy, back in Istanbul, Kennedy thought, 'and I'm up that church aisle with her pledging oaths to God and priests and in-laws in hats.' Don did not seem to have reached that point yet, Kennedy was kind of relieved to find out. He read in a gossip column that Don was shacked up with some other writer, who scribed for some upmarket mag; he knew just from reading her stuff that it was not going to last. She sounded way too sensible. He saw a photo of her and Don on a society page on the Internet, he red-eyed and she red-lipped, singing *We're in the Money* in pig Latin with Bret Easton Ellis and Donna Tartt. That was the kind of company a guy ought to keep, Kennedy guessed, if he wanted to stay inspired.

Anlong Road

Nolan Kennedy was inspired by the memorising of words that, basically, gave him a headache, but he had determined that he *would* learn Chinese, up its ladders, down its snakes. The city around him was full of words. What he could understand from them was that it was as fine a place as any in which to wind up. There were walks to walk, places to go, millions of people to avoid crashing into. He had to get used to them, and they in turn would have to accustom to him. There were books to read, movies to see, things to drink and eat and feel. It was not true that they cooked dogs there, but they cooked damn near everything else. It all went to make him a life to live, on Shanghai's Anlong Road.

He and Ling ate mooncake under the glorious round moon that smiled down on the Middle Fall Festival. There was cool, subtle music all around them, and Kennedy loved Ling and was certain that he always would. In China, people said, there were ten thousand ways to be happy. He and Ling were prepared to work their way through them all.

Ling held in her hand her keychain, on which was a little pink curly slipper to which she had taken a liking, Persian, and not Iranian. She sometimes took a long look at it, saying, 'We were both people overseas, then,' hitting a wistful note.

Now it was just Kennedy, she meant; there was an imbalance in their yin and yang that could be restored only with sacrifices, wishes, kisses and, eventually, leaving.

In the meantime, Kennedy liked to think China was for him only about the wishes and kisses, but he knew there was badness there too, just like there was anywhere, hidden by the smiles and the night, drowned out by music and voices and the sterling efforts of tree-fellers and construction workers. No doubt, he had the feeling, it would seek out Ling and himself, show them that there were ten thousand ways to be unhappy, too. Meantime, they muddled on, their days spelled out by Chinese characters. They met a whole lot of them, who told the pair with looks of both sympathy and cruelty that, as an item, they were doomed. Kennedy and Ling would never be convinced of that, though, would have to see it, live it; unbelieving romantics who knew only that there were plans to make and follow.

There were books to write too, Kennedy often forgot.

Nick Sweeney has collected (and paid) income tax, served drinks, washed glasses, taught English, and edited a million pages of text, most of it not his own. He has published short stories. This is his first novel. He lives and works in London as a musician, editor and writer.

I couldn't have got this book into the shape it's in today without the help, hindrance, encouragement, advice, inspiration and occasional ridicule from the following people: Martin Bax, Jerry Brahm, Mike Conway, Dru Conway, Bobby Darbyshire, Colin Grudz, Hilary Hodis, Robin Jones, Stephen Knight, Paul Lyon, Ron Maresh, Geoff Nicholson, Miriam Pinchuk, Joanna Podhajska, Jacqueline Sweeney and Zhan Ye.

Nick Sweeney

UNTHANK BOOKS

Unthology No.1

- Edited by Robin Jones and Ashley Stokes -

'The art of short stories is very much alive and kicking.'

Eastern Daily Press

Unthology No.1 is the first in a series from Unthank Books dedicated to showcasing unconventional, unpredictable and experimental stories. Containing seventeen pieces by brand new as well as established authors, this is a hard-hitting, hilarious and entertaining collection. Inside you will encounter motley of animals, objects and even humans. Relationships disintegrate and reform. Both domestic and global dramas unfold. A herringbone becomes an omen of impending doom. A boy waits to sit a sinister test he may or may not pass. A girl in a prison cell must write or die. These are tales that inject fresh venom into the shorter form.

Includes writing from: Viccy Adams, Sandra Jensen, Mischa Hiller, C. D. Rose, Melinda Moore, James Carter, Lora Stimson, Martin Pond, Deborah Arnander, Sherilyn Connelly, Sarah Dobbs, Jenni Fagan, Maggie Ling, Tessa West, Karen Whiteson, Ashley Stokes and Michael Baker.

ISBN: 978-0-9564223-1-6

Available from www.unthankbooks.com, The Book Depository, Amazon, Waterstones.com and all good booksellers.

UNTHANK BOOKS

Touching the Starfish

- Ashley Stokes -

'Crisp, witty and scalpel-sharp, *Touching the Starfish* doesn't miss a trick in its arch depiction of the orthodoxies and absurdities of Creative Writing Programmes and the many varieties of pond-life to be found therein. It's deadly accurate too on the often hilarious miseries of the writing life.'

Lindsay Clarke

'The work of an anarchic imagination stuffed with incident and mordantly humorous observations.'

Eastern Daily Press

'Comic writing doesn't get better than this.'

EssentialWriters.Com

Ashley Stokes's comic masterpiece stars Nathan Flack, a writer exiled in a backwater and teaching creative writing to a group of high-maintenance cranks and fantasists. When a very literary ghost by the name of James O'Mailer starts to haunt Flack, he was to ask himself: is he sinking into a netherworld of delusion, or is he actually O'Mailer's instrument?

ISBN 978-0-9564223-0-9

Available from www.unthankbooks.com, The Book Depository, Amazon, Waterstones.com and all good booksellers.